®

HELL ON EARTH

A Novel by Dafydd ab H[illegible]gh
and Brad Linaw[illegible]

Based on *Doom* [illegible]

POCKET STAR BOOKS
New York London Toronto Sydney

A Pocket Star Book published by
POCKET BOOKS, a division of Simon & Schuster, Inc.
1230 Avenue of the Americas, New York, NY 10020

Originally published in paperback in 1995 by Pocket Books

ISBN-13: 978-0-671-52562-0

First Pocket Books printing August 1995

20 19 18 17 16 15

Cover art by Robert Hunt

Manufactured in the United States of America

For information regarding special discounts for bulk purchases, please contact Simon & Schuster Special Sales at 1-800-456-6798 or business@simonandschuster.com.

The Entire Moon of Deimos Had Just Taken a Whirlwind Tour of the Solar System . . .

I swallowed hard; we were staring at Earth.

"I . . . guess we know their invasion plans now," I said, feeling the blood rush to my face.

Fly plucked at his uniform—Lieutenant Weems's uniform, except he'd pulled off the butter bars—like it had suddenly started itching. "Well, at least we stopped them," he said.

"Look again, Fly." The globe was flecked with bright pinpoints of light, flares of explosives millions of times more powerful, more hellish, than any we had ducked or lobbed back here on Deimos. I pointed to the obvious nuclear exchange blanketing our home, dumping a few billion tons of radiation, fallout, and sheer explosive muscle on—on everyone we had ever known.

"Looks like they've already invaded."

DOOM Novels Available from Pocket Books

KNEE-DEEP IN THE DEAD by Dafydd ab Hugh and Brad Linaweaver
HELL ON EARTH by Dafydd ab Hugh and Brad Linaweaver
INFERNAL SKY by Dafydd ab Hugh and Brad Linaweaver
ENDGAME by Dafydd ab Hugh and Brad Linaweaver

To Gail Higgins
for help at the penultimate hour

HELL ON EARTH

1

As we hit the roof of Deimos, I looked up.

The pressure dome was cracked. Of course. That made sense, the way things had been going. Next thing you knew, thousand-year-old Martians would come along and wink us out of existence.

Fly Taggart stared at the crack, and his eyes bugged out like a frog. I wish he knew a bit more physics; if I have one complaint about Fly, it's that he doesn't hold with higher education. The crack was small, and I could see it wasn't going to leak all the air out of the dome in the next few minutes. Days, more like; days, or even weeks. It's a *big* facility.

Then I looked past the crack and saw what that huge Marine corporal was really staring at: *we weren't orbiting Mars anymore!*

The entire moon of Deimos had just taken a whirlwind tour of the solar system. I swallowed hard; we were staring at Earth.

"I . . . guess we know their invasion plans now," I said, feeling the blood rush to my face.

Fly plucked at his uniform—Lieutenant Weems's

uniform, except he'd pulled off the butter bars—like it had suddenly started itching. "Well at least we stopped them," he said.

"Look again, Fly." The globe was flecked with bright pinpoints of light, flares of explosives millions of times more powerful, more hellish, than any we had ducked or lobbed back here on Deimos. I pointed to the obvious nuclear exchange blanketing our home, dumping like a few billion tons of radiation, fallout, and sheer explosive muscle on—on everyone we had ever known. "Looks like they've already invaded."

Fly suddenly latched onto my arm with a vise grip of raging emotion. I tried to pry his steel hands loose, while he hollered in my ear. "It's not over, Arlene!" PFC Arlene Sanders, United States Marine Corps: that's me. "We've already proven who's tougher. We won't let it end like this!"

Right. Me and Fly and nothing but weapons, ammo, and a hand with some fingers on it. We were going to *jump* from LEO down to the surface of the Earth. Or maybe we'd drive the planetoid down and land it at Point Mugu. I guess you couldn't consider Deimos strictly a moon anymore, since it appeared to be mobile.

We were stuck a mere four hundred klicks from where we wanted to be: but that was four hundred kilometers *straight up.* What's more, we were flying around the Earth at something better than ten kilometers per second—not only would we have to jump down, we'd better do one hell of a big foot-drag to kill that orbital velocity.

And after that we'd solve Fermat's Last Theorem, simplify the tax code, and cure world hunger.

That last one was easy enough to fix. The problem wasn't that there wasn't enough food; it was just in the wrong places and didn't last long enough. I once heard an old duffer say all we really needed was food irradiation, Seal-a-Meals, and a bunch of rocket mail tubes to plant the food in the center of the famine du jour.

Rocket mail tubes . . .

"Fly," I shrieked, jumping up and down. "I know how to do it!"

"Do *what,* damn it?"

Could we do it? I did some fast, rule-of-thumb calculations: our mass versus that of a typical "care package" from Mars, the sort they sent up to the grunts like me serving on Deimos; the Earth's gravitational pull compared to that of Mars—it's harder to fly up and down off the Earth's surface than the Martian surface. Maybe . . . no, it *would* work!

Well, maybe.

"I know how to get us across to Earth, Fly. Did you know there's a maintenance shed for unmanned shipping rockets on this dump of a moon?"

"No," he said suspiciously.

Of course he didn't. He was never stationed here, like I'd been. It was a garage where the motor-pool sergeant kept all the mail tubes, the shipping rockets. I had no idea why they were called "mail tubes"; we send our mail electronically, as the universe intended.

"A one-way ticket to Earth," I summed up, trying to penetrate that thick skull of his. "If we can find any kind of ship, we go home and kick some zombie ass. Again."

"All over again," he breathed, catching my drift at last. "Well, hell, we're professionals at this now!"

We continued looking at the familiar blue-green sphere of Earth, as the unfamiliar white spots appeared and disappeared all over the globe. An old piece of advice floated up from deep in my memory:

DON'T LOOK DOWN! We gazed upon white clouds so beautiful that they reminded me of what we'd been fighting to save.

Were we too late? Part of me hoped so, a part that just wanted to sit down and rest.

We'd fought those damned, ugly monsters until we were too tired to fight—and now it was looking like we had to do it all over again.

All at once I noticed a sprinkling of the flares all over California, my home state. "Oh, God, Fly," I said, my stomach contracting.

"Yeah. Terrible." Jesus, couldn't my best bud think of anything stronger to say when Armageddon came to your hometown?

I shook my head. "You don't understand. That's not what I meant. I mean *I don't feel anything.*" I trembled as I spoke.

Fly put his arm around me; well, that was more like it. "It's all right," he mumbled. "It's not what you think. There's nothing wrong with you. After what you've been through, you're just numb. Your brain is tired."

I let my head rest on his shoulder. "So my mind is coming loose. What about body and soul?"

Right then and there I decided we needed a new word to describe the state after you've reached exhaustion but had to keep going on automatic pilot.

Wherever that state was, Fly and I had been there a long, long time.

2

I put my arm around Arlene's shoulders, hoping she would understand it meant nothing but friendship. Oh don't be silly, Fly; of course she understands!

Where to begin? I was born at an early age, in a log cabin I helped my father build. I grew up, joined the *UnitedStatesMarineCorpsSir!*—went to fight "Scythe of Glory" Communist leftovers in Kefiristan, punched out the C.O., was banged up in the brig and sent to Mars with the rest of my jarhead buddies.

We up-shipped to Phobos, one of the moons of Mars—well, now the *only* moon of Mars—and discovered a boatload of aliens had invaded through the used-to-be-dormant "Gates," long-range teleporters from . . . from where? From another planet, God knows where. Arlene and I battled our way into the depths of the Phobos facility of the Union Aerospace Corporation . . . who started the whole invasion, turns out, by monkeying with the Gates in the first place.

It all rolled downhill from there. We ended up on Deimos somehow—and I'm still not sure how *that* happened!—and duked our way up one side and down the other, killing more types of monsters than you can shake a twelve-gauge at, finally ending up in a hyperspace tunnel . . . you'll have to ask Arlene Sanders (Exhibit A, the gal to my left) to explain what *that* is. But when we finally killed everything worth killing, we lucked into stopping the invasion cold. See previous report-from-the-front for full details.

In the end, we faced down the spidermind—the handy nickname chosen for the spider-shaped "mastermind" of the invasion, chosen by Bill Ritch, *requisat in pace,* a computer genius who helped us at the cost of his own life.

Right before defeating the spidermind, I'd thought there was nothing left in me. I was certain that I couldn't have continued without Arlene, a physical reminder of what we were fighting for, like old-time war propaganda. While she breathed, I had to breathe, and fight. Blame it on the genes. We'd had the strength to go on against hundreds of monsters. We weren't about to let a little thing like the laws of physics stop us now.

Arlene couldn't stop looking at California, so I gently led her away from the sight. "You know, Arlene, I feel really stupid that I didn't think of the shed; especially after using the rocket fuel to fry the friggin' spider."

She blinked her eyes and rubbed them. I could tell she was trying not to cry. "That's why you need *me,* Flynn Peter Taggart."

So we went spaceship shopping.

Of course, there was the little matter of adding to our personal armaments. We hadn't seen any monsters for a while. Maybe we neutralized all of them—but I wasn't about to count on it.

"Once, I was asked why I don't like to go out on the street without being armed," I told Arlene.

"Must have been an idiot," came the terse reply.

She'd regained her self-control, but she was still acting defensive. We were good friends, but that made it easier for her to be embarrassed in front of me.

"No, I wouldn't call her that," I continued. "But she'd lived a protected life; never came up against the mother of all storms."

"What's that?" Arlene wanted to know.

"Late-twentieth-century street slang for when the bad mother on your block decides it's time to teach you a lesson. At such times, it is advisable to carry an equalizer."

"Like this?" Arlene asked, bending down to retrieve an AB-10 machine pistol, her personal fave. Every little bit helps.

"If my friend had one of those in her purse—" I began, but Arlene interrupted.

"Too long to get it out. I like to carry on my person."

"Yeah, yeah. I was about to say if she had carried, she might be alive today."

Arlene stopped rummaging through the contents of a UAC crate and looked up. "Oh, Fly, I'm sorry."

"Sometimes you get the lesson only one time, and it's pass-fail." I playfully poked the air in her direction. "Welcome back," I said.

"What do you mean?" she asked, squinting at me the way she always did when I made her defensive.

"You can feel again, dear."

"Oh," she said, her body becoming more relaxed. "You're right. One person means something. Well, sometimes . . . if there aren't too many one persons."

"One's real. There's the body on the floor. A million is just a statistic, no matter how much screaming the professional mourner does."

She punched the air back at me. And she smiled. We didn't talk for a little while. We continued gathering goodies en route to the shed. It didn't take long to locate; the good news was that it was large and apparently well-stocked. It would take days to go through all the crates and boxes; but if the labels on the outside were accurate, we'd discovered a much larger inventory of parts than I would have imagined necessary for Deimos Base.

The bad news was a complete absence of ships in any state of assembly. There was nothing to fly!

"Well jeez, I *thought* it was a great idea," said Arlene. "Too bad it flopped."

Somehow it seemed immoral to give up hope while standing inside Santa's workshop. I began examining some of the boxes while Arlene kicked one across the room; but that didn't bother me, she was never meant for the modern age she was born into. She'd have been more homey as a freebooter in the days of blood and iron, when one physically competent woman did enough in her lifetime to breed legends of lost, Amazonian races of warrior queens. She had guts; she had cold steel will. She didn't have patience, but what the hell!

I didn't think I would face death as well as she. I'd go down in a very nonstoic way, kicking death in the groin if I could only line up my shot.

I looked inside those boxes—big ones, little ones, all kinds of in-between ones—and an idea grew in my head, a few words slipping out.

"I wonder if it still might be possible to seize the objective," I muttered.

Arlene heard, too. "Huh? What do you mean, seize the objective?"

I was only half listening. The little voice in the back of my head drowned her out with some really crazy stuff: "It seems ridiculous, A.S., but it could work."

3

The stoic qualities of Arlene Sanders were better suited to facing death than being irritated by her old buddy. "Fly, what the hell are you talking about?" She stomped to where I was going through a box of thin metal cylinders, perfect for the project growing inside my head.

"Yes," I said, "it really could work."

Using the special tone of voice normally reserved for dealing with mentally deficient children and drunken sailors, she said: "Tell me what in God's name you're on about, Fly!"

I lifted my head from the box. "When I was a kid, I wanted a car real bad. I mean *real* bad. Real real, bad bad."

"Here we go down memory lane," she said with a shrug.

"See, I couldn't afford the car," I said, "but I wanted one."

"Real real, bad bad?"

"I mean, I'd have taken anything with wheels and a transmission. If I couldn't have a six, I'd settle for four. Three, anything! But no matter how much I lowered expectations, I still couldn't afford a vehicle."

"Is this going somewhere, Fly, or do I need to hitchhike back home to Mother?"

"That's exactly right," I said. "I'm talking about transportation. I couldn't afford a car—but I *could* afford a spare part now and then, and you know how this ended up?"

She put her hands on her hips, head tilted to the side, and said: "Let me guess! You collected spare parts, and collected and collected, and finally you were able to build your own F-20! Or was it an aircraft carrier? Amphibious landing craft?"

I ignored her. "I *built myself a car.* Had a few problems; no brakes exactly, but it ran; and what a powerful sound that baby made when she turned over."

Arlene finally saw where I was headed. Memory lane dead-ended right here on Deimos. "Fly, you're BS-ing me."

"No, I really built an auto . . ."

"You *are* insane if you think you can build a freakin' spaceship out of spare parts!"

I literally jumped up and down. "You thought of it too," I said. "Great idea, isn't it? We can build a rocket and get off this rock."

She was very tolerant. "Fly, an automobile is one thing. You're talking about a spaceship."

I looked her straight in the eye. "After all we've been through, you going to tell me we can't do this?"

She looked me straight back. "Read my lips," she said. "We can not do this."

"We have nothing to lose, A.S. It can't be any harder than taking down the spidermind, can it?"

"You have a point there," she said grudgingly. "So how do you propose we start?"

She was always annoyed when I used reality to win an argument. I knew it was possible. But not without a manual.

"We need some tech," I said.

"Tech?"

"Plans . . . then we can give it to our design department."

"Don't tell me . . . *I'm* the design department."

I smiled. "You're the design department."

"And what are you, Fly Taggart?"

"Everything else."

We went looking for a manual. Ten minutes later we found one in the most logical place, which was the last place we looked, naturally: next to the coffee maker. I tried to get Arlene to make us a pot of coffee, but she stared at me as if I'd grown a third head.

So I made it myself; I'd forgotten that Arlene didn't indulge, but that was all right with me. I figured since I was the production line, I needed all the caffeine I could survive.

Next we inventoried everything we had to work with. Our best choice was to make a small mail rocket intended for one person, but capable of seating two, if they were really chummy. I wrote a list of parts needed and found almost everything within three hours . . . except for a thingamabob. I knew what it was really called, but I couldn't think of it. We spent another hour searching, and though we didn't come across it, we located more tools that would be of immeasurable value: a screwdriver, a drill bit, a magnifying glass, and a paper punch.

"Enough for now," said Arlene. "I'm sure the thingamabob will show up before we finish. We'd better get started . . . I have no idea how fast the air is leaking from the dome; we might have a month, we might have a couple of days!"

I wasn't going to argue with an optimistic Arlene. Hell, I hardly ever argued with the pessimistic one. "We haven't looked under all the tarps," I said, "and there are other rooms to check too. But there is one more shopping expedition required before we start work. We need enough food and water to hold us through the job; and all the spare liquid oxygen tanks and hydrogen tanks we can find."

Arlene nodded. We were in a race with a bunch of air molecules, and they had a head start. In addition to oxygen for fuel, we actually needed to breathe now and again over the next few days. Weeks, whatever. It would be cruel fate indeed if I screwed the last bolt and hammered the final wing nut, only to keel over from oxygen deprivation.

My brain was working overtime now: "The pressure is dropping so slowly, we're not going to notice when it gets dangerous. Can you rig up something to warn us when to start taking a hit of pure oxygen?"

"And regulate how much we should take. Yeah, it's a space station . . . I don't think I'll have much trouble finding an air-pressure sensor and rebreather kit."

She pulled a gouge pad out of her shirt pocket and started taking notes. She thought of something I'd missed: "I'll look for warm clothes too, Fly. The temperature will drop as we lose pressure."

"Won't the sun warm us? We're no farther away than Earth itself."

"We're underground. All this dirt makes a great insulator, unfortunately."

First day, we were good scouts, gathering supplies for our merit badge in survival. I regretted that we couldn't move what we needed to a lower level and seal off one compartment. That would stretch survival by another month. But hauling the tons of material we'd need to build a rocket was impossible.

Arlene scrounged a generous supply of food, most of it produced under the dome with considerable help from the Genetics Department. After watching the monsters produced assembly-line out of the vat, I hesitated even to eat our own—human experiments in recombinant-DNA veggies and lab-grown "Meet." But Arlene wasn't queasy. She preferred the Deimos-grown peas and carrots to the real delicacy, frozen asparagus from Earth.

"I despise asparagus," she insisted.

"All right; so I hate okra." The slimy stuff was one of my childhood loathings.

On the second day, we ran head-on into our first lesson in Spaceship Construction 101: namely, translating the manual from "techie-talk" into English. Here, what should we make of this?

> The ZDS protocol provides reliable, flow-controlled, two-way transmission of unenriched fuel-cell packet deliverables from nozzle to socket. It is a plasma stream (PLASM-STREAM) or packet stream (SOCK-SEQFUELPACKET) protocol. ZDS uses the Union Aerospace Corporation double-sequencing directed stream format. This format provides for *nozzle, spray, and extern-spray (socket)* specification.
>
> NOTE: see the definition for *ZDS-redirect* in Section 38.12.
>
> ACTIVE OR PASSIVE
>
> Sockets utilizing the ZDS protocol are either "active" or "passive." Nozzle processes must be directed into passive (external spray) sockets. They detect for connection requests from deliverable processes residing on the same or other nodes of the fuel-cell packet path. Socket processes broadcast requests for active (directed spray) nozzles. They sidestep nominal delivery in favor of reverse-directed (acknowledging) packet streams.

ALL CONNECTIONS BETWEEN NOZZLES AND SOCKETS MUST BE SET TO DEFAULT ACTIVE OR PASSIVE PROTOCOL DEPENDING ON THE ANTICIPATED FUEL-CELL PATH DELIVERY PROCESS.

WARNING! Failure to follow UAC active/passive nozzle-socket connection protocols may result in unanticipated fuel-cell path combustion with undesirable results.

I could translate the final warning pretty well: if we didn't figure out what the hell they meant by "active/passive nozzle-socket connection protocols," Arlene and I would become a rather spectacular fireworks display.

Arlene was better at figuring it out than I was; she had actually taken engineering night courses during her shore tours. I volunteered the use of my hands and a strong back if she'd turn the technical gobbledygook into the kind of instructions a Marine can follow: "Put this part here! Tighten that bolt, Marine!"

"Yeah, just like you to have the woman do all the *hard* work," she said.

"Just remind me to clean the carburetor before I work on the piston valves."

"It's not a car, you moron!"

"Huh. I guess in space no one can hear you make metaphors." Amazingly, she didn't shoot me.

Unfortunately, the rockets used by the Deimos facility—hence all the spare parts—were short-hop, lightweight supply rockets, never intended to carry a single human being, let alone two of us . . . and never intended to fight a gravity well like Earth's.

There were a couple large-bore rocket casings left

over from God knows when, back before we had the MDM-44 plasma motors developed by Union Aerospace, and this was the key: I figured I could hot-rod a 44 into a bigger cousin, cram it inside one of the old casings, and have enough juice to fling us off Deimos, burn into the atmosphere, and brake to a (messy) landing Somewhere on Earth.

My main goal was to keep from blowing us up. After frying our spider baby in JP-9 jet fuel, I had a new respect for the stuff. It beat the hell out of salad oil.

Arlene squatted on an uncomfortable stool translating technical paragraphs into something I could understand. My optimist projection was to finish the task in ten days!

Reality dragged ass.

Starting our *third* week, we ran into the first serious problem. Trying to jerry-rig parts we couldn't find into configurations we couldn't figure out was a bitch, and I insisted we needed to test-fire the motor when I finally got a working model. We didn't have much time, but the motor was life and death, a *must test.* We'd spent two days painfully assembling it, and I do mean "we." Arlene enjoyed an excuse to get off her stool; besides, it was a two-man job.

We finally ended up with a sleek beauty two meters long and a meter in diameter, *almost* small enough to fit inside the old-model rocket skin. Just a few odd pieces here and there where I thought I could supercharge the system—or where I couldn't find the correct part and had to substitute butter for eggs. A pair of start cables snaked into the machine from ten feet away, where a switch box was connected to twenty-seven fifty-volt ni-cad batteries.

I'd spent half a day welding steel bars together into a framework, sort of, kind of approximating the interior scaffolding in the mail tube. We bolted the motor inside, mooring it securely to the deck plates. Last, I attached a highly sensitive pressure sensor to the forward edge to measure the thrust. I'd trust Arlene to make the calculations and tell me whether we would make it into orbit or not.

"Want to say a prayer?" she asked before I switched it on.

"Yeah; I wasn't *always* in trouble with the nuns. Maybe I can collect on a few good deeds." Arlene stationed herself behind a bulkhead; I reached over and flipped the switch, then dived behind cover.

Superheated gases rushed out the back with a tremendous roar . . . and I could tell immediately it was too much force; I'd tweaked my rocket engine too good.

But I couldn't switch it off! It was just a model, designed to burn until the fuel was gone; no cut-off valve.

The scaffolding strained, groaning like a dying steam demon—whoops, remind me later—and I knew what was about to happen. "Get your head down!" I screamed. No use—she couldn't hear anything over the roar of the engine and the scream of steel twisting and ripping free.

The mooring tore loose with a horrible, grinding noise that for an instant even drowned out the 44. My beautiful, working rocket engine broke free, ate the pressure sensor with one gulp, and smashed through a dozen boxes of precious parts before making a smoking hole against the nearby bulkhead, leaving a perfectly straight series of holes, like a cartoon.

4

Destroying a bulkhead on a doomed base, or even some spare parts, was no cause for alarm. Destroying the motor was something else again. Arlene screamed something obscene, but I couldn't hear her over the ringing in my ears. We got off lucky. It could have struck the JP-9 and ended everything.

After we extinguished the fire and salvaged what we could of the motor, Arlene looked at me humorlessly. "Flynn Taggart, what deviltry did you do to those poor nuns?"

"Can you rephrase that, after what we've been through?" We were both a little punchy, getting by on shifts of four hours sleep. But no spiderminds were trying to kill us, no imps throwing a wrench in the machinery, no hell-princes setting fires worse than the one we'd just put out. It felt like we were on vacation.

All right, to fill in a bit: an imp is what we dubbed the brown, spiny, leathery alien that throws flaming balls of mucus. Hell-princes looked like the typical "devil" from my troubled youth in Catholic school—red body, goat legs, horns, and they too threw something noxious that killed you real dead; we pretty much decided it had to be an example of genetic engineering, since it was too close to a human conception of evil.

We had also killed demons, which I privately called pinkies, that were huge, pink, hairy critters with no brains but an awful lot of teeth; flying, metallic skulls with little rocket motors; invisible ghosts; and an unbelievable horde of zombies—spiritually, they were the worst, for oftener than not, they were our own buddies and comrades at arms, "reworked" into the living dead.

But the granddaddy monster of them all was the steam-demon, so called because it was a five-meter-tall mechanical monstrosity with a back rack full of rockets and a launcher where its hand should have been. When it moved, it sounded like a steam locomotive and shook the ground.

None of that was important compared to one fact: Arlene had completely changed her mind about building the rocket. "I'm sorry I ever doubted you," she said. "I guess it is possible."

But now I was the contrarian. "We did all the calculations right, A.S. We checked and triple-checked everything . . . How could the engine be so much more powerful than we thought?"

She smiled. "Because they obviously deliberately understated the capabilities in the technical literature—probably for security reasons."

"So all our calculations are worthless crap. How are you going to fly this thing?"

She didn't seem overly concerned. "Fly, the vehicle hasn't been built that I can't pilot."

"Um . . . well, this rocket *hasn't* been built, has it?"

"You know what I mean! If you build it, I will fly. I swear."

"Hm." I didn't know what to say. I had no idea whether she was or wasn't a hot-shot rocket pilot. We don't get much call for that in the Light Drop Infantry. But now that she believed in the rocket, nothing was going to stop us.

There were other motor parts, and we patched together something I figured was eighty percent ready. There was no time for better. The air was growing thinner and the temperature was dropping . . . the crack in the dome was finally taking its toll.

The pressure dropped so gradually, we didn't even notice. After a while I found myself panting for air after climbing a ladder, and Arlene had to rest after every heavy part she handed me.

Then a couple of days later, I realized my mind was wandering in the middle of a task. I focused, then wandered again.

Arlene was able to maintain her concentration; maybe being smaller, she didn't need as high a partial pressure of oxygen. But both of us were getting mighty cold.

When I saw Arlene shivering while working, I made her throw on a couple of sweaters and did the same. We wore gloves, except that I kept removing mine because it interfered with the work. Then my hands would turn to ice, and I'd put them back on to warm up before taking another stab at attaching the fine filaments that ran microvolts to the plasma globules.

Suddenly, the air-pressure sensor started screaming its fool head off. Arlene and I exchanged a worried glance, but we didn't need to be told twice. It was time to start hitting the raw stuff, O_2 neat. We took hits off the same oxygen bottle, trying to limit ourselves to a few breaths every hour or so, or when we started to get dizzy or goofy.

But we just didn't have that much bottled oxygen. Uncle Sugar packed a lot of air into a single bottle; but even so, even at the slow pace we used it, we'd run out of breathing oxygen in just a few more days. We had more bottles, but we needed them for fuel mixing.

And of course we'd need to breathe more frequently as the pressure dropped—paradoxically, it was dropping slower now, since there was less pressure in the dome to push the air out.

We stretched the bottles as long as we could, but they ran out while there was still plenty of work left. I'd done mountain climbing in my native Colorado before joining the Corps; as the air grew thinner, I tried to help Arlene deal with it. "Breathe shallowly," I said. "Rest, and don't talk except for the job."

The physical exertion wasn't any less, though. We'd have to stop frequently, gasping and panting. We tired easily and needed more sleep, but stayed on the four-hour rotations, creating a cycle of exhaustion we couldn't break. But sleeping longer would just make the job take longer, and the pressure would drop lower in the meantime.

Low pressure is insidious. There are obvious effects: exhaustion, trouble breathing, and cold. But there are other symptoms people don't often think about: your ears ring; it's hard to hear sounds (thinner air makes everything sound muffled and "tinny"); and worst of all, your mind can start to go. Our brains are built for a certain barometric pressure, and if it's too high or too low, we start getting strange.

Or in Arlene's case, *hallucinogenic.*

"Pumpkin!" she suddenly screamed, waking me after two hours of my allotted four. She grabbed a bump-action riot gun and pounded a shot over my head, so close it made my skull vibrate.

"Pumpkin" was our name for the horrible, floating alien heads—mechanical, I think—that vomited ball lightning capable of frying you at fifty paces. I threw myself off the table we used as a bed, figuring the vacation was over: the aliens had found us at last!

But when I dropped to my knees, Sig-Cow rifle at the ready, all I saw was the dark hole in the wall left by my overly enthusiastic motor test of a week ago.

Arlene ran down the passageway ahead of me, firing

wildly; firing at nothing. But those bastard alien "demons" could be fast! I had no reason to doubt my buddy as I joined her, ready to do what we'd done countless times during our assault on Phobos, Deimos, and the tunnel.

Then she ran straight into the bulkhead like it wasn't there, and I suddenly realized something was seriously wrong with her.

She knocked herself out. I couldn't look after her then; I had to make sure about the pumpkin.

Knuckling the residue of sleep from bloodshot eyes, I ran like a mother down the corridor, eyes left, right . . . not wasting a shot but ready for the enemy. For an instant I thought I saw a flying globe and almost squeezed off a shot. But it was a trick of peripheral vision, just a flash of my own shadow.

A cul-de-sac at the end of the corridor finally convinced me that there was no freaking pumpkin.

I stood for a moment, desperately trying to get nonexistent air into my burning lungs. Then I returned to Arlene, who groaned and panted as she started coming to.

"Pal, honey, I hate to do this . . . but I've got to relieve you of your weapon."

She stared uncomprehendingly.

"There was no pumpkin," I explained. "You're suffering from low-pressure psychosis."

"Oh Jesus," she said quietly. She understood. Sadly, she handed over the scattergun and her AB-10 machine pistol.

I felt like the bottom of my boots after walking through the green sludge. You don't relieve a Marine of his weapon, not ever. By doing so, I'd just effectively demoted her to civilian. And the worst part was, even she realized now that she'd been hallucinating.

She was crying when we walked slowly back to the

vehicle assembly room, a.k.a. the hangar. I'd never seen Arlene cry before—except when she had to kill the reworked, reanimated body of her former lover, Dodd.

"Hey," I said a few hours later, "can't we electrolyze water and get oxygen?"

Arlene was silent for a moment, her lips moving. "Yes," she said, "but we'd only get a few breaths per liter, and we need the water too, Fly."

"Oh." Not for the first time, I wished I knew more engineering. I vowed to take classes when we made it back home . . . if there even *was* a "back home" anymore.

I started having unpleasant dreams, so I didn't mind giving up more of my sleep allotment. It was always the same dream, actually. I loved roller coasters as a kid. They were the closest I could get to flying in those days. I lived only five miles away from a freestanding wood-frame monster. I thought I would love nothing better, until they built a tubular steel, eight-loop supercoaster.

I'd never been afraid on the old roller coaster. With all the courage of an experienced ten-year-old, I'd sit in the car as it slowly reached the top, the horizon slanting off to my left, and pretend it was the rim of a planet and I was an astronaut. As it went over the top, plunging down a cliff of wood and metal, I made it a point of honor not to hold on to the crash bar. I was too grown-up for that!

I was always interested in how things were put together and how they worked. So I asked about the new roller coaster. A man who worked at the amusement park told me stuff he wasn't supposed to say, stuff he knew nothing about—about how the forces generated could snap a human neck like rotten cordwood, how the auxiliary chain that gave the car acceleration had a lot of extra strain on it for an eight-loop ride.

As I started up the first hill of the new ride, I thought about what I'd learned. I didn't know it was all bogus crap made up to impress a ten-year-old.

The first loop, I worried about centrifugal force snapping my neck; the second loop, I sweated over velocity tearing me out of my seat; the third loop, I fixated on the damned chain coming loose; and the fourth loop was reserved for a ten-year-old having ulcers over the gears stripping. And then I threw up—not a good thing to do when you're upside down.

I wonder if that bastard ever knew what damage his misinformation caused?

As I grew up, I learned how *real* knowledge could banish fear. You play the odds. You focus on the job at hand. You don't want to mess up. The childhood trauma was behind me . . . until it came back now on Deimos as I tried to grab a little sleep. Instead of rest, I was back on that eight-loop metal monster, and now it turned into the arms and legs of a steam-demon. When the creature screamed at me and raised its missile arm, I would always wake up; so I didn't even have the pleasure of fighting or dying.

I didn't worry about my stupid dreams, though. It sure beat fighting the real thing. Besides, I was getting off easy compared to Arlene.

I knew things were bad when I tried to wake her up and she stared with unblinking eyes, not seeing a damned thing. I realized she was still asleep. I'd read somewhere that it's risky to wake a person from a trance state, and I didn't require medical training to know Arlene was Somnambulist City.

There wasn't time to go hunting for a medical library. A quick check of medical supplies produced a Law Book, wedged between the surgical bandages and antibiotics. I had to laugh. A text on medical malpractice had made it all the way to a Martian moon, and now, by way of a hyperspace tunnel, had almost returned to Earth.

I wasn't laughing as I returned to Arlene. She walked in her sleep, striking at the air in front of her. "Get away," she said to phantoms only she could see. "I won't leave you. I'll stay, I'll stay!"

5

If I shouldn't wake her, there seemed no reason I shouldn't try to communicate. "Arlene, can you hear me?"

"Quiet," she said, "I don't want Fly to hear you. He's depending on me."

"Why don't you want him to know about me?" I asked.

"Because you're evil," she said with conviction. "You're all evil, you bastards."

She walked slowly down the corridor. So long as she wasn't in danger of hurting herself, I saw no reason to shock her out of it. "Why are we bad?"

"You scare me. You make my brother do bad things!"

Up to that point I did not know that Arlene even had a brother.

It was weird—I thought we'd known everything

about each other's family life. She talked about her parents and growing up in Los Angeles all the time. I was uncomfortable pursuing the matter, but I rationalized away my moral qualms and decided to play out the hand. "Who are we?" I asked again.

She swayed drunkenly, delivering a monologue like those weird, old plays from previous centuries. "Bad things in the air, in the night, making my brother crazy. He'd never do bad things except for you. I thought I'd never see you again . . . Why'd you follow me into space, to Mars, to Deimos? When I grew up, I thought you weren't real, but now I know better. You followed me, but I won't let you get inside me; not inside!"

When Arlene had kidded me about going down memory lane, I took it in good humor. But if we were going to have to relive all the bad stuff from our childhood as the air leaked away, I was good and ready to say good-bye to Deimos now, rocket or no rocket, instead of later.

In the meantime, what was I going to do about Arlene? I couldn't let her wander the corridors, arguing with ghosts from her childhood. With time short and no way to send to Earth for a correspondence course in psychology, I went with common sense.

"Arlene, we'll make a deal with you," I said. "We'll stop bothering you and let you get back to Fly."

"In exchange for what?" she wanted to know, quite reasonably.

"Because we've moved back to Earth, and you can't touch us there."

"Fly and I are building a ship to take us to Earth."

"Ha, we don't believe you two will get anywhere near us. You'll be stuck on Deimos forever!"

"That's a lie!" she snapped, and stopped walking. "We'll fight you again." She stared right at me. "We're not afraid of your little genetic stupidmen."

"Big words!" I said.

She came right at me, fists raised, and started hitting me. As I fended off her blows—not too difficult, considering the difference in reach—I yelled, "Hang on, Arlene, I'm coming to help you. This is Fly, Fly!"

As I say, I never took any courses in psychology, but I acted in school plays. And to steal a phrase, it doesn't take a rocket scientist to go with the flow. I gave myself a magna cum laude graduation as her eyes came into focus and she recognized me.

"Fly? What happened?"

"We've been fighting monsters again."

She looked around the empty corridor and then back to me. I didn't have to spell it out. "How much longer can we take this?"

"Not a second longer than we have to."

Arlene started seeing weird colors after that—auras, shadows, and things she wouldn't tell at first. Sometimes she would put the tech documents down, sitting quietly with her eyes shut until the colors went away.

It scared me plenty, but it terrified her. She was losing her mind—and she knew it. So when I told her the engine was eighty percent finished, Arlene urged, "Fly, forget the other twenty percent. It's done! Let's blow this popcorn stand."

I had to be honest. "A.S., there are still a few systems I don't think are in really good shape."

"We can't wait. We've taken chances with worse odds than that the whole time we've been on this rock. Fly, I . . . I stopped being able to see color vision this morning. All I can see is gray—except when I hallucinate a rainbow-colored aura. And my peripheral vision is shot." She paused, licking her lips. "And Fly, there's something else."

She came close and spoke softly, seriously. "I want to confess something to you, Fly. What would your nuns think of that? For the first time I'm really afraid. I'm afraid I might kill you, thinking you're one of the monsters. I couldn't stand that."

The little voice in the back of my head had whispered that possibility when she first imagined the pumpkin. It was a chance I was willing to take. Even so, I was glad she, not I, stated the danger loud and clear.

I sped up preparations, insisting that Arlene sleep whenever possible. The air and pressure problems were getting to me as well, but I handled them better than Arlene.

Of course, the problem with oxygen starvation is that you are not the best judge of your own reason. But the best chance for both of us was to finish the rocket.

And we were close, tantalizingly close.

I suddenly got the creepy crawlies. I recognized the symptom: I was picking up the same psychosis as Arlene. "All right," I acquiesced, "we go in the next few hours. We have a chance, I guess; eighty percent is eighty points better than zero."

We got busy. We drank water. We ate a last good meal of biscuits, cheese, fruit, nuts. The Eskimos say that food is sleep, by which I guess they mean if your body can't get one kind of recharge, you might as well take the other.

Arlene abandoned me to work out the telemetry program that would (God willing) launch us, kill Deimos's orbital velocity, dropping us into the atmosphere, then take us down, at which point she'd hand over control to me to find a suitable spot to touch down. Fortunately, it was basically cut-and-paste; I doubt she could have written it from scratch . . . not in the condition she was in. The hand of God must have graced her, though she'd never admit it, for her to keep it together long enough to patch it together.

As we prepared to leave, I kept running the basic worries through my mind. The mail tubes were designed for Mars, which has only a fraction the atmosphere of Earth and a much lower gravity; the specific impulse developed by the rockets might not be enough to overcome Earth's gravity as we spilled velocity and tried to land. On the other hand, the thick atmosphere might cause so much friction that our little ship would burn up.

The launcher was a superconducting rail gun. Reminded me of the eight-loop wonder at the amusement park back in the Midwest. This time I hoped I wouldn't throw up. At least this piece of equipment didn't have an auxiliary chain . . . so what was there to worry about?

I grunted the launcher around to point opposite Deimos's orbital path. The rocket controls were simple to operate, thank God; throttle, stick, various navigational gear that I didn't really understand, and environmental controls, all ranged around my face in a tremendously uncomfortable position.

Then suddenly, a few hours before our scheduled departure, Arlene totally freaked out.

At first I thought she was joking. She strolled up to me and said, "Don't try to fool me; I know what you *really* are."

"Yeah, a prize SOB," I said distractedly. A moment later I was on my butt with Arlene's boot on my chest and a shiv—a sharpened piece of metal—against my throat. Looking into her eyes, I saw the blank look of a zombie . . . and for a moment, Jesus, I thought they'd somehow gotten her, reworked her!

But it was just the low pressure, or maybe slow

oxygen deprivation. I talked to her for five minutes from my supine position, saying anything, God knows what, anything to snap her back to some semblance of herself. After a while she dropped the shiv and started crying, saying she had murdered God or some such silly nonsense.

I wasn't going to abandon her, no matter what; but there was nothing in my personal rule book that said I had to make it any more difficult. We had Medikits in the shed. I gave her a shot. She struggled, coughed, and turned to me. "Why *can't* we eat our brothers?" she asked; then the drug took effect.

She'd be okay; in the mail-tube rocket, we've have more pressure, and more important, more partial-pressure of O_2. She'd be all right . . . I hoped.

I put her aboard the rocket, threw in a bag of supplies, and squeezed in next to her. It was like being in a sleeping bag together—or a coffin. I positioned myself so I could reach all the controls, took a deep breath and got serious.

Just before lighting the cigar, I remembered the stark terror of riding in the E7 seat of an S-8 sub-hunter "Snark" jet and coming in for my virgin landing on an aircraft carrier. Trusting entirely to the guy on the other end made me more nervous than the idea of landing on a postage stamp. Well, this time, for better or worse, I was the guy with the stick; considering that I'd never flown anything but a troop shimmy over some mountains, I almost wished I were back in the S-8.

I threw the switches, pushed forward on the throttle (oddly similar to a passenger airliner), and the rocket slid along the tube, launching at ten g's. Arlene was already out, of course, and missed the pleasure of blacking out with me.

Suddenly, I discovered myself in a strange room, a

faint hissing catching my attention. Black and white, no color . . . I knew I should know where I was, what all these things, this equipment around me, was.

I should know my name too, I guessed.

Then the sound cut back in; *fly,* someone said. A command? *Fly, fly*—"Fly." It was me, my lips, saying the word fly . . . the *name!* Fly, me; my name.

Then I saw color and recognized the jerry-rigged blinking lights and liquid-crystal displays of the mail tube. I'd installed them myself; the mail doesn't need to see where it's going, but we did.

Through the slit of a viewscreen, I saw deepest blue with faint, cotton-candy wisps, strings flashing past. I glanced at the altimeter—much too high for clouds. Ionized gases?

Then something socked me in the face, like a 10mm shell, and agony exploded across my face. At first it was bilateral; then it focused right behind my eyeballs, like God's own worst migraine. For a few seconds I thought my head literally was going to detonate. Then it faded as the blood finally repressurized my cranial arteries and rebooted my brain. I looked at the chronometer: the entire blackout had lasted only forty-five seconds.

It could have been forty-five years.

A low groan announced Arlene's return to consciousness. "Fly," she moaned, "good luck."

I was too busy to say anything. But it was good having her back again. The calculations she'd already worked out for our glide path were okay, and I used the retros to get us on her highway.

As we came in, the ride got bumpier and rougher. The interior of the little craft started heating up. Being so close together made us sweat all the faster. When it got over fifty degrees centigrade, beads of perspiration poured into my eyes, interfering with vision.

But the temp continued to rise. The mail tubes are supposed to be insulated—but the skin on this one was built for Mars.

In Earth atmosphere, we were being baked. The temp boiled up past *seventy degrees,* and I was gasping for air, every breath searing my lungs. My skin turned red and I could barely hold the controls. Another minute and we would be dead.

6

Fly!" Arlene screamed. "Blow the oxygen! We'll lose it, but it'll heat up and blow out the exhaust, cooling the interior!"

"Not again!" I said.

"Huh?"

"We'll be low on air again!"

"Do it, Fly, or we'll fry."

We took turns making the other face unpleasant facts. It was something like being married.

I did as she commanded. The cooling effect made a real difference. My brain was still on fire, but at least I could think again.

"So what systems still aren't working?" she asked next, still gasping from each searing breath.

This seemed like an opportune moment to be completely honest. "Now that you mention it," I mentioned, "the only one I'm worried about is the landing system."

"What?"

"The thingamabob would have come in useful for landing. What do they call it? Oh yes, the aerial-braking system."

She sighed. If there had been more room in our little cocoon, she might have shrugged as well. "By-gones," she said. "Sorry for the trouble I caused."

"Arlene, don't be ridiculous! I was having crazy dreams and was about to go off the deep end myself. You just went first because you're . . . smaller." It occurred to me that we were having more of a discussion than was wise under the circumstances.

"So how in hell do we land this puppy?" No sooner were these words out of her mouth than Arlene started yawning.

I figured we should try and set it down anywhere on dry land. Live or die, I wasn't in the mood for a swim. If we survived, we could get our bearings anywhere on Earth—pick a destination and then haul butt.

We didn't have any time to waste. Thanks to our stunt with the oxygen, the O_2 to CO_2 ratio was dropping. I was in even less mood for us to become goofy from oxygen deprivation after watching Arlene go nuts before—thanks, Mr. Disney, but I'm not going back on that ride.

I had to explain this to Arlene, but she was asleep again so I explained it to the Martian instead. He was a little green guy, about three feet high, and I was glad to see him. "About time one of you showed up," I said. "We always expected to see guys like you up here instead of all this medieval stuff."

"Perfectly understandable," he said in the voice of W. C. Fields. "These demons are a pain. But they're welcome to Deimos."

"Why is that?" I asked.

"Confidentially, it's an ugly moon, don't you think? Not at all a work of beauty like Phobos, a drinking man's moon. Speaking of which, you wouldn't have some whiskey on you?"

"Sorry, only water."

He was very offended. "You mean that liquid fish fornicate in? We Martians don't care for the stuff. You can drown in it, you know. Now ours is a nice, dry planet, rusty brown like that car of yours after you abandoned it to the elements. Mars is nice and cold, good practice for the grave. Are you sure you don't have any booze?"

I figured he was bringing up drowning just to scare me. If Arlene and I didn't burn up in the atmosphere, there was always a good chance of winding up in the drink and drowning like the Shuttle pioneers had in the 1980s.

Besides, he'd raised a certain issue and I wanted an answer. "Why does Phobos look better to you than Deimos?" I asked.

"My dear fellow, Phobos is the inner moon of Mars. Deimos was always on the outs even before those hobgoblins hijacked it. The outs is a bad place to be, and you are out of time and going to die and betray Arlene and betray the Earth, you puny little man with your delusions."

While he was talking, he was growing in size, and sharp teeth protruded beyond his sneering lips; the eyes flamed red, as the rockets flamed red, as the sky was underneath and overhead all at the same time. And I was screaming.

"You're one of them! You're a demon-imp-specter-thing. You tricked me."

"Fly," said a comforting voice from behind the Martian. "Fly, you're hallucinating."

"I knew that," I told her as the Martian faded from view. "I knew it all along."

A quick check of the cabin gave a head count of (1) myself, (2) Arlene, (3) no Martians. I checked again to make sure. Yep, just two humans. No monsters. No Martians. Not much air. Definitely not enough air.

"We've got to land this quickly," I said.

"Um . . . if it's all the same to you, Fly, I can wait until we can land it *safely.*"

The atmosphere got thick enough that I pulled the cord to extend our mini-wings. Instantly, we started buffeting like mad, shaking so hard I thought my innards would become outards. We rolled, pitched, yawed—triple-threat!—and it was all I could do to hang on to the ragged edge of Arlene's computer-projected glide path.

The screen displayed a series of concentric squares that gave the illusion of flying through an infinite succession of square wire hoops. So long as I kept inside them, I should go where she projected, somewhere in North America, she said; even she wasn't sure where.

But I kept cutting through the path, coloring outside the lines. I couldn't hold it! I'd yank on the stick and physically wrench us back through the wire frames and out the other side (they turned from red to black when I was briefly on the meatball). The best I could do was stay within spitting distance of my proper course . . . and naturally, we were running too hot, much too fast. We were going to overshoot our mark—possibly straight into the Pacific Ocean.

I barely hung on, abandoning retros to guide our two-man "cruise missile" by fins, air-braking to spill as much excess velocity as possible. The ship started shaking. An old silver tooth filling started to ache. Arlene leaned back against the seat, muscles in her jaw tightening, eyes getting wider and wider. I think she was starting to appreciate the *gravity* of our situation.

North America unwound beneath the window like a quilt airing out on a sunny day. We were over the Mississippi, sinking lower, falling west, descending fast. Then we entered a cloud bank. We weren't there very long.

"I know where we are!" shouted Arlene, voice starting to sound funny from the breathing problem. I placed it too. We'd popped out of the cloud bank about 150 kilometers due west of Salt Lake City. The Bonneville salt flats were ideal for a landing—a vast, dry lake bed, nothing to hit but dirt. Very hard dirt. But we had a chance.

"Spill the fuel!" she screamed, right in my ear, straining against the buffeting. At least we were low enough that we could breathe. I yanked the lever, dumping what little JP-9 remained in the tanks.

The cabin was getting hot again, the structure of the rocket shaking like we were in a Mixmaster, and it was now or never. "Hold on!" I shouted, thinking how stupid it sounded but needing to say something.

Arlene screamed like a banshee—a much more insightful comment.

We came down fast and hard, finally striking the ground at Mach 0.5. The ship shredded on impact, skipping like a rock on the waters of a salt-white lake. Then it rolled, and Arlene's elbow jammed into my side so hard it knocked the breath out of me.

End over end we tumbled, and my brains, already fried, scrambled so I didn't know dirt from sky. We shed bits and pieces from the ship—only the titanium frame was left, but still we kept rolling.

The ship finally skidded to a stop, on its side, with me underneath Arlene.

For a good five minutes, felt like five hours, we lay silently, dazed, wondering if we had made it or not . . . waiting for the world to stop spinning.

"Are you all right?" Arlene managed to ask.

"I think we're alive," I said.

The fuel was completely spent, which was just fine with me. No risk of fire or explosion. Now if we could just get out of the thing.

Fortunately, the door on Arlene's side wasn't jammed. In fact, it wasn't even with us anymore. Arlene stumbled out, falling heavily with a grunt. I followed somewhat more gracefully, which was a switch.

We'd suffered no injuries, thank God; I didn't want us to wind up sitting ducks. If aliens had taken over Utah—a belief held by one of my old nuns many years before the invasion—then we must be on our guard. Someone, or something, would come to find out what had just made a smoking hole in the salt lick.

We took a moment to enjoy being alive and in one piece, enjoying the dusk in Utah, breathing the best air we'd tasted in months. Then we took inventory. The food and water came through. But the weapons were trashed.

"You said we couldn't do it," she teased me.

"Never listen to a pessimist," I answered, adding, "and the world is so full of them you might as well give up." She laughed as she playfully punched my arm, numbing me.

Astonishingly, Arlene's GPS wrist locator was still working. That was one tough piece of equipment! I thought maybe I should buy stock in the company; then I wondered whether any companies still existed. Maybe the monsters had done what no government was able to do: end all commerce and starve the survivors.

She sat cross-legged and fiddled with the thing, trying to get a fix on our exact position. The satellite should have responded immediately, spotting us within a meter or two.

"Getting anything?" I asked, listening to the symphony of white noise coming off her arm.

"Nada," she said. "I'll bet the sat is still up there, but the Bad Guys must have encrypted the signal. Maybe so humans can't use them in combat."

"I wish they were all as dumb as the demons," I said.

"Yeah, one spidermind goes a long way. But who cares, Fly? We've beaten the odds again. We're alive, dammit!" She ran across the sand like a kid let loose at the beach. Then she gestured for me to join her. I ran over and grabbed at her. She threw me off balance and I took a tumble in the sand.

"Clumsy!" she said, sounding as young as she had when sleepwalking through her waking nightmare on Deimos; but now was a lot more pleasant.

"We don't have time for this, you know," I said, but my heart wasn't it.

"We don't have time to be alive, or to breathe air. But here we are, still in one piece. God, I didn't think we were going to make it. We got down from orbit with nothing but spare parts, spit, and duct tape, and our bare hands—hah!"

"Frankly, my dear, I had my doubts," I admitted. I couldn't help running after her. She was right. We kept coming through stuff that should have killed us twenty times over. We weren't indestructible, but I was beginning to believe in something I'd always hated: luck.

People who accomplish nothing in their lives always attribute the success of everybody else to good luck or knavery. I believe you make your own luck:

"Chance favors the prepared mind." But in combat, there are too many random factors to calculate. Arlene and I were feeling cocky. We had plenty of reason to be thankful.

"I wonder what the radiation level is here," I said.

"Do we have to know?" she asked, skipping. "It didn't look like any bombs were going off in this area."

"Not while we were watching," I pointed out.

"There's no reason to nuke a desert. It's already a wasteland."

"You nuke military bases, Arlene. And don't forget the nuclear testing that's gone on in areas like this."

"Human wars, Fly; and human preparation for war. Besides, we don't know for certain we were seeing nuclear weapons going off; they could be some other kind of weapon without fallout. Makes it easier to take over later."

"Some of these beasties seem to thrive on radiation."

She stopped playing in the sand and sat down. She didn't say anything at first, as she poured sand out of her right boot, but then had an answer for me as she began unlacing her left one: "The radiation levels on the base weren't healthy for humans, but they weren't anywhere near what you'd get from a full-scale nuclear exchange."

The lady had a point. "You're probably right. You can thank me for going to such lengths to bring us down in this location."

"Ha," she said. "Pure luck. You brought us down where you could."

"Skill and perseverance, dear lady. One of these days, I'll explain my theory of luck to you."

7

For the moment, I was glad to join her, sitting in the sandbox. I ignored the little voice in the back of my head that worked overtime to keep us alive. It said we didn't have a moment to waste; the monsters of doom could be upon us any second, burning away our little victory faster than the setting sun.

Comes a time when you have to say the hell with it, if only for a moment. Arlene and I had recently faced the worst thing anyone can face, worse than the monsters or dying in space. We knew what it meant to lose your sanity . . . and come back to yourself again.

Arlene started whistling "Molly Malone." She'd picked one of the few songs to which I knew the words. I sang along. All that was missing was a bottle of Tullamore Dew, the world's finest sipping whiskey. As it was, our duet seemed to transform the lengthening shadows of dusk in Utah into the cool glades of Ireland. I wondered if doom had come there. Were there demons in Dublin? Did the men there see little green leprechauns instead of Martians in their moment of madness? I wondered about the whole world, and it was too much for me.

Right now the world was a stretch of desert in Utah. What we could do for ourselves, for the human race, for the world, would be determined here, as it had been on Deimos, and before that, Phobos. We'd take it one world at a time.

I lay back happily for a few moments, watching the stars wink into existence in the darkening sky.

As night fell, we spotted a glow, due east. That was the way to bet—Salt Lake City, I guessed. We gathered together what had survived the crash and followed the light. We took a break at nine P.M., another at midnight.

"How long do you think this is going to take?" she asked.

"Not sure, but I'm glad we brought the provisions." The bag survived the crash just as nicely as we did. We had water. We had biscuits and granola bars. We had flashlights (which we wisely didn't use). But I sure as hell wished we had some weapons, other than one puny knife in the provisions bag.

We trekked at night and slept by day. Hell, I saw *Lawrence of Arabia.* After Phobos and Deimos and nearly splattering ourselves over old terra firma, after all we'd survived, I'd be damned if we were going to cash in our chips here. Hell, we could go to Nevada to do that!

The water held out better than the food. We huddled together in the cold during the day, when we slept. We could have made a fire, but no point giving away our location with unnecessary light. And there was one thing about the situation creepy enough to encourage caution, even though we hadn't run into any trouble yet.

Arlene was the first to notice it: "Fly, there are no sounds."

"What do you mean?" I asked. We crunched along in the night, heading toward a glow that seemed barely bigger than it was three days ago.

"The night creatures. No owls . . ."

"Are there owls in the desert?"

"I don't know, maybe not. But there should be something. No bugs. No lizards. No nothin'."

I thought about it. "If we've seen the collapse of civilization, you'd expect wild dogs."

"There's no coyotes. Nothing. Even out here, there ought to be *something*. Unless everything was killed by the weapons."

"No, that can't be right. We'd be puking up our guts by now from poison or radiation. That light suggests somebody's still in business."

"I hope so," she said. "So you think that's Salt Lake City."

"Should be."

"Salt Lake City, *Utah?*"

"Unless it's wintering in Florida."

She was silent for a hundred paces; then she cleared her throat. "Fly, I have to confess something to you. Again."

"Anytime."

"I sort of have a problem with the Mormon Church," she said.

Making out her face in the dim light wasn't easy. I wished we had a full moon instead of the sliver hanging over us like a scythe. "You were a Mormon?" I asked.

"No. But my brother was, briefly."

"You blame the church for . . . for whatever happened?"

She shook her head. "No, I guess not. He had problems before he joined the Church; had problems when he left."

"Do you think he might be here?" I asked.

"Nah. We lived in North Hollywood. He left for Utah when he became a Mormon; but after he left the

Church, I don't know what became of him. I don't care if I ever see him again."

"I'll never bring it up," I said.

"There's another reason I'm telling you this," she went on. "I became obsessed with Mormonism while he was with them. I read books by them and against them. I even read the Book of Mormon."

"Maybe that could come in useful," I suggested.

"I doubt it. It just makes me more prejudiced. Look, Fly, if we find living human beings at the end of this, we must stand with them and fight with them. I'm promising you right now I won't discuss religion with any of those patriarchal . . ."

She paused long enough for me to jump in: "I get the picture."

"Do you have any opinions abut them?" she asked, quite fairly.

"Well, I read an article about them having a strong survivalist streak; that they stockpile a year's supply of food and stuff like that. You'll get a kick out of this! When I visited L.A. once, I took in the sights: Disneyland, the La Brea Tar Pits, Paramount studios, the Acker Mansion, and I even found time to go into their big temple at the end of Overland Avenue. There's an angel up top with a trumpet; I mistakenly called him Gabriel."

"They must have loved that; it's the Angel Moroni."

"Well, *now* I know."

"Heh. I used to drop the *i* off that name when I used it."

I took a deep breath. "Arlene, I'm going to hold you to that promise not to talk theology with them."

"Scout's honor," she said.

"Were you ever a Scout?"

She didn't answer again.

We kept the flashlights off; the glow on the horizon was the only illumination I wanted in that desert. It was easy to follow the direction at night. We made sure that we didn't waste opportunities.

"You're burning night-light," Arlene would say when it was her turn to wake me up. Then she'd snicker. Something amused her, but she didn't let me in on it.

Turned out that we ran out of food, but we had more water than we needed. It took us five days to get to Salt Lake City, the center of what once had been the Mormon world. And by God, it still was!

We lay on our bellies in some brush, shielding out eyes from the sun, leaning against a side-paneled truck.

"They're people!" marveled Arlene as we watched hundreds of men on the streets in the early dawn. They relieved other men who'd obviously been doing the night shift.

"Where do you think the women are?" I whispered.

"Home, minding the kids. Mormons are so damned patriarchal."

"Arlene . . ."

We were in a good spot to see plenty, behind a wrecked truck on a rise. As the sun crawled up the sky, shafts of light came through the broken windows like laser beams, one blinding me for a second. We positioned ourselves to see more. There was plenty to see.

The streets of this garrison town had over a thousand men with guns, and to my surprise I made out a few women and teenage girls toting heavy artillery. Arlene gave me one of her funny looks.

I didn't make her take back anything she'd said; when a society is threatened, it will do what it must or go down fast.

"You don't think they might be working with the aliens?" asked my buddy. I had the same thought. But they didn't act zombified, and we'd learned that the monsters preferred human lackeys in that condition. The spidermind had made only one exception when it needed knowledge in the human brain of poor Bill Ritch.

We had to make contact with these people, but I preferred doing it in a way that wouldn't get us shot. While I was formulating a plan, Arlene tapped me on the shoulder.

I turned and found myself staring down both barrels of a twelve-gauge duck gun. It had gorgeous, inlaid detail work running all seventy-five centimeters of the stock and barrel . . . and it was attached to a beefy hand connected to a large body with a grinning, boyish face topping it off. Twenty-two, twenty-three, tops.

"How do?" said the man. His buddy was a lot thinner, and he held an old Ruger Mini-14 pointed at Arlene.

He caught my expression and grinned at me as if he could read my mind. Here was proof positive we were facing honest-to-God, living humans: they had pride in a good weapon.

"Hi," I said, moving my eyes from man to man.

"Good morning," said Arlene.

"Hey," said the other man by way of greeting, noticing how my eyes kept drifting to his piece. "Took me quite a while to get one of these," he said conversationally.

"Beautiful weapon," I said, noticing that the beefy guy was still calm.

The thin one nodded and said, "They are compact, easy handling, fast shooting and hard hitting." He paused, then added: "Don't you agree?"

Thunk. The penny dropped. They were testing us.

"Oh, yes," said Arlene, jumping in. The thin guy looked at her a little funny and waited for me to say something.

"One of my favorite weapons," I said. "Hardly any kick. Not like the bigger calibers."

Finally the big guy spoke again: "Jerry, these people don't want a lecture."

Jerry squinted at him. "They're military. Look at their clothes." We weren't asked to confirm or deny anything, so we kept our mouths shut. Jerry had plenty of words left in him: "They're interested in a good weapon. Aren't you?"

He looked straight at me and I answered right away: "I sure am, especially that one you've got."

Jerry smiled and went on: "Albert gets tired of hearing me go on about what a good model this is. They were even reasonably priced until they were outlawed."

"Not a problem now," said Arlene. "I'm sure there's plenty of squashed zombies you can take one off'n."

Whenever she spoke, the men seemed a bit uncomfortable. I had the impression she was getting off on it.

Arlene looked over at me and winked. We'd fought enough battles to read each other's expressions and body language. Her expression told me that things were looking up as far as she was concerned, but she couldn't resist getting in the act: "I like an M-14," she said.

Jesus, it was like going shooting with Gunnery Sergeant Goforth and his redneck buddies!

The men started to warm to her a little. "Good choice for a military gal," said Albert. We all just kind of stood there for a moment, smiling at each other, and then Albert broke the ice by changing the subject.

He asked, in the same friendly tone of voice: "You wouldn't happen to be in league with those ministers of Satan invading our world?"

"We were wondering the same thing about you," said Arlene. I gave her a dirty look for that.

The beefy kid with the double-barreled duck gun chuckled. "Don't mind her saying that, mister. It shows a proper godly attitude. I hope you both check out; I like you. We talk the same language. But we can't take any chances."

They searched us both thoroughly, found the knife, and impounded it. We were weaponless. In a way, I was glad. These guys weren't acting like amateurs . . . which meant they had a chance against the invaders.

"Okay," said the man with the bird gun, "we'll take you to the President of the Council of Twelve."

Arlene grimaced, which told me she knew what he was talking about; but she kept her promise. Not a word came out of her about the religious stuff. The title sounded impressive enough to tell me that the Church of Jesus Christ of the Latter-Day Saints was still in business *big-time.*

Maybe she was right, and they were a cult; but I don't know any difference between a cult and a religion except as a popularity contest. They had survived, and we needed allies against the monsters.

I knew one more thing about the Mormons that I hadn't mentioned to Arlene during our little chat in the desert. A friend I trusted with Washington connections told me that a good part of Mormon self-reliance was to *really* prepare for every eventuality. After their tumultuous history, extreme caution was understandable. Result: there were a lot of Mormons in the government . . . in the FBI, in the various services, in the CIA, even in NASA. God help anyone who tried to play Hitler with the Mormons as the Jews! The Mormons should be ideal allies against a literal demonic invasion.

Arlene and I would find out soon enough.

8

As we were led through the streets of SLC, I allowed myself to hope that Arlene and I had lucked out by landing here. If I were still a praying man, I'd burn candles and say a few Ave Marias that we wouldn't find a spidermind sitting in the Mormon Tabernacle . . . which loomed closer and closer, obviously our destination.

The people in the street gave us a wide berth as we passed, but they didn't act unfriendly—just cautious. No one acted like an idiot. I hoped it stayed that way.

Suddenly, a man on a big motorcycle roared over to us and stopped a few inches away, kicking up dust. He wore a business suit. "Hey, Jerry," he said.

"Hey, Nate," said Jerry. "Folks, this is my brother, Nate. I'd introduce you, but I don't know your names."

"Now, Jerry," said Albert, "you know better than that. The President of the Twelve hasn't interviewed them yet. They should give their names to him."

"Sorry."

"Sounds like they know your names already," said

the man on the cycle, taking off his helmet. These guys were twins.

Although Arlene kept her promise about not discussing theological matters, she leapt into any other waters that gurgled up around us. "That's a bad machine," she said.

Nate proved to be his brother's brother: "You like this?" he asked with a big grin.

"They have good taste in guns," said Jerry, spurring them on. Albert groaned.

Nate was on a roll: "BMW Paris-Dakar, 1000 cc's . . ." He and Arlene went on about the bike for a few minutes.

Part of me wanted to strangle the girl; but another part appreciated what she was doing. Putting the other guys at their ease is a critical strategy. There were a lot more men in the street than women, but our captors—hosts?—remained respectful and polite in Arlene's presence. A very civilized society.

". . . and the glove compartment can hold five grenades!" announced Nate, topping off his presentation.

"That does it," said Albert. "If these nice people are spies, why don't you just give them mimeographed reports?"

In the short time we'd been prisoners, I'd learned that there was no genuine military discipline here. I had mixed feelings about this. The good thing was that I couldn't believe these casual people had been co-opted by the invaders. They still talked and acted like free men. Very loquacious free men!

As far as getting their president to cooperate with us, it could go either way. In the land of the civilians, the Marine is king . . . or a fall guy. I was impatient to find out which.

"Oh, I almost forgot," said Nate. "I have a message for you. The President hasn't returned yet."

"You should have told us that right off," said Albert peevishly. "We'll take them to Holding."

We entered the Tabernacle. It was nice and cool, with a fresh wood smell that was clean and bracing. The floors were highly polished. You wouldn't notice anything different from the world I'd left on a court-martial charge that now seemed to belong to a different universe.

Arlene wasn't the only one with a lot of reading under her belt. I didn't know a whole lot about the Mormons, although I knew a bit more than I told her—but I'd read the Bible all the way through, enough to recognize things the Mormons took for inspiration from what they accepted as the earlier Revealed Word.

In addition, the nuns taught a little about comparative religion, probably so we'd be better missionaries. I remembered that God was supposed to have given Moses directions for the construction of the Tabernacle. The structure was to be a house constructed of a series of boards of a special wood, overlaid with gold, set on end into sockets of silver. In other words, it wasn't Saint Pete's, but it was no Alabama revival tent either. The Mormons adapted the idea for a permanent standing structure.

Right outside the Tabernacle were some more conventional office buildings. We entered one, and were led into an office by Albert. "I'll bring you something to eat and drink," he said. I was hungry and thirsty enough to settle for bread and water. A minute later Albert returned with bread and water, then left us alone.

"Damn," I said; "I was hoping for a more splendorous galley."

I walked over to a small table, and picked up the sole object on it: the Book of Mormon: Another Testament of Jesus Christ. I felt puckish and decided to tease Arlene a bit. I thought she'd pushed the envelope too much, encouraging the more talkative of our captors.

"Bet you can't remember all the books in here, Arlene."

She gave me that look of hers. "Will you bet me the next decent weapon we find?"

"Deal," I said.

"Okay," she replied, and rattled them off: "First and Second Books of Nephi, Jacob, Enos, Jarom, Omni, the Words of Mormon, Book of Mosiah, Alma, Helaman, Third and Fourth Nephi, Book of Mormon, Ether, Moroni. You're not getting out of this, Fly. I get first pick on the next piece!"

"Damn!" I said, thoroughly impressed.

"Watch what you say near a holy place."

"Don't worry about it," came a third voice. Albert had rejoined us without knocking.

"Don't you knock?" asked Arlene.

"As soon as you're no longer prisoners," he said, closing the door behind him. "I just wanted you to know that I don't think you're spies for the demons."

"We call them aliens," I said. The medieval terminology didn't bother me when Arlene and I were using it to distinguish the different kinds of monsters. It seemed very different when talking to a deeply religious perseon. These things from space could be killed. They were created by scientific means. In no way should they be confused with immortal spirits against which all the firepower in the galaxy would mean nothing.

"I understand," said Albert. "Would you mind telling me who you are and how you came to be here?"

"Won't the President ask us that?" I asked.

"Yes."

"Then why should we tell you?" asked Arlene.

"Because I don't have to be as cautious, and I'm a fellow soldier."

"So you should tell us about yourself," I said.

"In time. You don't have to tell me anything either, but you should consider it."

"Well," I said, thinking on my feet, "if we talk to one Mormon, we should probably talk to the leader."

Albert laughed. "We're not all Mormons here," he said. "Just most of us."

"Oh?" I said, unconvinced.

"Uh, *I* am," he cautioned. "Think about it. We're fighting the common enemy of mankind. We don't care if you're Mormons. We care that you can be trusted."

"Makes sense," admitted Arlene in a tone of voice so natural that I realized she'd been subtly mocking them before.

"I'm of the Church," continued Albert, "but Jerry and Nate are Jehovah's Witnesses."

"I thought they didn't fight," said Arlene, surprised.

"They are not pacifists, but neither are they of the Latter-Day Dispensations," he said as warning bells went off in my head. I prayed I could count on Arlene's promise to keep her trap shut . . . but she pressed her lips pretty tight.

"Latter-day what?"

Albert was more succinct than his friends: "They believe all the world's governments are works of the devil. They won't fight their fellow man at the command of a state. But they can fight unhuman monsters until Judgment Day."

"I get it," I said. "Draft protesters in World War Two—"

"But volunteers for this," Albert finished.

"What do you mean by, uh, 'dispensation'?"

He laughed. Apparently we'd fallen into the hands

of someone lacking in missionary zeal, for which I was grateful. "The United States Constitution was ordained by God. That's why we didn't like seeing it subverted. We never know if a governmental person is good or bad until we see where his loyalty lies. But you two made a wonderful impression on the Witnesses; I think you'll do fine with the President. If you change your mind about chatting with me, you will find me easily enough." He left us with the promise we would see the President soon.

Three hours later we were led to the office of the President of the Twelve. A clean-shaven, elderly man with pure white hair, a dark tan, and a tailored suit got up from behind a walnut desk and rested his hands on his blotter. He kept his distance. He had a judge's face, carved in stone. If we were assassins, he was giving us a clear shot at him. But Albert and Jerry continued to baby-sit, fingers on triggers.

Mexican standoff. He sized us up. We did the same to him. He reminded me of a senior colonel in the Corps, a man used to giving orders.

Finally, he coughed. "I'm the President here," he said.

"You make it sound like President of the United States," I said.

He didn't seem to mind. "Might as well be," he said, "under the circumstances. Who are you?"

We gave him name, rank, and serial number. Being a gentleman, I let Arlene go first. Then he asked the sixty-four-trillion-dollar question: "How is it you come to be here?"

Arlene laughed and let him have it: "Fly, here—that's his nickname—Fly and I single-handedly kicked the spit out of the entire Deimos division of the alien demons. They moved the Martian moon into orbit around Earth, but we cleaned their clocks."

The leader of the Mormons said, "This is a time for mighty warriors. We have many prophecies to this effect. In the Book of Alma there is a verse that I find indispensable for morale:

> "Behold, I am in my anger, and also my people; ye have sought to muder us, and we have only sought to defend ourselves."

He smiled, pausing before continuing.

> "But behold, if ye seek to destroy us more we will seek to destroy you; yea, and we will seek our land, the land of our first inheritance."

"Those words were spoken by Moroni. We must gird our loins for battle against the ultimate enemy. At such times as this even women must be used in a manner unnatural to them. Do you know how much Delta-V is required to move a *moon,* even one as small as Deimos? Why should I believe you?"

I blinked, nonplussed by the change in subject. Glancing quickly at Arlene, I saw she was controlling her reaction to the "unnatural" crack, her face impassive. *Good girl!*

"We, ah, fight the same enemy," I said.

"This is what you purport. You also claim to have hopped out of orbit and landed on your feet. Pray that we may prove both to our satisfaction. Until such time, we must be careful. If what you say is true, you will be able to demonstrate this to us on a mission. Only then, if you earn our trust, will *you"*—he pointedly stared at me, ignoring Arlene—"be allowed access to our special wisdom. The audience is over, and good luck to you."

I worried that Arlene might say something stupid

when I saw her mouth open and the danger sign of her eyebrows rising faster than any rocket. Hell, I was worried about myself. But we were ushered out of there without any disasters.

"As far as I'm concerned," said Albert, leading us back to our room, accompanied by Jerry, "you just flunked spy school."

"Huh?"

"I don't imagine a spy would concoct so ridiculous a story and annoy the President so thoroughly."

I said nothing; privately, I thought that was exactly what a spy might do. It worked, didn't it?

We felt tension leaking from the corridor, like air escaping from the dome on Deimos. At least the President was taking some kind of chance on us. He didn't realize how big a chance he'd taken talking that way to Arlene.

"We belong to the brotherhood of man," Albert said. "If you think you have problems now, just wait until people begin believing your story. Then we'll start treating you like angels!"

9

I guess they believed our story, somewhat at least. Fly and I were left alone at last when that rugged stalwart, Albert Whatever, scurried off on some errand.

Fly gestured me close. "We really should report in," he whispered in my ear.

"Report in? To whom?" A good question. If the country were as devastated as we'd been led to believe, there wasn't much of a military command structure left to report to anybody.

If . . . I saw at once where Fly was coming from.

"How much do we really know about these guys?" asked Fly, confirming my cognition. "Whose side are they on?"

"You'd have a hard time persuading me they're demon-lovers," I said.

"All right . . . . maybe. They're patriots. But are they *right?*"

Wasn't much I could say to that. Fly had a point . . . as patriotic and pro-human as these Mormons might be, they still might be wrong about the extent of the collapse. "You're saying they could be deluded by their apocalyptic religion."

He raised his brows. "Mormons aren't apocalyptic,

Arlene. I think you're confusing them with certain branches of Christianity. I'm only saying that they're pretty cut off from information . . . the whole government might look like it's collapsed from this viewpoint; but maybe if we contacted somebody somewhere else, in the Pentagon or at least an actual Marine Corps base, maybe we'd get a different picture."

"All right. Who, then?"

"Chain of command, Arlene. Who do you think we should contact?"

I'm always forgetting about the omnipresent chain. Usually, all I see are enlisted guys like me, maybe one C.O.—Weems, in our case. I'm not used to thinking of the Great Chain of Being rising above my head all the way up to the C-in-C, the President of the United States. Guess that's why Fly makes the big bucks (heh) as a noncom, while I'm just a grunt.

"Um, Major Boyd, I guess. Or the great-grandboss, Colonel Karapetian."

"Hm . . . I'm betting this is a bit above m'lord Boyd's head. I think we should take this up with God Himself: the colonel."

"I agree completely. Got the phone number?"

"Yeah, well, that's the next problem. Surely in a facility this size, there has to be a radio room somewhere, wouldn't you think?"

We did a lot of thinking over the next hour; we also did a lot of quiet, careful questioning, staying away from those obviously "under arms," questioning the less suspicious civilians instead. But what we mostly did was a lot of walking. My dogs were barking like Dobermans long before we found anything radio-roomlike.

The "compound" actually comprised a whole series of buildings, different clumps far away, and included a large portion of downtown Salt Lake City. There were other buildings and residences all around, of course; SLC is big. Well not compared to my old hometown of L.A., of course, but you get the idea.

"The compound" might include two buildings and *not* include the building in between them; it wasn't defined geographically.

However, we quickly discovered we were restricted to a small, two-block radius surrounding the Tabernacle. An electrified fence cut that central core off from the rest of the facility (and the rest of the city); guards patrolled the fence like a military base; there were even suspicious pillboxes with tiny bits of what might have been the barrels of crew-served weapons poking out, and piles of camouflaged tarps that might conceal tanks or Bradleys. And the guards were as tight about controlling what *left* the core as they were about what entered.

I saw a lump that looked suspiciously like an M-2/A-2 tank, state of the art; I turned to point it out to Fly, but he was busy staring at the tall office building at our backs. "What's that up top of that skyscraper?" he asked.

"Skyscraper? You've lived in too many small towns, Fly-boy."

"Yeah, yeah. What's up top there? That metal thing?"

"Um . . . a TV aerial."

"Are you sure? Look again."

I stared, squinting to clear up my mild astigmatism. "Huh, I see what you mean. It could be, but I'm not sure. You think it's a radio antenna, right?"

"I don't know what they're supposed to look like when they're stationary, only what they look like on the box we carry with us."

"Well, you have an urgent appointment, Fly? Let's check it out."

"Sure hope they have a working elevator," he said,

surprising me; I thought after our experiences on Deimos, he'd never want to look at another lift again.

There was an armed guard at the front entrance of the building, which was a mere fifteen stories tall . . . hardly a "skyscraper." The rear entrance was barricaded. The guard unshipped the Sig-Cow rifle he carried. "Ayren't you the two unbelievers who claim they stopped the aliens cold on Deimos?"

"That's we," I said, "Unbelievers 'R' Us."

Fly hushed me. He always claims I make things worse in any confrontational situation, but I just don't see it.

"The President sent us on an inspection tour," said Fly with the sort of easy, confident lying I admired so much but could never pull off. "Supposed to 'familiarize' ourselves with your SOPs." He rolled his eyes; you could hear the quotation marks around *familiarize.* "As if we haven't had enough military procedures for a lifetime!"

The guard shook his head, instantly sympathetic. "Ain't it the truth? Few weeks ago, you know what I was? I was a cook at the Elephant Grill, you know, up at Third? So what do they make me when the war breaks out? A sentry!"

"You know this building well?"

"Well, I should! My fiancée worked here. Before the war."

"Look, can you come along with us, show us the place? I come from a small town, and we don't have buildings this size. You're not stuck as the only guard, are you?" There were no other guards in sight; I'm sure Fly noticed that as well as I.

" 'Fraid so, Corporal."

"Fly. Fly Taggart."

"I'm afraid so, Fly. I can't leave. Look, you can't get lost. It's just a big, tall square. See the Tabernacle there? Anytime you get lost, just walk to the windows and walk around until you see the Tabernacle. You can't miss it."

"You sure it'll be okay?"

"You can't miss it. No problemo."

"Look, if I get in trouble, is there a phone I can call down here on?"

"Sure, use the black phone near the elevator, the one with no buttons. Just pick it up; it'll ring here."

"Thanks. This way? The elevators over here?"

The helpful sentry showed us how to get to the elevators. They were actually behind some partitions; we might not have found them . . . for several minutes.

We climbed aboard, and Fly said in a normal speaking voice, "Don't trust these elevators. May as well start at the top and walk down, floor by floor, familiarizing ourselves with the procedures. Then we can report back to the President and tell him where we'd do the most good."

To me, he used hand signals: *Start top; find radio; broadcast report.*

The antenna was atop the roof, of course; but that didn't mean that's where hte radio room would be. We wandered around every floor, trying to look official. Early on, I found a clipboard hanging on a peg in the rooftop janitor's shed, where they kept all the window-washing stuff. Fly took the clipboard and made a point of officiously writing down reports on everybody in every office, with me trailing along behind looking like his assistant.

It worked; people tensed up, stopped talking, worked diligently, and not a one confronted us to ask us who the hell we were. It helped that Fly had been inventory control officer for a few months. He stirred them up and made them sweat.

Finally, twelve floors down from the top, we found the damned radio room. Two operators, both civilians. One had a pistol; we were unarmed, of course.

Fly strode in like Gunnery Sergeant Goforth on the inspection warpath. "On your feet," he barked; the startled operators stared for a second, then leapt to their feet and stood at a bad imitation of attention. "Classified message traffic from the President," he snarled. "Take a hike."

"Sir, we're not supposed to—"

"*Sir?* Do you see these?" He angrily pointed at his stripes. "Do I look like a God-damned pansy-waist gut-sucking ass-kissing four-eyed college-boy *officer* to you?"

"No sir! No—ah—"

Fly leaned close, playing drill instructor. "Try COR-POR-AL, boy. Next time you open that *hole* of yours, first word out better be *Corporal Taggart.*"

"C-C-Corporal Taggart, sir! I mean, Corporal Taggart, we're not supposed to leave."

"Did you hear what type of message traffic I said this was?"

"Classified? Sir—Corporal!—we're fully cleared for all levels of classification."

"Do I know that, boy? You got some paper you can show me?"

"No, not on me."

"Then take a hike, dickhead. Go back and get something from your C.O. We'll wait right here."

The man dithered, looking back and forth at the door, the equipment, and his partner, a small, frail-looking man who pointedly looked away, saying *No, way, bud, this is your call.* "All right. You won't touch anything while I'm gone, will you?"

"Scout's honor," sneered Fly. Was he ever a Boy Scout? I couldn't remember.

The man slid sideways past Fly and almost backed into me. I glared daggers at him and he split. After a couple of seconds Fly turned to the mousy companion. "What're *you* still doing here? Get after your partner!"

Meekly, the man turned and darted out of the room.

"Fly, what's going to happen when they get across the street and find out there's no message traffic from the President?"

"Well, we'd better hurry, A.S., so we're done before they get back!"

Fortunately, they'd left the equipment on, because I had no idea how to *turn* it on. It was some new, ultramodern civilian stuff I'd never seen before. I found a keypad next to a small LED display. At the moment, it showed the frequency for Guard channel, plus another freak above that.

I tapped at the keypad; they hadn't locked it out, thank God. I typed the freak for North Marine Corps Air Base, office of the SubCincMarsCom, Colonel George Karapetian. It was no great trick remembering it; I was the radioman for Major Boyd when we were stationed on Deimos on TDS to the Navy.

I wandered all over the band from one side to the other, looking for the carrier. Finally, I found it; it was weak and intermittent, as if the repeaters were blown and I was picking up the source itself. But I boosted the gain, and we were able to pick out the words from behind the snow.

I engaged the standard CD encrypter, digitally adding the signal to a CD of random noise from background radiation; they had an identical disk at North—if we were lucky, they'd figure out that the signal was scrambled and pull their encryption online.

"Corporal Fly Taggart, commanding officer of Fox Company, Fourth Battalion, 223rd Light Drop Division, to SubCincMarsCom, come in, Colonel Karapetian."

Fly broadcast the message over and over, and I started to get nervous . . . both about the time and about the lack of response. Finally, a voice sputtered into life on the line. I recognized it; it was the colonel himself, not some enlisted puke.

"Fox, connect me to Lieutenant Weems. Fourth Battalion, over."

"Fourth Battalion, Weems is dead; I am in command of Fox."

"Who is this?"

"Corporal Taggart, sir."

"Corporal, give me a full report. Over."

Fly gave the colonel the verbal cook's tour of everything that had happened to us in the past few weeks. When he finished, Karapetian was quiet for so long, I thought we'd lost the carrier.

"I understand," he said. "Now where the hell are you? Can you get back here, like yesterday?"

"We're at a resistance center in Salt Lake City," Fly said. Suddenly, I got an uneasy feeling in my stomach; should we be spilling this much intel, even to the sub-Commander in Chief of the Mars Command?

"Use rail transport," ordered Karapetian. "Get your butts to Pendleton as fast as you can. We've got to talk face-to-face about this. Got that, Corporal?"

"Aye, sir."

"Good. Then I'll expect you tomorrow at—"

With a loud thunk, the entire system died. All the dials, all the diodes, all the cool flashing lights.

I looked over my shoulder; Albert towered over us, his face set in a mask of concrete. On one side stood our friendly guard from the entrance; on the other was the radio tech Fly had bullied, holding a remote-control power switch in his hands.

I gasped; framed in the light, Albert looked like he had a halo.

"I'm afraid you're going to have to come with me," Albert said.

"Where?" I asked.

"To the President. Only he can decide cases of high treason against the Army of God and Man United."

10

With a heavy heart, I brought our two miscreant warriors to the President of the Twelve. I tried to keep angry thoughts from my mind; judgment and vengeance are the Lord's prerogatives, not ours.

Besides, I genuinely liked Fly Taggart, and I even believed his wild story about fighting the alien demons on Phobos and Deimos. And Miss Sanders, now . . .

No, that's wrong. I had no right; I didn't even know her.

I brought them into the chamber of justice to find the President and his mast already seated. He wore a suit; I sighed a hearty prayer of thanksgiving to the Lord that this was to be mast, not a court-martial; the President would have worn his robe for the latter.

"Sit," I commanded, putting a heavy hand on each prisoner's shoulder and pushing him into the waiting chair.

"Who speaks for the outsiders?" asked Bishop Wilston. He was a stickler for legalities.

"They can speak for themselves," said the President, "this isn't a formal trial. I just want to find out what the devil happened—and to find out whether the devil himself was responsible."

"Or just the imp of stupidity," I said. The President glared at me; but I learned my manners under his predecessor, who would listen to even the youngest child with a mind to speak. This new fellow was from out of state and a personal mentor of our old President, may he rest in peace.

"You're rude," said the President, "but you may be right. Corporal Taggart, as the responsible NCO, what on Earth possessed you to start broadcasting all over the globe from our radio room?"

"Well, um . . ." Fly looked distinctly pink. "It seemed like a good idea at the time."

"Why are you so flipping surprised?" demanded the woman. "Why *shouldn't* we report to our C.O.? We just got back from a mission. What the hell did you expect?"

For a moment I thought the President was going to burst a blood vessel. We all turned in annoyance to Fly; couldn't he control his woman? His team member?

He was not a stupid man; he spoke up quickly: "Arlene is tired, upset—you know how women get." Now it was Arlene's turn to turn angry-red, opening and closing her mouth like she wanted to say something devastating but couldn't even find the words. Wisely, she pressed her lips together and said nothing.

A soft answer turneth away wrath, says the proverb;

or again, *Even a fool, when he holdeth his peace, is counted wise.* The President was mollified and chose to take the question seriously.

"Miss Sanders—"

"Private Sanders, if you will," she said, voice betraying the seething emotion within. Her red hair flamed like a burning house, setting off her green eyes.

"Private Sanders, the 'why' is because the entire military structure of the erstwhile United States, from top to bottom, has been co-opted by the demons. Our former government has capitulated . . . they *surrendered,* to put it bluntly, two weeks ago."

"Oh, really! Maybe everybody but the Marines. Semper fidel—"

"Even the Marines," said the President softly. The sudden change from loud and angry to quiet and cold lent him an air of authority, as was befitting. I must admit, the man had the mark of divine awe; the Lord definitely moved through the President, when he let Him.

"Do you two know what you've done?" asked the bishop. "Even the broadcast itself might have been traced. But to actually tell the forces of darkness where we are . . . ! That passes understanding."

"Look, maybe I shouldn't have done that. But they must already have known this was a pocket of resistance."

Don't dig yourself a deeper grave, Fly, I thought urgently. Outwardly, I kept my face impassive; no need to draw the judges' attention to the attempt at blame-shifting.

"But Corporal," said the President, voice at its quietest and most dangerous, "they did not know that *you* were here. If you still maintain that you and your—your comrade aborted the division invading through Deimos, don't you think you might have incurred a special wrath, a wrath now transferred to us? Perhaps they consider you Demonic Enemy Number One. Did that cross your mind?"

Fly remained silent. Good man. So did Arlene.

I stared at the woman; she was not at all bad-looking, not what I would expect of a female Marine. I had never served with one in my three years of active duty service; she looked tough, but not like an American Gladiator.

In fact, the swell of her breasts and hips was quite womanly; she would be a sturdy woman, well able to bear many children and face the rigors of life under siege. I could almost see her standing in a doorway, babe in arms . . . or lying bare on the bed, awaiting me—

Ow! My conscience hammered on my head. *What are you DOING, you godless sinner!* Here I was, in the presence of the representative of Jesus Christ Himself, and I was mentally undressing this woman!

> Get thee behind me, Satan: thou art an offense to me: for thou savorest not the things that be of God, but those that be of men.

I concentrated on verses from the Bible and the Book of Mormon, mentally reciting them so quickly I lost all track of the trial and Miss Sanders.

When I blinked back, Fly and Arlene looked chastened, humble. They clearly repented of their foolish act and had found their way back to friendship with God. Pride and Arrogance were banished—well, for the moment.

The President sighed heavily. "Go and be stupid no more. And prepare for an attack, for surely one arrives within an hour or two." He nodded to the bishop, who, as General of the Armies of the Lord, had primary responsibility for readying our defenses.

I already knew my station: Jerry and I manned the dike west of the city, along with two thousand other stalwarts.

I had an idea. "Mr. President," I called. He turned back, pausing at the door. "Sir, I'd like to suggest that Taggart and Sanders be assigned to the defense alongside me."

He stared at me, and I squirmed. "Any particular reason? They've already had their chance and botched it."

"That, sir, is the reason. Let them atone for their mistake. They may have cost the lives of righteous men; let them at least stand beside those men and put their own lives on the line. Let them be at peace."

I glanced at Fly and Miss Sanders, and was tremendously relieved to see a grateful look on their faces. I was right about them: stupid, maybe; but they had honor, and they probably felt like children whose rough play accidentally killed the pet dog. I sure would.

The President was a hard man; but he was a just man—else the Lord would not have allowed him to serve as President of the Twelve; the Father has His ways of making His pleasure known. He shook his head, but said, "I think you're too forgiving a man, Albert; but you know them better than I ever could. Take them, if your C.O. approves."

The bishop was smiling, though not in a friendly way. "He'll approve," he prophesied.

Less than half an hour later we were at the line. I took care to see that both Fly and Miss Sanders were armed, so they would know we still extended our trust. It was part of the healing process. And the President's prophecy came true, albeit a little late: in fact, it took the forces of darkness two hours to mass and attack, not one.

Squinting into the distance, I saw first a column of

dust at the ragged edge of vision. We watched for several minutes before even hearing the sound; you can see a long, long way in the Utah desert, where ten miles seems like one. The dust came from a column of Bradley Fighting Vehicles, the same type in which I had trained as a gunner before going to sniper school. Thank the Lord they hadn't yet had time to scrounge any M-2 tanks!

As they roared up, we surprised them: the antitank batteries opened up at two klicks. In the still air, the artillery captains had the eyes of angels; they dropped the first load of ordnance directly on the advancing line. The laser spotter-scopes helped.

Once the troops knew they were not up against cowed, frightened refugees, they separated and advanced while evading. I took a risk, standing atop the dike and focusing through binoculars mounted on a pole. It was the BATF in the vanguard, as usual, backed up by FBI shock troops. Reporting the battle order over my encrypted radio, I saw the gold flag of the IRS and realized we would doubtless have to face flamethrowers and chemical-biological warfare shells. The bastards. Regular Army filled in the gaps and supplied most of the grunts—cannon fodder, as we called them.

They brought a contingent of brownies and baphomets, but no molochs, praise God. Probably didn't have any nearby. But I'd bet my last bullet there'd be molochs and shelobs aplenty before the week was out.

There were a few of the unclean undead, but most of the soldiers, horribly enough, appeared to be living allies of the demons. I hoped to spare Fly that knowledge, that our own species would willingly cooperate in the subjugation of men to demons from another star; but maybe it was better he find out now.

I guess he realized how wrong he was . . . but it was a horrible way to find out.

Contact was established a quarter hour later, on the north side of Salt Lake City. Within a few minutes battle was joined in my quadrant as well.

Fly and Arlene acquitted themselves admirably; they were no cowards! I especially enjoyed watching the girl in combat, too busy and scared even to worry whether my interest was righteous or sinful. She loped forward to the out perimeter and spotted for the mortars; my heart was in my throat—if they spotted *her,* that beautiful body would be blown to tiny pieces in seconds.

Bombs and shells exploded left and right, but our positions were secure; except for the occasional lucky shot, the evil ones hit only stragglers. But I was very glad for my earplugs; Fly had refused a pair, but Arlene took them.

We threw back the initial blitzkrieg; the demons simply weren't prepared for that savage a level of resistance. They'd probably never encountered it before. Like the heroic Jews of the Warsaw Ghetto, who stood up to the Nazi butchers, without despair, we forced the bastards back and back, until at last they withdrew and formed a circle around our force, three klicks back—out of range, they thought.

After two more hours passed without movement, Arlene and Fly took a chance and returned to me.

They looked shaken. I wanted to put my arm around Corporal Taggart, cheer him up; how could he have known? But the gesture would not have been appreciated. He stepped across the dead bodies of righteous men to come to me; he knew what he had done, and the last soul to forgive him would be himself. He would probably carry guilt to his grave, unless he found a minister to unburden himself.

I had the vague thought that he was a Catholic. I would never condone such a perversion of the teachings of Christ—in normal times; but in this world, even to call oneself a Christian is a courageous step. I hoped he would find a priest and confess; otherwise, he might never give himself absolution.

"We seemed to have scored a temporary stalemate," he said, sounding defeated.

"We kicked ass!" argued Arlene.

"You're both right," I said, ever the diplomat.

"But how long can we hold out?" asked Fly. "A few days? A week? Two weeks? Eventually they'll get reinforcements and overrun us." He didn't add *and all because of me,* but I could tell he thought it.

"Eventually," I agreed. "In about five or six *years.*"

"Years? What the hell do you mean?"

I winked. "We've been preparing for this sort of war for a long time, my friend . . . we just never realized we'd be fighting literal demons!"

"Jesus . . . who were you expecting to fight?"

The blasphemy angered me, but I let it slide. He was an unbeliever and might not even realize what he'd said. "Exactly who we are fighting; the forces of Mammon. We'd hoped to avert the crisis by engaging in the world, steering it toward the righteousness of the Constitution ordained by God Himself in 1787. We sent our members out into the world, joined the Army, the FBI, the Washington power structure. We increased our numbers within the IRS and even within NASA. But in the end, all that effort bought us only advance warning and some spies and saboteurs within the enemy ranks."

Fly shook his head, dazed. He said nothing.

"Now we are the last stronghold in the continental United States. There is but one major enclave left on the planet for humans and the godly; there centers the Resistance."

"Where?"

I chuckled. "Even if I knew, Fly, I wouldn't tell

you. Your interest rate on keeping secrets isn't very high right now."

He smiled sardonically. "I guess I wouldn't tell you either, if you'd just done what we did. What *I* did."

"We," corrected Arlene. "You were right the first time. I stood right beside you and helped you report to Karapetian."

He shrugged, neither confirming nor denying.

"Are there plans to get to the Resistance?"

"If there are, we haven't executed them yet. We can send brief messages—too quick to triangulate or decrypt. But we can't send people."

"Why not?"

"There is some sort of energy barrier that prevents us from leaving the continent . . . and at times, even from leaving an urban center. Los Angeles has one; you cannot fly from L.A. to anywhere else unless the demons drop the wall—which they do only for their own, of course."

"But if you go around the barrier?"

"We've tried; we can't find an edge. It seems to be everywhere. What we need to do is find the source or the control center and *shut it off.* At least long enough to get our people out, join up with the Resistance. Otherwise, eventually, we *will* fall; we have years worth of food and medicine, but not decades worth. And after a while they will mass enough troops against us to overrun us in any case.

"Worst-case scenario, you two, we lose this city after a four-month siege. That's if they throw everything in the world at us."

"Are you kidding?" demanded an incredulous Arlene. "What about missiles? Nuclear bombs dropped from airplanes?"

"Our agents were heavily involved in the Strategic Defense Initiative . . . remember?" I winked. "And we have anti-air defenses too. We're not worried about nukes; we're more worried about tanks and undead soldiers. None of our defenses were erected with molochs in mind."

"Molochs?"

"What you called steam-demons, I believe."

Suddenly, the radio phone buzzed. The radioman answered, listened for a moment, saying a string of "yessirs." He turned to me. "Albert, the President wants to see your charges."

"Now?"

"Tonight. The captain says he has a mission for them . . . something to prove themselves after their incompetence . . . no offense, guys; I'm just quoting."

"None taken," said Arlene, highly offended. My eyes began to dwell longingly on her curves and swells again, and I brutally forced my gaze to the dead and wounded littering the battlefield . . . even *their* dead. The corpsmen were already busy, collecting the casualties for transportation to hospital.

"Got a time?" I asked.

"Eighteen hundred," said the radioman. I didn't know his name, even though he knew mine; it made me uncomfortable.

I nodded. "Okay, you heard the man. Fly, Arlene, start polishing your brass. We've got three hours before your mission briefing. And guys?"

They waited expectantly.

"Try not to hose it up. This time."

Arlene Sanders flipped me the finger; but Fly just looked down at his boots, brushing the mud off with his hands.

11

Arlene, Albert, and I sat in our little room like old friends. "Albert, you were right," I said. "We should have asked you before charging off to report to Karapetian."

"The fact that you had to sneak around and concoct an absurd fairy tale should have told you something," he said, smiling faintly. I caught Arlene looking at him with an interest I hadn't seen in her eyes since she first began getting close to old Dodd. Could she . . . ?

Nah; that was a silly thought. Not with how she felt about religion in general—and Mormons in particular. Not after her brother.

She spoke, her voice tight and controlled. "Albert, can you tell us what on Earth happened? I mean here on Earth."

"Gladly," said Albert.

Evidently, even with only half an invasion force, the urban areas of Earth had fallen quickly. Albert suspected that high-ranking U.S. government officials and their counterparts in other governments, the federal and state agencies and even the services themselves—the U.S. Marine Corps!—actually *collaborated* with the aliens.

I guess there wasn't much argument I could make . . . not after seeing *living human beings* on the march against us in the siege. If I cared to climb up to the roof, I could see them still. I didn't care to.

The monsters promised a peaceful occupation and promised each collaborator that his own government would be given the top command slot. A tried and true approach, with plenty of terrestrial examples: it worked for Hitler and Stalin; now it worked for a bunch of plug-uglies from beyond the planets.

Naturally, the aliens screwed the traitors, killing hundreds of millions . . . utterly destroying Washington, D.C., and demolishing much of New York, Paris, Moscow, and Beijing. The Mormons knew the invaders were really serious when all the stock exchanges were wiped out in two hours.

"They control all the big cities now," Albert reported.

"So at least some things will feel the same," said Arlene. Our newfound friend laughed uproariously. He was taking to Arlene's morbid brand of humor.

"What's the Resistance like?" she asked, hanging on his every word. I started to resent her interest. Maybe I was only her "big brother," but shouldn't that count for something?

Albert turned up his hands. "How should I know? We know only that they exist, and they have a lot of science types, techies. They're working on stuff all the time . . . but so far, they haven't been able to shut off the energy wall from outside—and the only way to get to it from the inside is to mount an assault . . . or infiltrate."

"Maybe that's what the President wants us to do," I speculated; I don't think Albert had any more idea than I, though.

Jerry joined us again; now he too was in a dark suit, though still heavily armed with a Browning Automatic Rifle. It reminded me of a "Family" war between Mafia soldiers. I began to feel distinctly underdressed.

"What about the countryside?" I asked.

Albert nodded and answered: "That's the local resistance, such as it is. At least we are not alone. For a little longer, at least."

Jerry volunteered a comment: "They seem more interested in taking slaves from the rural areas than conquering the territory."

Albert concurred: "It gives us a fighting chance, they being so slow expanding their pale."

"What is this 'special wisdom' the President offered to share before the attack?" I asked. "Can you give us a hint?"

Albert and Jerry exchanged the look of comrades in arms. "Don't worry about it," said Albert. "He's less worried about what you know than what you see."

Albert insisted that Arlene and I rest and bathe. The only choice offered was a cold shower, but that was fine with us. We found clean clothes.

Then we got the "fifty-cent-tour" from Albert, the tour that wouldn't get him in trouble.

Albert took us down to the hidden catacombs they'd constructed beneath the Tabernacle complex. The trip began with an elevator ride. The metal was shiny and new. Everything was air-conditioned. The doors slid open to reveal something out of the latest James Bond movie. But somehow I was not surprised at the vast complex they had constructed. We walked under a gigantic V arch to bear witness to dozens of miles of secret shelters. We were not taken behind the locked doors to see the contents, but Albert told us they had millions of rounds of ammunition, stores, heavy military equipment, a whole factory, and more. It was survivalist heaven.

"I wonder what kind of heavy equipment?" Arlene whispered in my ear.

"Tanks and Humvees," I whispered back. "The rest when he trusts us."

"I'm sure he'll trust us plenty after we've died for the cause," she concluded.

"Can't hardly blame him." I could kick myself for such self-pity, but I couldn't get my stupidity out of my mind.

We took a turn in the passageway and reached another elevator marked for five more levels down. "Jesus!" said Arlene, followed by: "Sorry, Albert."

He only shook his head. Even Albert was probably cutting her some slack for being female. Arlene could always sense a patronizing attitude, but she had too much class to throw it back at someone working so hard to play fair with her.

"Why would you have all this?" she asked.

He didn't hesitate in answering, "To equalize our relations with the IRS."

"Man, all I had was Melrose Larry Green, CPA," marveled Arlene.

"I'll let both of you in on something," he said, "because it hardly matters today. All you saw today were ground troops; but did you know the IRS had its own 'Delta Force,' the Special Revenue Collection Division?"

We shook our heads, but once again I wasn't really surprised. "In case of another Whiskey Rebellion?" I guessed.

"An interesting way of putting it," he said, and continued: "They had an infantry division, two armored cav regiments, a hidden fast-attack submarine, a heavy bomber wing, and from what I hear, a carrier battle group."

Somebody whistled. It was Yours Truly. If the Mormons knew about that, could they have wound up with some of it? This was an obvious thought, and would make full use of an installation this size; but I wasn't going to ask. Arlene and I were lucky to be learning this much.

"How'd they finance it?" I asked.

"The IRS can finance anything?" suggested Arlene, as if a student in school.

"Well, even *they* had to cover their tracks," said Albert. "Jerry thinks they hid the military buildup inside the fictitious budget deficit. Unfortunately, the Special Revenue Collection Division was seized by the demons."

"Aliens," Arlene corrected, almost unconsciously.

"Whatever."

This seemed a good moment to clear up the nomenclature: "Actually, Albert, we named the different kinds of aliens to keep them separate. We call the dumb pink ones the demons."

"How did the aliens get their claws on all that IRS equipment?" Arlene asked.

"Hm. Because Internal Revenue was the very first group to sell out Earth," he answered. This was definitely *not* a day of surprises.

"Do we get to ride on the other elevator?" I asked.

"Later," he said. "And I'm sorry I can't show you behind the doors."

"No, you've been great, Albert," said Arlene. I could tell she was impressed for real, no joke. This was rare. "Why don't you tell us about your checkered military past?"

"That's next on the agenda," he said, "and the President will want to brief you on the mission, if he's picked it yet."

We took the elevator back up to face the boss. I promised myself that no matter how much I wanted to do it, I wouldn't say, "Howdy, pardner."

Three more bodyguards surrounded the President. These guys didn't seem friendly like Albert or Jerry. He led us to the auxiliary command center (I supposed the real command center was at the bottom level of the complex), where we learned that the nearest nerve center of the alien invasion was Los Angeles. The monsters had set up their ultra-advanced computer services and war technology center near the HOLLYWOOD sign. I didn't want to ask who sold out humanity there. I was afraid to find out.

The President didn't waste time coming to the point: "Two highly trained Marines who fought the enemy to a standstill in space; then floated down out of orbit, would be better qualified to lead a certain mission we have in mind than our own people. This is assuming that we haven't been subject to a certain degree of exaggeration. A man and a woman alone could only be expected to do so much against hundreds of the enemy."

Arlene was behaving herself, but it dawned on me that I hadn't made any promises to keep my mouth shut. This wasn't about religion. This was about doubting our word after we'd swum through a world of hurt to get this far.

I reminded myself that we needed this man; I reminded myself we'd already hosed the job . . . but stupidity had nothing to do with dishonor!

"If the two of you could get to Los Angeles," the leader continued, "and make it into the computer system, download full specs on their most basic technology, and get it back to the United States War Technology Center, it would aid our defense immeasurably."

"What's that?" I asked.

"The War Tech Center was created a few weeks ago, hidden—west of here. You'll be told where when the need arises. When you get the download."

I thought for a moment. It couldn't be as far as Japan or China; Beijing and Tokyo were both destroyed. He must mean Hawaii.

I couldn't resist being a smart-ass; the President

brought that out in people. "It's either Wheeler AFB, Kaneohe Bay Marine Corps Air Station, or Barber's Point Naval Air Station, all on Oahu," I declared. "Do I win anything?"

"I love Hawaii!" said Arlene. "Great weather. Hardly any humidity."

"But those prices," I answered.

It was a trivial little protest against the man's pomposity and skepticism, but it made us feel a whole lot better.

"Please," said the President, his face turning positively florid. "As I was saying, if you can penetrate the enemy stronghold and bring the specs to the U.S. technology center, there are scientists there who can do something with it. We have refugees from ARPA, the Lockheed 'skunk works,' NASA, MacDAC, hackers from many places." It sounded to me like the President of the Twelve had been boning up on other subjects besides theology . . . and finance. "Has Albert told you about the force field?"

"He said something about an energy wall."

"You have to find a way to shut it off . . . otherwise, you're not going anywhere. You get offshore about fifteen miles, then call an encrypted message in. We'll vector you to the War Technology Center."

"If we can pull this off," said Arlene in her serious, engineer's tone of voice, "and a computer expert can dehack the alien technology, we might come up with shields against them. Defenses, something."

"The first problem is to crack Los Angeles," said the President.

"Then we're your best bet," I said. "After Phobos and Deimos, how bad can L.A. be?" Even at the time, this sounded like famous last words.

"Yes, my point exactly," he agreed languidly, still frosted; "how much simpler this would *have* to be than the Deimos situation." He paused long enough to annoy us again. "This is more than a two-man operation." Translation: we needed keepers. Well, that was all right with me. "You'll be infiltrating, so we're not talking about a strike force here."

"Stealth mission," said Arlene.

"Two more people would be about right," I said.

The President's first choice was excellent. Albert wanted to go. "By way of apology for being the one to turn you in," he said, holding out his big paw of a hand. I took it gingerly; he hardly had anything to apologize for. He winked.

"If you'd been one fraction less of a hard-ass, I wouldn't want you on this mission anyway."

"This is probably a good time to tell you about Albert's record," said the President. "He was a PFC in the Marine Corps, I'm sure you'll be pleased to hear. Honorably discharged. He won a medal for his MOS." Military operational specialty.

"Which was?" I asked Albert, eye-to-eye.

"A sniper, Corporal," he answered. "Bronze star, Colombia campaign. Drug wars."

"Sniper school?"

"Of course."

"God bless," said Arlene.

Albert was fine; we both dug Albert. Couldn't say the same about the second choice, who Nate ushered into the ops room: she looked like a fourteen-year-old girl in T-shirt, jeans, and dirty sneakers.

"Fly," Arlene said, staring, "does my promise apply to bitching about personnel decisions?"

"Say your piece."

She shook her head in incredulity. "I'd never have expected this kind of crap from this bunch of sexist—"

"Uh, no offense," I mumbled to the President,

feeling pretty lame. My face flushed red-hot, as if I'd just taken niacin.

He chose to ignore the editorial. "I hate sending her. Unfortunately, she's the best qualified."

Arlene stared at the girl, a foxy little item ready to stare back. "I never thought I'd say these words," Arlene began, "but there's a first time for everything. Honey—"

"My name is Jill," she said defiantly.

"Okay, Jill. Listen closely. Please don't take offense, but this is no job for a girl."

"I *have* to go," she said. "Live with it."

"Honey, I don't want to *die* with it."

"What's this joke?" I demanded.

"I told you. She's the best, uh, hacker, I think it is, that we've got. But you deserve an explanation." He turned to her and asked, "Do you mind if I tell them?" She shrugged. He went on: "I apologize for her sullen attitude."

I don't know about Arlene, but I didn't see anything sullen about the kid. The President never seemed to look directly at her but kind of sideways.

"Back in the life, before her family moved here and accepted the faith, Jill was arrested twice for breaking into computer systems. She served six months in a juvenile detention center in Ojai; then her parents joined the Church and moved here."

All the time he was talking, he kept sneaking glances out of the corner of his eye. He seemed to be looking at the top of her head. She was pretending not to be interested but hung on every word.

"Jill was embarrassed and ashamed of her arrest and conviction," the President said very slowly, as if coaching, watching her all the time. "She was locked up with a girl who was a prostitute and drug dealer—"

"She didn't want to be a junkie-hooker," said Jill, speaking about herself in the third person.

The President pretended not to hear. "She still loves computers, but wants to be a security person now." He took a breath, then concluded, "The aliens killed her parents, and only missed her because she was covered with blood and they assumed she was dead. She was frightened by the aliens, of course—"

"I hate them," she piped in. "I want them all dead."

"Good girl," said Arlene, half won over.

The Mormon leader approached Jill but was careful not to touch her. At least he finally looked at her. "You don't like your former hacker buddies, do you?" he asked.

"I hate them."

"Why?"

She was uncomfortable about talking but couldn't keep the words from spilling out. "Because they don't care about what happens to anyone else. They don't give a rat's ass if they hack a hospital computer and destroy a patient's records, by accident, or as a joke."

"Some joke," said Arlene.

"They'd only be upset if they did a sloppy job," the girl replied, her voice monotonous. "They suck."

"God bless you, Jill," said the President. "And you know what the aliens are?"

Jill sure did. "A million times worse. I've got to kill them all."

Mother Mary, a regular little parrot! Did the President write the script out for her? I wondered. Or was she just adept at ad-libbing what he wanted to hear, what would get her on the job?

"Don't you think you should leave the killing to Albert and this other man?" asked the President.

"That does it," said Arlene, hackles smacking the ceiling.

"I'm sorry, but there's no alternative to taking her along," said the President.

"That's not what I meant!" Arlene gave me her special look. I sighed, but didn't shake my head or give her the shut-up signal. I'd had about all of the President I could take.

"Mr. President," she began, speaking slowly as if to a child—I realized we still didn't know his name—"I respect your beliefs, even though I don't hold them myself. But we are in a *situation* where every able-bodied individual must do his or *her* best. There are armed women outside."

"Yes," he answered. "Adult women."

Arlene turned to Jill. "I apologize for doubting you," she said. "I think you'll do fine." She glared back at the President, who shook his head sadly.

I smiled, suddenly realizing we'd been had: he had put on the whole "Mormon patriarch" act just to get us to accept a little girl as a teammate! It was masterful . . . and I didn't say a word to Arlene. Let her keep her illusions.

"If you succeed," concluded the President, "you will have redeemed yourself thrice over."

"And if we fail?"

"You'll be dead. Or undead. Either way, you'll never have to think about your error again."

Gee. Thanks a lump.

"What weapon do you have?" Arlene asked Jill. The fourteen-year-old picked up a slim box from the table; took me a moment to recognize it as a CompMac "Big Punk" ultramicro with a radio-telemetry port. That was some nice equipment; did she come with it, or did the President hijack it for her?

"You'll train her in the use of firearms," the President said, turned on his heel and walked away.

"I've fired guns before," said Jill.

Arlene touched the girl on the shoulder. Jill didn't pull away. Arlene didn't talk down to her. In a casual tone she asked, "Do you think there might be some pointers I could give you, hon?"

The fourteen-year-old smiled for the first time. She didn't answer right away. Then she said in a firm voice, "Want some pizza?"

Now that she mentioned it, my mouth began to salivate.

12

I took my cue from Arlene and reluctantly accepted the kid. The Mormon leader guaranteed the girl's bona fides. Given the way he felt about the female of the species, if he wanted Jill on this mission that badly, that was good enough for me.

"Welcome aboard," I said, approaching Jill and putting out my hand. I didn't expect anything, but she surprised me by shaking hands and smiling. Smart kid. She knew when she'd won a victory.

"Thanks." Jill sized each of us up, letting her glance stay on me a little longer—not exactly pleased with the effect, I noticed. "I won't let you down," she said to all of us.

"How do you know?" asked Albert, but he wasn't being belligerent about it.

"Yeah," said Jill, not losing a beat. "They talk that way around here. I won't get anybody killed on purpose."

Arlene bent down and patted Jill on the head. The girl didn't pull away, but acted surprised. Affection was something new in her experience. I hoped she would live long enough to experience a lot more of it. But I didn't kid myself: once we entered Los Angeles, the mission was everything, and we were all expendable. It had been that way since the first monster came through the Gate on Phobos.

"Come on," said Arlene, taking Jill by the hand. "Your training starts now."

Jerry had stayed with us after the boss sauntered off. "There might not be time for that," he said. He didn't say it as if he liked it. So far, the only person I'd met who impressed me as something of a jerk was the leader, and even he was no fool.

Arlene kept her voice even and calm. "We'll *make* time," she said. "Training is not a luxury."

Looking at the man's face, I could see that he didn't like arguing with facts. He shrugged and didn't say another word.

"How about it, Albert?" I asked the other member of our team. "What kind of time do we have?"

"Plenty," he said. "I've seen Jill shoot. She'll do fine."

"Do I get a gun of my own?" asked Jill.

"Does she?" Arlene asked Albert.

"Sure as shootin'," he said, letting a moment pass before we responded to his wordplay. He enjoyed the double take.

We went to an aboveground arsenal. Seeing what they kept up top made me more anxious to see behind those doors downstairs. As it was, they wouldn't notice the absence of Jill's weapon of choice, though it was a little strange seeing the fourteen-year-old holding an AR-19 like she was used to it.

Jill noticed my expression. "We need all the firepower we can get," she said.

"You're right. Let's see what you can do with it." And thank God she didn't have her heart set on an AK-47. The kick would knock her on her butt. At least the AR-19 was a small enough caliber.

There were plenty of places to shoot. We went to a makeshift range where someone had gotten hold of old monster movie posters. Jill chose one already pretty badly shot up: a horns-and-tail demon from an old British movie. It looked a lot like a hell-prince. One of the horns was shot out, but the other was still intact.

"I'll take the bone on his head," she announced. She missed with the first burst, pulling up and to the right; but she nearly shredded the target anyway.

Arlene went over and whispered something in her ear. Jill smiled and tried again. This time the bursts were shorter and stayed on target. The demon's second horn was history.

"What did you tell her?" I asked Arlene. I always appreciate a few well-chosen words.

"Girl talk," she said, arching her dark eyebrows.

"Kind of a shame to destroy these collector's items," I observed when we ran out of ammo.

"No problem," said Albert. "We have hundreds of these. The President used to visit the church in Hollywood, and we have a lot of contacts."

"How did I do?" asked Jill, bringing us back to the original point of the exercise.

"I thought I'd need to teach you something," said Arlene. "Guess you're mostly ready. Mostly." The day was shaping up nicely. We could do a whole lot worse than Jill.

I was still in a good mood when we had dinner with the President that night. They set a good table, and he boasted how they could keep this up for a long time.

After dinner, Jill toddled off to bed in the female-teens quarter. Albert wanted to spend time with an older woman we'd been informed was an aunt, and I managed to get Arlene alone in the presidential garden.

Although night had fallen, the security lights in the garden were bright, thanks to the generators of our hosts. I saw Arlene frowning in thought. "Albert may have an extra mission," she said, "scouting out new converts for the Church."

I laughed. "Hey, don't make it sound so sinister. We should ask any survivors to join us, male or female."

"Unless they've gone insane," she said, "and there are parts of Los Angeles where it would be difficult to know."

"Well, I'm glad we have Albert and Jill with us."

She brightened. "Me too. That young lady impresses the hell out of me. Maybe she's lucky to be going off with us to face demons and imps."

Arlene never lost her ability to surprise me. "Lucky?" I echoed. "Why do you say that?"

"She's past puberty, Fly. They'd probably marry her off to one of these . . ." She didn't finish.

I recognized that the conversation was on the slippery slope to more trouble than a barrel of pumpkins. Arlene's prejudice against anything and everything religious, and especially against Mormons, was disturbing; the people in this compound, Mormons and others alike, had done nothing to warrant such anger. Time for a strategic retreat. "So, what do you think of the President?"

"What do you think?" she threw it back at me.

"Well, as I've said before, you don't have to like

someone in power to recognize that you need cooperation from the boss. This man is no fool; he's playing his own game."

Arlene shook her head, but it wasn't because she disagreed with me. "I always understand a leader," she said. "It's the followers who confuse me. This man is a master of transferring authority. His followers won't argue with someone who says he gets his marching orders direct from God."

"Yeah, but in the war we're about to fight, let's hope God really *is* on our side. Or we're on God's side, I mean."

She took a stick of gum out of her pocket, popped the contents in her mouth, and gave forth with her considered opinion: "Agreed. Any god, any goddess, anything to give us an edge is fine by me."

I ignored the blasphemy. Honestly, she does it just to needle me. "Where did you get the gum?" I asked.

"Jill," she said between chews. "Want a stick?"

"No thanks." Gum is not one of my vices. But I was impressed with how quickly Arlene had been won over.

We went back in the compound, expecting to return to the room we'd been in before. A matronly woman we hadn't seen before greeted us. "Hello, my name is Marie," she said. "I'm here to show the young woman to the female quarters."

Arlene and I exchanged knowing glances. I think we both did a commendable job of not bursting out laughing. I couldn't remember the last time I'd slept without Arlene taking watch. We'd already been through the sexual-tension zone and popped out the other end with the understanding that we were buddies, pals, comrades.

But now we were back in the Adam and Eve department. The only question that really mattered was, did we trust these guys to keep us alive while we slept? The fact that they were still here was pretty good evidence.

"What kind of security do you have here?" I asked the woman.

She didn't understand. "Good enough to keep you out of the henhouse," she answered with a slight smirk.

I rolled my eyes. That wasn't what I meant, but—ah, skip it.

"See you in the morning," I said to Arlene.

For the first time in a long time, I was alone. Maybe the President still had doubts about me, but they put me on a long leash.

Suddenly I realized I didn't know where I was supposed to sleep. The room we'd been in before made sense. We'd been allowed to use it when we freshened up, but we were under guard then. I wished I'd thought to ask the woman if that was where I was supposed to go.

I didn't know anyone in the hallways, but they didn't pay any attention to me as I went past; they weren't afraid . . . what a strange concept that had become. I could have asked them about a men's quarters, but I wasn't in a rush to have the old YMCA experience if I could avoid it. If I wasn't going to bunk with Arlene, then I wanted to be alone.

Privacy suddenly exerted a strong appeal: to be alone without a hell-prince stomping on my face, to sleep without worry of a zombie who used to be a friend cuddling up next to me and sharing the rot of the grave, just to enjoy silence and solitude, without spinys fudging it up. Yeah, the more I thought of it, the better I liked it.

I retraced my way back to the room. After the corridors on Deimos, this was almost too easy. The door wasn't locked. Then I noticed that the lock had been removed. Now that I thought about it, there were no locks anywhere. But the room was empty, gloriously empty, and that was good enough.

I went in, closed the door, flipped on the light. There was a miracle. The light came on. No conservation or blackout measures in this small, windowless room. Which meant I could do something more important than sleeping.

The book was where I'd left it. Normally, the Book of Mormon would not be my first choice of reading material; the sisters would not approve. Under the circumstances, I was grateful to have it.

I started at the beginning, with the testimonies of the witnesses and the testimony of the Prophet Joseph Smith. This told the story of the finding of the gold plates with the Holy Book written thereon. Reminded me of the old joke about the founding of the Unitarian Church: a prophet found gold plates on which was written . . . absolutely nothing!

As I read, I remembered an old Hollywood movie about Joseph Smith and Brigham Young, founders of the Church of Jesus Christ of the Latter-Day Saints. Hollywood . . . where we would be going. Hollywood was in the hands of the monsters. Vincent Price starred in the Mormon movie and also in a million monster movies. I was sure this all meant something.

I started the first book, made it to the second and the third; and kept reading until I reached Chapter Five in the Book of Alma, Verse 59:

> For what shepherd is there among you having many sheep doth not watch over them, that the wolves enter not and devour his flock? And behold, if a wolf enter his flock doth he not drive him out? Yea, and at the last, if he can, he will destroy him.

That seemed like a good place to stop because I doubted I would find a more agreeable sentiment anywhere else in the Mormon scriptures.

13

"Did you sleep well?" Arlene asked, winking.

"Not bad," I said. "I think it's the first night I didn't dream about monsters."

The sun was up, the sky was clear, and for a moment it was possible to believe that none of this had ever happened. A dog ran by, a healthy mutt that someone was feeding—not a sign of impending starvation, but perhaps an overgenerous use of resources.

"Guess what?" she said with an impish smile. "I didn't dream about monsters either. But I did dream."

Teasing was simply not Arlene's style. She really surprised me. "Maybe that's why they segregate the boys and the girls," I said. "To make everyone think about it."

"We can't keep any secrets from you," said Albert, joining us outside the main cafeteria.

"Except the ones that count," I replied, not altogether innocently. I was still thinking about secrets and closed doors, and an unknown, upcoming mission.

"Where's Jill?" asked Arlene.

"Already inside, having breakfast," he said. "We should join her. Afterward, we'll receive our briefing."

It had been a long, long time since I'd eaten pancakes, with real maple syrup yet. I didn't think I'd be able to get coffee in Salt Lake City, but there was plenty of it for those with the morning caffeine monkey on their back. This was a pretty trivial monster in the grand scheme of things.

And then we got down to business. We returned to the ops room from the day before. The President was waiting for us dressed in a conservative black suit. He could've passed as an undertaker, not the most inspiring image to send us off to California.

"The entire state of California is in enemy hands," he said, then led us over to a map of the relevant states. Red lines marked all the existing train tracks. "There used to be a high speed train between L.A. and Salt Lake City. We destroyed the train to prevent the aliens from sending us a cargo of themselves. I refuse to refer to those creatures as soldiers. We also thought the train might be used to send us an atomic bomb."

"Would they even know how to use the trains?" asked Arlene.

"You fought them, didn't you? They can use anything we can. Machinery is machinery. It offends me how they used our own, God-given atomic weapons against us. We are fortunate the radiation and poisons have not contaminated this area. God has intervened." Atomic, not nuclear; an interesting word choice.

"We'll be going into radiation?" asked Jill. She had not thought of this until now.

"You'll be entering undestroyed areas, and our scientists tell us that the invaders have neutralized much of the fallout in the areas they control."

Arlene interrupted, as usual. "When we fought them on Phobos and Deimos, they were comfortable with higher radiation levels than a human being; but that doesn't mean they could survive H-bomb fallout."

For a moment I thought the President was going to bite her head off, but then he controlled his temper. "We have antiradiation pills for you to take and wrist bands that will glow red if you get a near-lethal dose. In addition, you'll have some protective gear if you require it. And any weapons you can bear, of course."

"How do we get to L.A.?" I asked.

"Take the train," answered Albert.

"Great. How do we get to the tracks? I thought they were all ripped up."

"Not all the track was destroyed," said the President. "You can take one of our Humvees south, following the railroad track to a good spot for getting aboard the train." *Getting aboard* . . . How easily he breezed over that slight difficulty!

And another small difficulty. "Um . . . the aliens are going to let us drive right out in a Humvee?"

Albert snorted. The President glowered at him, then returned to the question. "Of course not. You'll leave here and pass underneath enemy lines. The Humvee is hidden in a safe location—Albert knows where it is."

"I do?"

"Where you hid after blowing the tracks three weeks ago."

"Ah." Albert nodded, remembering the spot. Well, that made one of us.

"Underneath the aliens," I asked, "you have a tunnel?"

"It's always wise to build in a way to expedite escape," said Albert. "All our safe houses use them—

including this facility. Usually exit from a basement, dive down thirty or forty feet, then continue a long way, miles perhaps."

"How did you build all that without anyone knowing?"

"We had a lot of time on our hands." He grinned. "And a lot of members in street maintenance positions."

"You must ride the train into Phoenix," continued the President, producing a pointer and stabbing Phoenix.

"Why Phoenix?" asked Arlene.

"The train that goes from Phoenix into L.A. can't be stopped and can't be boarded; Phoenix is under demonic possession. If you stow away *before* Phoenix and escape detection, you might not be boarded. Then it's smooth riding all the way into L.A." He put down the pointer with a flourish.

Jill laughed. She sounded a lot older than she was, listening to the scorn in her laugh; it suggested a lifetime of frustration.

The President did not act as defensive as I would have expected. "I know it's a long shot," he said. "I'm open to any better suggestions."

"I wish I had one," said Albert.

I expected Jill to launch into a tirade, but instead she kept her mouth taped.

"The plan sounds workable to me," I said. "Everything is a long shot from now on."

At no point had anyone talked about who would lead this mission; I suspected the President would want his own man in charge, and I prepared myself for an argument.

Then Albert surprised me: "*Corporal* Taggart is in charge, of course." He surprised the President too, who started to object, then bit off whatever he'd been about to say. Leadership was clearly already determined.

The President allowed us to pick our own weapons: a double-barreled scattergun for me, and a .41 caliber hunting rifle with a scope for long-range work. Arlene was back to her perennial AB-10 machine pistol and a scoped .30-30. Albert surprised me by picking some foreign-made Uzi clone I'd never seen before; I didn't think a Marine would go in for that kind of flash. But I guess it wasn't really different from Arlene's AB-10, though a bit bigger; and even that might give it more stability in a firefight. Albert said he would just use Arlene's .30-30 for any sniping . . . and Jill already had her AR-19, of course.

We also took pistols, ammo, grenades, day-to-night goggles—we had to be careful to conserve the battery power, using them only when absolutely necessary; no recharges—and one of the more exotic energy weapons I never liked; not a BFG, which they'd never heard of, but a gas-plasma pulse rifle. We packed food and blankets and other useful items, including a complement of mountaineering (or wall-scaling) equipment: knotted rope, a grappling hook, crampons and pitons, the usual usual.

The Humvee waited—God and Albert knew where. Would we find it? Would it run if we did? I tried not to think about such questions as, with great solemnity, the President of the Twelve led us through the inner compound to a small, cinder-block building . . . and to the escape tunnel.

14

Other members of the community gathered around us before we departed. Somewhere back in my mind, I wondered why we weren't hearing a heroic anthem to speed us on our way. Where was the brass band? Where were the speeches? In my mind, I heard fragments of the speech: "Never before have so few faced so many in the defense of so few." Well, that wasn't exactly right.

There were a large number of heavy barrels of fuel oil in the building, seemingly stacked somewhat haphazardly. A pair of soldiers approached one particular barrel carrying an odd tool that looked like a giant-sized jar opener.

They lowered the prongs over the barrel and pushed levers forward, running steel rods through the lip. Then they put their shoulders to the two ends of the "jar opener" and walked counterclockwise. Rather than tip over, the barrel *unscrewed* like a light bulb; they lifted the heavy, false barrel from the narrow tunnel, just barely wide enough to admit a single man of my size.

Arlene took point. She *tchked* and winked at the President and blew him a kiss; his face flushed bright red. Then she held her AB-10 pointed straight down and dropped out of sight. Albert followed, then Jill; I went last.

We dropped into what looked at first like pitch-dark; then, as our eyes adjusted, we found the slight ambient light adequate to see a few meters ahead and behind.

The light came from phosphorescent mold, and the tunnel was deliberately carved to look natural, a fissure meandering left and right but mainly going straight northwest. It was wide enough for two abreast, and Arlene and Albert walked the point—Albert because he alone knew the route. I took tail-end Charlie, leaving Jill reasonably protected in the center.

Before we started, I cautioned the crew: "From here on, *no talking,* not even for emergencies. We'll use the Marine Corps hand language; Jill, you just watch me. They may have listening devices, hunting for tunnels. Let's not make it easy on them, all right?"

The tunnel was cool and dark, a relief from the hot sun of the Utah desert; at night, I hoped it would also insulate us from the freezing overnight temps. We could be underground for . . . how many klicks?

Eight kilometers, signed Albert in response to my silent question.

Six passed by at breakneck speed . . . well, as breakneck as you can get shimmying through underground caverns with rough, natural-hewn floors in limited light. Took us more than six hours, in fact, not much of a speed record. But the end was in sight, metaphorically speaking. We had just finished our fourth rest and were ready to tackle the final quarter.

As Arlene ducked and stepped under an archway, I heard a sound that chilled me to the marrow: the startled hiss of an imp.

We were not alone.

Reacting to the sound, Arlene backpedaled; she stuck her arm out and caught Albert on her way back, knocking both of them to the ground.

The move saved their lives; a flaming ball of mucus hurled past where they had stood but an instant before and splattered explosively against the wall. Arlene didn't bother rising; she raised her machine pistol and fired from supine. I swung my shotgun around and unloaded the outside barrel; between the two of us, we blew the spiny apart.

It had buddies. As Arlene and Albert scrambled to their feet, and the latter fumbled his Uzi clone, swearing under his breath in a most un-Mormonlike manner, I pushed Jill to the ground and unloaded my second barrel, decapitating a zombie who wielded a machete.

I cracked and reloaded; Albert finally got everything pointed in the right direction and loosed a volley of lead.

We had surprised the bastards, and now they weren't even sure where we were shooting from. To make things worse, the zombie troops had zeroed in on the imps, catching them in a cross fire with us.

I pushed Arlene forward, and she charged, taking advantage of the distraction. Yanking Jill to her feet, I followed; but we were several steps behind our teammates.

Arlene broke left and Albert kept on straight, taking after the two clumps of spinys—who made the fatal mistake of turning their attention to their own pathetic troops.

To my horror, I realized what this resistance meant: *the tunnel was breached;* if the aliens knew about the tunnel, then soon troops would come pouring down the pipe, lurching directly into the heart of the last human enclave for hundreds of klicks!

Albert must have realized the terrible danger at the same moment. He took advantage of a lull to flash a frantic sign: *explosives—tunnel—blow up—hurry!*

I got the message. The Mormons had intelligently lined their own escape tunnel with high explosive; if we could somehow find the detonator, we could collapse the tunnel, saving the compound.

But how? Where? I doubted even Albert knew where the nearest fuse lay—and wouldn't blowing the tunnel blow *us* up as well?

But considering that it was I who brought this trouble upon them, it was clearly my duty to do it . . . even at the loss of my own life in the explosion.

But first we'd have to take care of these brown, leathery bastards.

Arlene had gone left and Albert straight; but one imp suddenly lurched out of the darkness to our *right* out of nowhere. I caught it out of the corner of my eye.

"Jill!" I shouted, violating my own orders. "Look out!"

Fortunately, like Rikki Tikki Tavi, she knew better than to waste time *looking.* She hit the deck face first as I unloaded both barrels over her body.

The imp landed nearly on top of the girl. If it had, it probably would have crushed her to death: those damned demons mass 150 kilograms!

Arlene and Albert finished killing their targets, and I started to relax.

Then I noticed what the imp I had just killed held in its claws. Damn, but it sure looked suspiciously like a satchel charge.

For an instant I froze, then that little voice behind my eyeballs whispered, *Fly, you know, standing like a statue might not be the best career move right about now . . .*

"RUN!" I bellowed, bolting straight forward, picking up Jill on the fly. I ran right up to the imp and right over it, gritting my teeth against the expected blast.

It didn't blow up. Not until we had all made about ten meters down the tunnel.

The explosion was loud, but not deafening; it was the sequence of seven or eight explosions *after* the satchel charge that rattled my brains.

We kept running like bloody lunatics as we heard the loudest report yet. It sounded like it was directly over our heads—and the tunnel began to collapse.

A million tons of rock and dirt crashed down on my head, and something hard and remarkably bricklike cracked my skull. I was hurled to the ground by the concussion . . . and when I swam back to consciousness, I found myself lying half underneath a huge pile of collapsed tunnel roof. Had we been just a few footfalls slower, we'd have all been buried under it.

A steel brace arched up from our position, slightly bent. About five meters overhead I saw daylight; but ahead of us there was only rubble.

"Congratulations," gasped Arlene, picking herself up and choking in the dust. "You found the only door frame for a hundred meters in each direction! You *sure* you never lived in L.A., say during an earthquake?"

No one was crippled; Jill needed first aid for a nasty cut on her forehead, and I needed about five or six Tylenols.

Albert stared forward into the collapse, then up at the sky. "Course correction, Corporal," he said. "I think it's time we rose above all this."

We made a human ladder: I stood at the bottom, then Albert on my shoulders, then Arlene on his. Reaching up, she caught hold of the bracing beam and held herself steady for Jill to climb like a monkey up and out. She secured a rope and threw the end back down for the rest of us.

Outside, the sun was just setting, a faint flash of green in the western sky. The exploding, collapsing tunnel left a long, plowed furrow running jaggedly along the hard-packed dirt of the desert floor.

We hurried away from the site, found a rocky hill and lay on our bellies on its top. When the stars appeared, Albert sighted on Polaris, then pointed the direction we should journey. "The ranch is another four klicks yonder," he said. "We ought to be there before midnight."

Three hours later we skulked onto the deserted, burned-out ranch. Near the barn was a huge haystack. Inside the haystack, covered in a yellow, plastic tarp, was a surprise.

Ordinarily, I'd have rather run during the night and holed up in the daylight; but the aliens were more active at night. And more important, we were all utterly spent. Arranging a three-way watch over Jill's protest, we collapsed into sleep. Despite her threat, Jill didn't awaken until Arlene shook her the next morning.

The engine of the Humvee groaned into life, the coughing gradually diminishing. The thing might actually run, I thought. Jill almost jumped up and down with excitement as the machine started to move. She was a kid again, forgetting all the crap of the universe in the presence of a new toy. The little things that bothered her sense of dignity vanished.

She was why we would win the war against the monsters, no matter how many battles were lost. And no matter what happened to us.

"Here we go," said Albert, holding an Auto Club map as if it were a dagger. He was a lot more dashing than the President.

"Let's kick some monster butt," said the old Arlene.

After two hours of a steady, off-road seventy kilometers per hour, we'd seen no signs of the changed world; but I knew this illusion couldn't last. While it did, I enjoyed every minute of it. An empty landscape is the most beautiful sight in the world when it doesn't contain smashed buildings, burning remains of civilization, and fields of human corpses. Of course, it would have been nice to see a bird, or hear one.

There was a long line of straight road ahead, so I asked Jill if she would like to drive the Humvee.

"Cool," she said. "What do I do?"

I let her hold the wheel, and she seemed satisfied. A Humvee is a big horse, and I wasn't about to put the whole thing in her charge. But she seemed comfortable, as if she had driven large vehicles before . . . possibly a tractor?

Our first stop was for a bathroom break. That's when I saw the first evidence that Earth wasn't what it used to be: a human skull all by itself, half buried in the dirt. Nothing else around it—no signs of a struggle. But dislodging it with my shoe revealed a small patch of clotted scalp still on the bone. The ants crawling over this spot provided the final touch. What was this fresh skull doing here all by itself?

"Ick," said Jill, catching sight of my find. I could say nothing to improve on that.

"What's that odor?" asked Arlene.

"It's coming from up ahead," observed Albert.

It was the familiar, old sour lemon smell . . . unmistakable bouquet of finer zombies everywhere.

As we resumed the journey, the terrain altered. There were twisted shapes on the horizon made of something pink and white that glistened in the sun. They reminded me of the flesh blocks that might still be pounding endlessly up and down on Deimos.

These were shaped more like the stalagmites I'd seen in my spelunking days. They didn't belong out here.

The whiff of sour lemon grew stronger, which meant zombies shambling nearby or rotting in a ditch somewhere close. My stomach churned in a way it hadn't since Deimos.

The sky altered as well. The blue slowly shaded into a sickly green with a few red streaks, as if pools of green sludge were leaking into the sky.

We were all quiet now, fearing that to say anything was to ruin that last glow of quiet friendship before the storm. I glanced at Jill. She wore a determined expression better than the President of the Council of Twelve wore his gun.

Arlene and Albert checked out the ammo and guns, more for something to do. Jill was content to stay up front and help drive the vehicle.

Arlene finally broke silence: "You know, Fly, they gave us more than we can pack with us when we dump the Humvee, if we're going to be able to stow aboard the damned train when it slows down."

"Yeah," I said. "Take what you can."

Jill looked over her shoulder. "Can I help?" she asked.

"We're doing okay," said Albert.

"You're not throwing out my machine gun, are you?" she asked suspiciously.

Albert laughed, the first sound of happiness since we crossed over into what I was already dubbing Infernal Earth. "Honey, we'll toss food and water before we let go of a good weapon."

"My name's not—" she started to say, then noticed Albert's friendly expression. Context and tone of voice made a difference. I wouldn't be surprised if we weren't the first people in her life to treat her like a person.

There was the sound of an explosion to the west. "Is that thunder?" asked Jill. She stared to the right, but there was nothing to see.

"No," I said. "Someone is playing with firecrackers."

"Something, more likely," said Arlene.

"Behold," said Albert in a low voice, obviously speaking to himself, *"that great city Zarahemla have I burned with fire, and the inhabitants thereof."*

Jill suddenly surprised me by turning around and facing Albert, asking: "Are you saying the monsters are a judgment of God against the human race?"

"No," he said, "I think it is a testing."

Arlene had promised not to talk religion with the boss. Now the circumstances had changed. Albert was a comrade. She'd talk about anything to a comrade.

"Would you say what the Nazis did to the Jews was a testing?" she asked angrily.

"The most important lesson from what Hitler did to the Jews," he said calmly, "was that at the end of the war, they were still in the world. I'd call that a testing, one they passed by surviving when the 'Thousand Year Reich' was destroyed. If they'd been destroyed, it would have been a judgment."

Arlene fumed at Albert, but didn't say anything. Obviously, his answer irritated her at some level, but she couldn't think of an intelligent response.

"In space," she said finally, "on Phobos, we found a giant swastika." She let her observation hang in the air, waiting for the Mormon to respond.

"What do you think it means?" he asked.

Arlene sighed. "I don't know; except it's a reason for me to hate them more."

"I would hate them just as much," said Albert, "if you had found the cross up there, or the flag of the United States, which I believe was also inspired by

God. A symbol used by aliens means nothing to me. We know them by their fruits."

"Oh, fug," said Jill. "This is like being back in class. Don't give me a test, Albert."

I figured it was a good time to move on. "I'm with Albert," I said. "Symbols mean nothing outside of their context. But I never expected to hear that from a religious guy!"

"I'm full of mysteries," he said.

I was glad for our little debate. It took our mind off the fact that the sky kept changing. It was now completely green. Made me think of fat frogs and mold. The lemon stench was bad enough that it seemed the same as back on Deimos and Phobos. I had forgotten how after a while you get used to anything and then you could ignore it.

Albert reminded us he was in charge of the map by pointing out we were nearing the sabotage point. "I'd say we're a mile away," he said.

"Let me take the wheel back, Jill." The kid didn't argue, glad to say. I started slowing down the Humvee.

"We need to tip it over on the tracks just past that curve," said Albert. "We don't want to derail the train."

"Right," I said. "They should see it in plenty of time after they come around the bend."

"Have you given any thought to how we're going to tip this monster over?" asked Arlene. "It must weigh a couple of tons."

"I sure have. That's why I brought along—Block and Tackle in a Drum!"

She didn't seem to appreciate the humor.

15

"No, really, A.S. I'm not joking."

"I'm not laughing."

I held up the drum.

Arlene squinted. "C-4? Plastic explosive?"

"Just a soupçon. A bit of spice for an otherwise drab mission."

The others stood back at a safe distance as I parked the vehicle next to the tracks, molded a goodly glob on both front and rear left tires, then rolled it forward until the C-4 was against the ground. I fused both bunches with identical lengths of det cord, lay flat and closed the connection.

Jill covered her ears; clever kid.

The Humvee is normally one of the most stable-wheeled vehicles ever built; but even its wide body and long wheel base was never meant to stand up to a double charge beneath the left side. With a flash and a bang, the C-4 did its job: the wheels blew off, but not before the entire vehicle jerked into the air and rolled along the longitudinal axis, landing upside down on the rails. I held my breath as it skittered and spun—but it came to rest still blocking the tracks.

I even had more C-4, just in case we'd needed a slight adjustment.

"That wasn't too tough," declared Arlene, standing with hands on hips, surveying the undercarriage.

"Of course you'd say that," I complained, "after letting me do all the work."

"You! You mean you and Charlie Four!"

"What do we do now?" asked Jill.

"We guard the gear," I said, "and hurry up and wait. Hey, welcome to the armed forces."

"Inconsiderate of the fiends not to post their schedules for us," said Albert.

"Amen," agreed Arlene, to Albert's amusement. I had expected her to say something sarcastic in reply, but she patted him on the arm. They really seemed to like each other. Maybe their argument over Judgment Day was a test for each other.

The idea, of course, was for us to climb aboard when the train stopped to clear the tracks. We'd stay back until it started to move again; then we'd take a running leap and catch the ladders, humping up to the roof.

I was worried about Jill; I had no idea whether she could make the jump; and if she missed . . . But she was a wiry kid and looked like a tomboy. All the same, I quietly removed everything heavy from her pack, including her CompMac ultramicro; couldn't afford to let her drop it under the wheels . . . or drop herself.

"Can I put my ear to the track and listen for the vibration?" asked Jill. "I saw that in a movie."

"You don't think you'll fall asleep?" I asked back. "It could be a long wait."

She assumed the position and managed to stay down for a good twenty minutes before flipping over and trying the other ear. Fifteen minutes after that she decided that it could be a long wait and joined us over by the stuff, around the hill.

"Why do they have to change the sky?" Jill asked.

"I don't know," said Arlene, "but it makes me appreciate the night. At least we won't see the green then."

Albert passed around some beef jerky. We had plenty of water and didn't have to worry about rationing yet. We carried chlorine pills to purify the water, which wouldn't help much if the aliens poisoned it with some nerve toxin.

Jill poked Albert. "Why do you think these are demons if they can be killed?"

He looked at me, raising his brows.

"Don't give me a hard time," I said. "I haven't discussed it with her. She can think for herself, you know."

"There are greater and lesser powers," he said. "There is nothing wrong with viewing these creatures as alien invaders as our Marine friends do. But we believe they would not have taken on these guises unless they were directed by genuine demonic forces."

"Then why don't we exercise them?" said Jill.

Arlene smiled. "You mean exorcise, Jill."

"I like exercise better," I interjected. "Some of these monsters seem out of shape to me. We should capture one and PT the hell out of it."

"Speaking of which—" Albert began, but he didn't have to finish. The train whistle was high and loud, a lonely call from the remnants of our world. "I don't think you'll need to place your ear to the track," I told Jill.

First, there was the rumbling. Then it came around the bend, bigger than life, the engine the head of a dragon, each car behind it a segment of spinal cord. Thousands of tons rushed toward our little Humvee, lying across the dark rails like a sacrificial offering.

"It's not slowing down," whispered Jill.

There was no way the man or monster in the engine couldn't see the obstacle in the path of the train. The natural reaction was to slow and stop.

Instead, they chose the *unnatural* reaction—dispelling any doubts about what sort of creature was driving. The monsters were among us.

The damned train sped up! The drone of the giant diesel electric motors drowned out the world, sinking our great plan beneath drifts of sand as if drowning in that dry ocean.

Jill moved forward, still going to give it a try; but no way would I let her commit suicide. I grabbed her arm hard and shouted, "Back off, everyone!" If that behemoth came off the tracks, it could explode and obliterate us like bugs. I had other plans, foremost among them to stay alive.

We ran, the roaring of metal-on-metal and groaning diesels directly behind us. We felt the impact of the collision before we heard it, as the vibration tuning-forked through the desert into the soles of our feet and up to our hearts. The sound ripped through my head, made my teeth ache, and squeezed my lungs with the weight of the crash.

Bible stories ran through my head, the good old King James version, with the Old Testament warnings and massacres. Lot's wife looked behind her after the Lord God told her not to. She was too curious for her own good—my kind of woman. I couldn't resist a backward glance either.

The train plowed through the Humvee like it wasn't even there except as a sound effect. Pieces of our transportation flew at us, and I realized there was a certain wisdom to Bible stories. This crap could sever our necks and smash us to pulp. You could actually hurt an eye.

We kissed dirt, and something whizzed past my right ear, but I had no curiosity to see what it was. Finally, the dangerous sounds went away.

Standing up to see the remains of our vehicle, I checked that my three buddies weren't bleeding or buried under hunks of twisted metal. The receding train reeled drunkenly from rail to rail, like an Iowa farm boy with a snootful on his first night of liberty. I half expected to see a fat, red demon riding in the caboose, leaning out and giving us the finger. Then again, a good number of these beasties lacked the digits and dexterity to perform such a feat.

"So," said Arlene, after a long, dramatic pause. "What's Plan B?"

Jill occupied herself spitting out a mouthful of dirt, while Albert helped her to her feet. "Liabilities," I said: "no Humvee; no train."

"Assets?"

"We're alive; we still have our weapons."

"Feets do your stuff," said Albert.

"We'll hike into Phoenix," I said. "It's already late afternoon. Better for us to travel by night anyway, especially on foot."

"Great," said Jill, but when she didn't continue the complaint, I let it slide. A little bitching from the troops can have its salutary effects.

Whatever the green crap in the atmosphere was, it didn't prevent the stars coming out, although the twinkle was a bit weird. Footsore and weary, we took our first rest stop at midnight.

"My first girlfriend lived in Scottsdale," said Albert. "I always enjoyed Arizona."

"Was she a Mormon?" Arlene blurted out.

"No; I'm a convert. We didn't believe in much of anything, not even each other."

"Why do you like Arizona?" asked Arlene.

"The desert is clean. The mountains are clean. And best of all, there's no humidity."

"You sound like a travel folder," I said.

"Not anymore," he sighed.

"We'll get our world back, Albert," said Arlene.

An attack of commanditis seized Yours Truly: "If we're going to save the Earth, then we need to sleep, in shifts." I took first watch so everyone else could sleep, but Jill joined me.

"I can't sleep," she said, "so don't try and make me."

"No, I'm glad for your company," I said. "I hate wasting the rest of the night, and I'm not tired either. When Albert and Arlene wake up, I'm thinking we should move on."

"Fine with me," she said. "I think they're sweet on each other."

I stared at Jill, wondering where the hell that comment came from. I didn't say a word, but the teenager had given me something to think about besides how many rounds it took to put down a spidermind.

Absolutely nothing else happened for four days, except Arlene and Albert spent a lot of time arguing, leaving me to debate computer ethics with the fourteen-year-old net-cop of the month. Jill was down on even the slightest infraction against privacy . . . by *anyone.*

It was dawn on the fifth day when we arrived on the outskirts of Phoenix. A number of buildings were rubble, but some were still standing. We decided to hole up in one of those. With weapons loaded and in hand, we moved in. I was pleased to note Jill handled herself well. This was good. If anything happened, I'd be too busy to hold anyone's hand.

In the first alley we entered, we ran into an appetizer of three pathetic zombies. Albert, Arlene, and I acted so quickly that Jill didn't even get off a shot—but it was her first contact with the enemy.

We rounded the corner and found ourselves in the enviable position of staring at three zombie backs. It was two males and a female; one of the males a civilian, the other an Army sergeant, and the woman used to be a cop in life.

Any qualms I had ever had about shooting women in the back were burned out of me up on Phobos. Phobos meant "fear," and fear was a marvelous teacher. Without a word, I swung my double-barreled shotgun up to my shoulder, sighted as if aiming for a clay pigeon, and let fly with the outer trigger.

The living-dead female cop pitched forward without a sound, her head vanishing in a haze of red and green blood and gray brain matter. The other two growled and started to turn, but the soldier-zombie took two taps in the head from Arlene before he got even halfway around. She kept her AB-10 on single-shot; no sense wasting ammo.

The third zombie was armed only with a stick of some sort; it looked like it used to be a gas station attendant. It shambled toward us, unafraid, of course; its only desire was to beat us into a bloody pulp and perhaps eat the remains.

Jill whimpered and sank to one knee, fumbling her AR-19 around. Her numb, nerveless hands shook, and she suddenly had not even the strength to pull back the T-bar and cock the weapon.

Well, no reason to dump a death on her conscience, even a zombie death; she'd have plenty more chances. Sparing her a friendly glance, I raised my shotgun again, the outer barrel still unfired. But Albert beat me to the punch, expertly firing a quick, three-round burst that caught the zombie in the face, destroying it instantly. The guy was good: he had literally fired from the hip on rock 'n' roll and tapped it perfectly.

I stole a look; his face was grim, determined. I had no trouble believing he had been a sniper.

The soup course consisted of five imps who were attracted by the noise. Given the time of day, thinking of breakfast would be more appropriate. Time to fry the bacon.

They came shuffling around the corner, already wadding up balls of flaming snot. One was a fast mother; it heaved its flame wad before we could get off a shot, and Arlene had to hit the deck to evade.

I heard a snik-click, as Jill finally ran the slide, cocking the hammer and slamming a round into the chamber.

I discharged my remaining barrel, knocking an imp to the dirt; it was still alive. I crabbed sideways, cracking the breech and sliding two more shells inside, while Albert fired short bursts, alternating between the nearest imps. Each burst drove the target backward a few steps.

Then a dead-eye spiny from the back ranks chucked a mucus ball over the front ranks, catching Albert on the shoulder. It splattered across his armor, still burning, and he yelped and dropped the Uzi clone.

Arlene got to one knee, clicked the lever one notch down, and began firing bursts at the still-advancing imps. She focused fire on one imp at a time, taking them down.

One of them slid by us somehow; none of us saw the damned thing. All of a sudden I turned and it was in my face, hissing and screaming like death on two legs.

16

I backpedaled but took a piece of flame wad in the face anyway. Blinded and agonized, I dropped the shotgun to the pavement and grabbed my face, screaming. I heard *and felt* the 180-kilogram monster looming over me, and I steeled myself to take a savage swipe to the ribs.

The swipe never came. I heard the high-pitched "rim shot" sound of the AR-19 discharging on full auto, and the monster pitched forward against me. I rolled to slip it as it fell; I sure didn't want to get crushed underneath.

By the time I was able to blink my eyesight back, the rest of the spinys were room-temp . . . and Jill stood over the body of her very first kill, managing to look simultaneously triumphant, sick, and scared to death.

"Congratulations, girl," I croaked, still grimacing at the pain, "virgin no more."

"Thanks." She looked as ambivalent as she probably would in a couple of years, when she lost the other form of virginity . . . unless I'm showing my age by presuming she hadn't already.

My mistake; one of the critters wasn't quite dead. When we huddled to assess damages, it leapt to its feet and took off down the alley. Arlene, the Hermes of the group, bolted after the thing, Albert hot on her heels.

We raced the imp. I'd never seen one move this fast before. Was it that this one had the sense to be afraid, or had the genetic engineering made some improvements?

The imp scooted around a corner. Arlene followed, then Albert, and finally Yours Truly. Jill was somewhere behind.

We spied an open door across the alley, and Arlene and Albert made a beeline for it; but I noticed a nearby trailer was rocking back and forth, as if someone had just entered.

"Over here!" I yelled. I wasn't used to an imp doing something as clever as opening a door to mislead his pursuers before doubling back to his real objective; but then I hadn't expected the imp on Phobos to talk either.

The door was locked, but a trailer door hardly merited the waste of ammo. As I started to kick it, I heard a familiar sound. Once you've heard the humming-whizzing sound of a teleporter, you never forget it.

One good thump and we were in; a few sparks of light hung in space over the rectangular piece of metal. "Damn," I said.

"Shazam!" said Arlene.

"Huh?" asked Albert.

"Just making a little joke before your time," she said.

"Hey, I've had friends who take that stuff," Albert countered. "It's bad stuff, ma'am."

"We'll get into the cross-cultural discussion later, kids," I said. "Right now we have more important problems. Like, should we follow this one or leave well enough alone?"

"If we follow," said Albert, "it might put us in the center of this thing."

"I think we *shouldn't* follow, exactly because it might put us in the center of this thing," said Arlene.

They both had a good point. There was no questioning Albert's courage; but Arlene and I had the experience.

I felt a disturbance in the Force behind me. Jill squeezed in, her face hard, cheeks streaked where she'd been crying. But she was in control, the mask tight.

"Let's vote on it," she suggested, demonstrating she'd picked up some vile, egalitarian habits from somewhere.

"Sure," I said. "A show of hands for all those who think we should follow the imp through the teleporter." Albert and Jill raised their hands. "Now, those against." Arlene raised her hand.

"If you vote with her, it's a tie," said Jill, proving she'd taken some courses in the Higher Arithmetic.

"It's not necessary for me to vote," I said, "because Arlene's vote counts as three. The nays carry."

"Oh!" exclaimed Jill, frustrated. Albert merely shrugged.

"Let's put a guard on the grid," I said. "The spiny could return with reinforcements: hell-princes, pumpkins—"

"Maybe even a steam-demon," Arlene added. We could tell that the new monster fighters weren't exactly following the conversation.

"There's lots of different aliens," said Arlene.

"I know that," said Jill, a touch defensively.

"I'll take first watch," said Albert. "If we're not going to follow, I'd suggest we hide out in the trailer . . . but maybe that's not such a good idea. Instead of teleporting, the—imp?—might drive up with a tank column. Are we waiting until night before we leave?"

"On foot we'd wait," I said, "but in this truck, the Bad Guys will probably just assume we're members of the club. Who but a monster or zombie would be driving in this region now? Besides, Albert is right; we have to get out of here like now."

"Assuming zombies can drive," mumbled Arlene.

"If they have brains enough to shoot, they have brains enough to drive," I said.

"Can I drive the truck?" asked Jill, eyes wide. "It would really be cool."

I've created a Frankenstein's monster! I thought. "Can you drive a stick?" I asked. She nodded. "A big rig like this, double-clutching, multiple forward gears? *Have* you ever?"

"Well, not this big," she admitted. "But I'm sure I can handle it."

Normally, that wouldn't be good enough. But this time, I wanted all three seasoned fighters in the back in case the imp came back with a beastie battalion.

"Wait a minute," I said. "Maybe we can take the truck and not be stuck with the damned teleporter." I went back to it, crouched down and examined it thoroughly. It was literally melded to the steel floor; the only way to leave it would be to ditch the entire trailer. But we still had to get to a place of safety before we could stop long enough to unhitch cab from caboose.

"How about I go up front and look for the keys," said Jill, growing happier by the second. She wasn't about to let this opportunity slip by her.

"I'm going with you," I said, praying the monsters would not choose this moment to invade.

There were no keys in the cab, but I found a set in one of those little magnetic holders outside, underneath the left front fender. This bothered me. If the monsters were using the truck, why would they hide the key? Or had they not even used this vehicle as a vehicle since they attached the teleporter?

I didn't know how long we'd use the cab—maybe only long enough to hop the next train, assuming we could warp back to the original plan. But in the field, no plan was any good that didn't adjust instantly to reality. If the truck could get us a good piece of the way, we should go for it. If it caused more problems, then we could always switch back to playing hobo.

Jill opened the glove compartment and found a map showing the most direct route to L.A.—good old I-10; the best truck stops were marked for convenience. The original driver had been most obliging. If we were lucky, some of these stations might be abandoned, with stocks of fuel waiting for us. I could do without demonic attendants offering free human sushi with every fill-up. I'd definitely go with self-service, even if I had to shoot it out for the privilege.

Jill started the engine and I gave her a lecture about reading gauges. As if I had any idea what I was doing! But you can't let kids think you don't know.

This led right into a few more lectures about overheating the engine, dust storms, fatigue factors, and highway hypnosis.

At no point did Jill try to shoot me. Her self-control was exactly what you demand of a good Marine.

"At least there won't be many cars for me to run into," she predicted. If I didn't know better, I'd think she wasn't trying to cheer me up.

"Go west, young lady," I said as a parting shot. "Find us somewhere safe to park and disconnect. I don't like hauling around this reinforcement roach coach."

"See you later," she answered.

I returned to the back and caught Arlene grinning like the Cheshire cat that just ate the bird store. Albert seemed amused by something as well.

"You were up there a long time," she said.

"Looking for the keys," I answered solemnly.

"You took a long time getting back here since the engine started," said Albert.

I wouldn't let them get to me: "Giving her a few helpful tips, that's all. I'm sure she'll do fine." At that precise moment the truck lurched forward and stalled. Everything in the back shifted forward, except for the teleporter pad. The teleporter pad was just fine.

Arlene laughed. At no point did I try to shoot her; if Jill could hold it, so could I. I'm trained, a professional—a Marine.

Jill finally got the hang of shifting—I suppose she *had* had some training—and we were on our way. She proved herself a teenager by driving too fast; then she swerved suddenly, creating a new mystery to solve: what the hell was she avoiding?

Being thrown around inside gave me motion sickness; I hadn't felt this bad since the last time I was on a friend's boat and got seasick. But I wasn't complaining. Not me.

Besides, just about the time I would have risked Arlene's mirth, the spiny sent us a Christmas present.

There was a brief moment of warning, the humming and the glow. We trained our weapons on the spot, allowing for a split second of identification. There was always the remote possibility of a human escaping from hell.

Then the thing materialized. It wasn't a recruit for humanity's army. And it wasn't a zombie, an imp, or any other old friend. The bastards had sent us a new monster.

There was something especially odd about the appearance. This sucker wore clothes! He had on red shorts and a white T-shirt. At a quick glance, it looked like a living skeleton in lederhosen. There wasn't time for a closer look—we already delayed firing a second too long. The idiotic wardrobe threw us off.

The thing jumped at me, picked me up with one hand and threw me at the wall. I rolled with the impact and scrambled to my feet, still holding onto my twelve-gauge; but before I could fire, the monster had Arlene in one claw and Albert in the other. Thin as it was, we were like rag dolls in its hands.

Jill was shouting through the partition, wondering what was wrong. I would have loved to tell her, but I was otherwise occupied, waiting for a clear shot.

The skeleton flung Albert down, but kept hold of Arlene. The angle made Arlene a shield, so I started maneuvering around, trying to maintain my footing with Jill's increasingly panicked driving. As I tried for a better position, the damned bone pile turned and *punched out Albert!*

I mean, it hauled off and slugged him, and he went down for the count. The stupid red shorts suddenly seemed like boxing shorts. If the invaders were developing a sense of humor, I knew the true meaning of horror.

Adding to the fun, Jill started swerving left and right. Maybe she thought she was helping. She wasn't. I heard a horrible crunching sound, and I was thrown to the floor . . . but Red Skeleton remained planted as if it had grown roots. Jill must have run into a car—but from here, it was impossible to tell whether it had been parked or was tooling down the road with Satan himself at the wheel. At the moment, I didn't care about anything except dismantling that freaking skeleton.

Back on my feet, duck gun in hand, I shouted loud enough for Jill to hear: "Keep steady and keep going!" I was afraid that if she came to a sudden stop, it would be an advantage for Mr. Bones. I needed my opening.

Then the dumb monster gave it to me. He put

Arlene down so he could slug her. I let him place her out of the line of fire, and the minute she was down, I got in close to the thing and introduced its mouth to both barrels. The mouth opened just like a human one. I made sure it would never close again. I blew its head clean off.

This slowed it down. Unfortunately, decapitation was not the last word with this guy. He'd spent so much time throwing us around like preteen sparring partners, I hadn't even noticed the pair of rocket launchers strapped to its back—until now. In its death throes, Bones bent forward like a hinge and fired a rocket from each tube.

Its head was pointing toward the front . . . and that's where the rockets went.

The thing splintering into constituent bones, but Arlene was up from the floor in time to scream *"Jill!"* I was already out the trailer door and scuttling along the running board before the echo died away.

17

The rockets blew through the front of the trailer and the back of the cab, passing on either side of a white-faced Jill while she was driving. Either side. By some miracle worthy of every Holy Book ever written, both rockets missed her.

"Jesus and Mary!" I shouted. I slid through the hole

where the cab wall used to be and sat down next to Jill. She was white as cotton, shaking like an AK on full-auto, gripping the wheel so hard I half expected her to leave indentations. First Rule of Talking to the Driver When the Driver is in Shock: "It missed you, Jill; you're all right."

She nodded very slowly, but didn't speak. I tried another tack: "Wouldn't you like a break from driving?" She nodded again. "Well, why don't you pull over, uh, there," I said, pointing to a tree-lined side street. There was nothing around here; we could pull the plug on the teleporter trailer. Jill pulled over.

"Would you stay up here on watch while I return to the others?" I asked.

She finally spoke: "Yes. I will. Fly." I patted her on the shoulder, glad she'd addressed me that way. I suspected she would be driving more conservatively after this. I decided not to ask her about the car.

As Jill parked and sobbed, I crawled back into the trailer. "Our new convenient, modern cab," I said, "lots of ventilation makes it easier than ever to move back and forth."

My attempt at gallows humor fell on adder's ears. "Fly," said Arlene, voice shaking, "maybe we should acquire another vehicle."

"Why?" I asked. She stared at me dumbfounded. "Let's take a closer look at our new critter," I continued.

On first contact it appeared to have no skin at all. But close examination showed a thin layer of almost transparent epidermis. Close up, it looked a man in the terminal stages of starvation.

"I'd hoped we wouldn't see anything like this," said Arlene.

Albert started to get the drift and asked: "You never saw one like this in space?"

"No," I answered, "but we saw a place where they manufactured creatures on an assembly line."

"And living blocks of flesh," said Arlene. "I'm certain it was human flesh—experiments creating human flesh."

"The evils of science," said Albert.

I saw Arlene tense up, but this time it was my turn. "There's no putting that genie back in the bottle, my friend. We master everything the universe offers, or we're wiped out, another failed experiment. No happy medium or ignorant bliss."

He held up his gun. "Maybe you're right," he said. "This weapon would be black magic to Joseph Smith. I should pick on the engineers instead of the scientists. Some scientists say that some things we can do, we must never do."

"Such as?" asked Arlene.

"Godless genetic manipulation," he answered. "That's what we're fighting, isn't it?"

"Scientists who talk that way are the worst traitors to the human race," said Arlene. "I don't really mind religious people being afraid of new discoveries," she said, "but scientists are supposed to know better. This enemy's greatest power is biology. They've turned it into a superweapon. If that means we have to learn to use it ourselves, then we have to . . . otherwise, we're disarmed."

"You'd turn us into monsters like that?" asked Albert, pointing at the dead one. "Or our children?" he added.

"No, of course not," she said. "But why should you object to genetically engineering *angels?*"

"Because they already exist and will help us in the hour of need."

"Mexican standoff," I said. "This head-cutting is officially declared a tie. Now, shall we return to the matter at hand?"

"Well, Fly," purred Arlene, "whose turn is it to name this sucker?"

"I'm sure it's yours," I lied.

She must have already decided, because right away she said, "That's easy; a bony."

"Brilliant," I said. "Don't you think so?" I asked Albert.

"I guess," he said. "I guess we should be able to tell them apart."

"Albert, would you mind checking on Jill?" I asked. He was happy to get out of there. As Arlene and I started decoupling the trailer, I whispered in her ear, "So what do you think?"

"I think they're getting closer to copying our real, human form. Even the stupid clothes are a dangerous advance. A goal of the aliens is probably to create false humans; if they succeed, they can infiltrate the areas not under alien control . . . like Salt Lake City."

"We can expect better frauds as time passes," I said. "Now let's get to the next town along the railroad line, hop a train, and continue to L.A."

Albert and Jill were glad to hear the new plan. While Arlene and I were busy worrying each other, Albert had helped calm Jill down to the point where she insisted on doing whatever driving remained.

Fortunately, it was a sleeper cab for partnered driving; we squeezed in, Arlene and Albert in the back, me up front with Jill, and set off down the road. We passed a score of alien patrols, but the truck must have had the mark of the beast on the grill, for none of them threw us a second glance.

The next town along the line was Buckeye. We ditched the truck cab, then waited for night. We found an alley and enjoyed the busy sounds of night life in this modern world: troop trucks every few minutes, the tramping of little zombie feet, screams of pain, howled orders from hell-princes, and the occasional earthshaking tread of steam-demons. Even more soothing to our shattered nerves were mechanical sounds that reminded me of the spidermind, evidently a smaller model. I wondered if this one got better mileage.

"Have you noticed an odd thing?" whispered Arlene.

"You mean besides everything?" I replied.

"The aliens generally seem to know when humans are around," she said.

I hadn't thought about it before, but the facts supported her. "How?"

"Remember that lemony smell of theirs, right?" she continued her line of argument. "What if we smell as bad to them? They might detect us by the odor we give off."

"Maybe they deliberately give the reworked zombies that odor so they can tell them apart from living humans?"

"You know, A.S., if the aliens start manufacturing infiltrators, they sure as hell can't smell like zombies. That would be a dead giveaway." My heart bled for the technical difficulties faced by the alien imagineers.

The importance of having Arlene and Yours Truly on this mission was the background we brought with us. Remembering how we had turned the monsters against each other upstairs, I figured we could try it again when the time came. In fact, it should be even easier to turn the monsters against the new infiltrators: they wouldn't smell *wrong* enough.

Meanwhile, there was the little matter of our immediate survival and carrying on to L.A. . . . and that meant hopping a freight as soon as possible.

"I have another plan," I told my loyal troops. I hoped it would sound as good to me as I was about to make it sound to them.

We waited for another truck to go by before settling

down to the conference. It was easy to size up the strengths and weaknesses of our little foursome. Jill was brainy but callow; Albert was forthright, strong, reliable, stalwart, and no dummy. But he had yet to show the special kind of intelligence and instincts needed for command (another reason for the President of the Twelve not to press about who would command this mission). Arlene was cynical and sophisticated, the best woman soldier I'd ever known. But at some deep level she lacked a certain badness that was so much a part of Yours Truly that I didn't have to think about it.

The reason for me to be in charge was that I wouldn't hesitate to sacrifice all our lives if I thought it would make a difference in winning a crucial battle in this war. Arlene could make the same deision, but she'd hesitate where I wouldn't. In a strange way, I was the safest of the adults to befriend the teenager because no friendship or emotional ties would cloud my military judgment. With all that Arlene and I had faced up to this point, I counted myself fortunate that we had survived. I was also glad that I hadn't needed to be a perfect bastard. *Yet.*

The truck passed, and they waited to hear the plan. "You all know that we must infiltrate the train station and stow away on an outgoing train. The risk will increase once we do this. Let me point out that until we reach the enemy computers, *Jill is the only one not expendable.* After she retrieves the data, everyone is expendable, so long as one of us survives to get it through to the War Technology Center. Get it out to Hawaii; they'll find you."

"Yes," said Arlene calmly. Albert nodded. Jill stared wide-eyed as my words registered.

I continued: "I noticed a number of abandoned grocery stores as we were working our way in. I don't know if zombies still eat human food, but I doubt it. And I'm certain the monsters don't."

"Maybe the aliens can't digest what we eat," said Albert.

"Well," mused Arlene, "they can eat *us;* and we are what we eat." She was being her usual, grisly self; but I was the only one who smiled.

"Whatever," I said. "So here's the plan. Albert, you buzz to one of these stores and collect all the rotting lemons you can."

"I get it," he said. "That'll smell like those zombies we gunned down . . ."

"Like all zombies," said Arlene.

". . . and confuse their sniffers," he finished his thought. "Arlene—would you come with me?" He paused, as if surprised at what he'd said. He looked at me, remembering our informal chain of command.

"Is it all right if she comes with me?" he asked. "I mean, if it's okay with her." He stared at her a little sheepishly.

"I was going to assign you one of us," I said. "So long as there are four of us, it's crazy for one to go off alone. We'll always pair off when we have to separate."

"I'd like to go with Albert, then," said Arlene in an even tone of voice, betraying nothing.

"Fine," I said. "Jill and I will wait here until you return. We'll assume you've run into trouble if you're not back by, hm, 2200." Among items I was grateful for, we still had functional watches. Who gave a damn what day of the week or month it was any longer? The importance of a wristwatch was to coordinate activity.

Jill and I watched as A&A checked their weapons and moved out. They ran across the open space, Arlene first, Albert bringing up the rear, and then I could breathe again.

"When do we move out?" asked Jill.

"In a moment. We're still safe here."

The word "safe" triggered something in her. "I hadn't thought about it until what you said, but I don't like being more . . ."

"Critical to the mission."

"Uh-huh. Critical. It feels weird."

"Don't worry," I said. "After you've done your hacker bit, you have permission to die with the rest of us." I tried for a light tone of voice but the words sounded wrong.

"I'm not afraid to die," she said.

"I know you're not. You did great in the truck, the way you kept driving. I'm proud of you." Her whole body relaxed when I told her that.

I figured she could handle some more of my deep thoughts. Arlene and I had been through so much together that there were things I could say easier to the new recruit: "Cowardice is usually not the problem in war, Jill. Most people have more guts than they realize. Most can be trained to do all right."

"What's the problem, then?" she asked through slitted eyes.

I looked up and down the alley. We were still alone, and it was a pleasure to hear the sounds of demonic industry muffled and distant. The danger was at arm's length, a good place to keep it as long as possible.

"In a way, we're lucky to be fighting monsters."

"Lucky?" she half shouted.

"Keep your voice down!"

"Sorry."

"Fighting monsters makes it easy. Up to now, all the wars on Earth have been between human beings. That's much harder."

Her face scrunched up as she pondered what I said. It was like watching thoughts march across her face.

"I could never hate human beings the way I hate the demons," she said.

"You're lucky to feel that way," I said.

"How does fighting monsters make it easier?" she threw at me. "They're harder to kill than people."

"We don't take any prisoners," I said. "We don't have to worry about any of that. And if we did take one, we don't have to decide whether we should torture him. Hell, we don't even know if they have a nervous system like ours."

"Torture?" she asked, wide-eyed again. Then she thought about it. "I could torture them."

"To get information?" I asked.

"To pay them back for what they've done."

"Could you torture humans if they'd done the same things?"

"I don't know," she said. "What kind of torture?"

Looking at her, I remembered an officer who briefly passed through Parris Island as my class officer before moving on to Intelligence, maybe even the CIA (who knows?).

He took a whole slate of medical courses, though he had no interest in being a doctor. He had a weak, limp handshake. He probably couldn't fight his way out of a revolving door. He scared the living crap out of me. I figured I'd given a fourteen-year-old enough to chew on for one day.

"Any kind." I didn't elaborate.

"I think I could torture any humans who join the aliens," she said.

"Then you're home free," I said. "I don't think the enemy is doing any recruiting except for zombies."

She brightened. "And we know what to do with them, don't we, Fly?"

"We sure do." I tried out one of my playful punches on the kid's arm, like I did with Arlene. She pulled away at first, then sort of apologetically punched back. She gave off all the signs of having been abused once. By human beings, probably. Human beings always confuse the issue.

Now it was time for us to hurry up and wait.

18

I kind of felt bad leaving Fly and the kid to go traipsing off with *this* geek.

The first time I saw Albert, I thought he was a trog. Maybe it was the way he held his weapon against the head of the only other man in my life besides Wilhelm Dodd who's ever been really worth a damn: Flynn Taggart, corporal, United States Monkey Corps. As I joined this Mormon beefcake on the grocery store expedition, I found myself sneaking glances at his profile, and finding strength where I'd first suspected weakness.

I've always loved strong men. That's how I remember my father. He died when I was only ten, so I may not remember him with complete objectivity. But that's the way I want to think of him. I grew up defending his memory against my brother, who acted like a snot and said Dad deserted us.

I hadn't thought about my family since the invasion began, except when Fly got me going on my brother and the Mormon Church. I'd be happy to keep it out of my mind and off my tongue, except that Albert asked me: "You don't like Mormons much, do you?"

We were in an alley outside a likely grocery store, taking a breather. Zombies were unloading bread from a bread truck, an eighteen wheeler. Bet the boxes didn't contain bread; and I wasn't sure I wanted to know what was really in them.

"I have a problem with all institutional churches," I said. "It's nothing personal." Of course, it was personal and I'm not a very good liar.

"If you don't want to talk about it, I'll understand," said Albert diplomatically. The big dork had some smarts.

Maybe I should talk to him. Fly and I were so close that we couldn't verbalize everything there was between us. He had a little-boy quality that was attractive in a friend but definitely *not* what I wanted in a lover. Maybe it was part of the Mormon conditioning, but Albert projected father qualities.

The one time I let myself be talked into therapy, back in college when my family was exploding, I dropped hundreds of dollars to be told what I already knew. My ideal male friend would be the brother I never had. Fly was just what the doctor ordered. My ideal lover was Daddy. The therapist was a Freudian so he didn't have much imagination.

The women's group I hung out with for one summer had a lot more imagination. It wasn't my fault that the experiences of my youth fit the Freudian pattern better than they did the theories of the sisterhood. It just came down that way.

So I saw the concern in Albert's face, a guy who wanted to be a pillar of strength to some All-American Gal, and it was hard not to cut him some slack. Here we were, huddled down together in a dark, smelly alley, ready to save the human race from all the

like a guy; I mean a girly-man kind of pretty. You know, delicate features, pale skin, long, beautiful lashes like a girl."

"Big guy?"

"Yeah, right. When I was twenty, I outweighed him by ten pounds—I mean, five kilograms . . . gotta be military here."

"Ow. That can be rough."

"It got worse. A lot of the older guys in the theater—he did stage-crew stuff for the Spacelings—they kind of came on to him. Real aggressive, gay stuff; sometimes the theater can get like that, and anybody who says it can't never did theater in L.A. or New York. I don't even know if they were serious, or of they just wanted to freak him; but Buddy—"

"Buddy?"

"Heh, blame him for that. He was named Ambrose, so he called himself Buddy. Buddy got real scared that he was, you know, gay. It wouldn't have mattered if he were; he would've said, 'Hey, like, that's it,' you know? But he wasn't. He wasn't really anything; so he totally bugged."

"I don't know what to say. I've never had that problem. I've always known I was a flaming heterosexual."

"So he kept always trying to prove his manhood . . . you know, shoving little girls around, sticking his zinger in any doughnut hole he could find. He even once . . ." I hesitated.

"With you?" asked Albert, suddenly too perspicacious for words. Damn it.

"It was pathetic; really negative zone. I took him down so fast he cracked the sound barrier between vertical and horizontal. And it wasn't too long after that he fell in with a bad crowd and suddenly decided he would convert to Mormonism."

"What were you before that?"

"What do you expect? 'Sanders,' Episcopalian, as close to the Church of England as you can get in the U.S."

"How long did he stay with us?"

"Eight months; he moved to SLC, moved back to Hollywood half a year later. I think he showed up at the Overland church a couple times, then found a new savior: a drug called tank. Ever hear about it?"

"Nope. 'Fraid I'm not up on the drug culture . . . not from the using perspective. Your brother's problems are his own making," said Albert. "Would you feel the same way about the Catholics or Lutherans or Baptists, if he used them as a rest stop on the road to hell?"

That made me smile. "Albert, I had no idea you were so eloquent! I admit I'm prejudiced; when I'm *thinking* about it, I'm pissed at all organized religion; but only the Mormons cut into my guts like that. I think church enables aberrant behavior."

Albert laughed, and I had to admit I sounded pompous. "Temples too?" he asked.

"Oh, right," I said. This man had debated at some point in his life. "All religion, especially the ones that pretend not to be. They all say theirs is a way of life or an ethical system or a personal relationship with God—it's only the other guy who has a religion."

"Arlene, I'd like to ask a favor of you. Please don't tell Fly about our talk. I like things the way they are right now between all of us. I don't want to do anything to distract Taggart from doing the fine job he's doing."

"I keep confidences. You listened to my story, that's all."

He shifted his bulk against the wall so he could sit more comfortably. "You mentioned your brother getting involved with drugs. So did I, from the other side. I don't like to talk about being a Marine sniper; it's a private thing between me and the Lord. But one week, I was assigned to kill a woman who was *suspected* of being the primary money launderer for the Abiera drug cartel in Colombia."

"No great loss," I said, far too quickly.

He moved closer, as if he thought the monsters might overhear and report his confessions to Satan Central. "Arlene, I said she was suspected, not proven."

"Oh," was all I could think to say. I said it with sincerity.

"I'd never killed a woman before. They call it termination, but it's killing. I don't make it easier by playing with words."

"There goes your career in the military," I said, liking him better all the time. "So you were to terminate this woman with extreme prejudice because she was a suspect."

He nodded, unable to speak for a moment. "Strong suspect. But I had a lot of problems with it. It went against my moral learning."

I was having an attack of sarcasm and couldn't keep it bottled up. I hit him with: "Killing all the suspects in the hope you get the target? The Church of Central Intelligence makes that a sacrament."

"No, I mean killing a woman. In the end I decided if I couldn't justify killing *her,* then how could I justify killing a guy who was supposed to be a renegade colonel from Stasi? I did him the month before."

"Now who's playing with words?"

"Killed him the month before. He was training Shining Path terrorists to be sent over to Kefiristan to help the Scythe. It came down to one thing: either I trusted my superiors knew what they were doing, or I didn't."

He wanted to be frank with me, but the words choked in his throat. I helped him along. "You killed her," I said.

"I killed her, yes. I still *think* she was guilty."

Suddenly, I chuckled. He looked at me as if I'd completely lost my mind. "No, no, Albert, it's not what you think. I'm laughing about all the trouble America went to trying to protect fuck-ups like my brother."

My use of the past tense brought both of us back to the immediate nightmare. "I think we're all sinners," he concluded. "We all deserve to die and be damned; we earned that fate when we disobeyed the Lord. Which is why we need the Savior. I take responsibility for the blood on my hands, even if I let Him wash it clean. I don't blame the Church, the Marines, my parents, society, or anyone or anything else."

"We have a difference there, my friend," I told him. "I blame God."

"Then you blame the nature of things."

"Yeah, I guess I do. 'The nature of things' is waiting for us beyond this alley with claws and horns, lightning and brimstone. My only regret is that I won't meet God when I have a rocket launcher." I knew I was getting worked up and discussing religion; but I was talking to a human being, not the President of the Twelve.

And really, Arlene Sanders, are you sure you're not trying to wash away the blood on your *hands, the blood of a whole compound of innocents who might die because of your stupid mistake, sending a radio message to co-opted Colonel Karapetian?* I shuddered and shut off the thought.

"You can't blow up God, Arlene," he said in an annoyingly tolerant tone of voice. I expected my blasphemy would get more fire out of him.

I tried one last time, while I still had my mad on: "He made Himself flesh once, didn't He? If He'd do it again . . ."

"I think you'd find the cross a heavier weapon to carry than a bazooka, Arlene. Somehow I don't see you nailing anyone to a cross."

I almost told him about the row of crucified hell-princes the pumpkins had used to adorn Deimos and how I'd happily do the same; then I made myself shut up instead. I'd said enough. More than enough. The quiet, easy way he was dealing with my outburst told me that Albert was a man of faith so strong I couldn't crack it with a BFG. Besides, I had the feeling he would start praying for me if I didn't cool it.

"Thank you for telling me about Colombia," I said.

"There's no one I'd rather talk to than you, Arlene. Now let's get back to work."

Damn if I wasn't becoming attracted to honest Albert. For the first time in weeks, I thought about Dodd, my—my guy, who was zombified; my lover whose body I put out of its misery.

A small glimmer of guilt tried to build up into a fire, but I doused it with anger. We all had our problems. We were all human. I was sick and tired of thinking about all the things I did wrong or could have done better. Humanity was not a weakness; it was a strength, and our job was to win back our world, and damn it, *why did I hesitate* to think "lover" when I thought about Willie? Was it because it had the word "love" in it?

Darling Dan's Supermarket was the next battlefield. The zombies finished unloading the crates of whatever and drove off in the bread truck. Now the coast was clear.

"Come on," I said.

"Right behind you," he said.

19

We slipped into the supermarket through the back delivery door and worked our way toward the front. Lights were flickering on and off with the same irritating strobe effect that Fly and I had to deal with on Deimos so friggin' often. Maybe these guys weren't sloppy, slovenly, indifferent creeps; maybe it was some kind of aesthetic statement. All I knew was flickering light gave me a headache and made me want to unload a clip at the first refugee from Halloween who happened across my path.

"Come on," said Albert, a few steps ahead of me now.

I loved symmetry as much as the next guy. "Right behind you," I quoted. It was the next best thing to dancing with him.

Inside the main part of the store, the fluorescent lights were on and burning steady. But the refrigeration was off, and there was a rotten smell of all kinds of produce, milk, and meat that had been let go before its time.

"Ew," said my Mormon buddy, and he hit the center of the bull's-eye. The meat smelled a lot worse than the bad vegetable matter. And oh, that fish!

If I hadn't been wide awake on adrenaline—compared to which caffeine is harmless kid stuff—I would never have believed what I saw next. Nothing on Phobos or Deimos had the feeling of a fever dream compared to the spectacle of . . .

"Hell in the aisles," breathed Albert.

The grocery store was as busy as a Saturday afternoon in the good old world. Mom and Dad and the kids were there. Young lovers wandered the aisles. Middle-class guys with middle-sized guts in ugly T-shirts pushed shopping carts down the center aisle with no regard for who got in the way. Nothing had changed from the way it used to be . . . except that everyone was dead.

Zombies on a shopping spree. Eyes never to blink again. Mouths never to form words, but to drool foul-smelling, viscous liquid worse than anything in an old wino's stomach. Hands reaching out to grab anything or anyone that fell in their path.

The sour lemon odor was so concentrated that I had trouble breathing and Albert's eyes were watering; my throat was filling with something unpleasant.

The nearest zombie to us had been a big man once, a football player would have been my guess. Thick blue lines stretched across his face; I couldn't tell if they were veins or grooves or painted on. Next to him stumbled the remains of a cheerleader whose long hair she'd probably taken good care of a long time ago in the world lost way, way back . . . in the previous month. The zombie girl's hair looked like spiders had tangled themselves up in their own webs and died on her head.

These two were the best-looking zombie couple. The nearest family was disgusting; especially the thirteen-year-old boy (what had been a thirteen-year-old boy). Part of his head was missing. It looked melted, as if a big wad of caramel had been left out in the sun and gone bad on one side.

A thin, bald man looked like a scarecrow with a

laughing skull on top. His right cheek was missing and the few teeth that hadn't fallen out on that side made me think of kernels of uneaten corn or keys on an unpolished piano.

Two zombie Girl Scouts carried filthy boxes in their pale hands. One dropped a box and several fingers spilled out. A man dressed as an undertaker fell to his knees and shoveled the fingers into his mouth where they stuck out like pale worms. A dead priest groped at the attaché case of a dead account executive over a pile of fish left to rot on the floor. The zombie odor was so pronounced that I could barely smell the week-old fish.

"Are you all right?" asked Albert. I nodded but didn't look at him. "You're staring at them."

Albert's words were like an echo from Fly. My old buddy always gave good advice, like not focusing on any details that wouldn't help the mission. But this was the first time I'd seen so many of these human caricatures this close when I wasn't engaged in taking them apart.

"I'm okay," I whispered, pulling Albert back in the shadows. "We're doing fine. The stink in here is so bad they couldn't smell out live humans to save their—"

"Lives," he finished my inappropriate image. "Let's get the lemons and get out of here."

There's never any arguing with good sense. But as we took another look-see, the zombie density inside the store was worse than a minute ago. "Where the hell are they all coming from?" I asked.

"Probably," Albert agreed.

The scene was becoming even more surreal. Zombies pushing baskets up and down the aisles, grabbing cans and boxes of junk food (which would take a lot more than the end of the world to go bad). Some of the zombies were engaged in what seemed to be purposeful activity, moving items from one shelf to another and then back again.

They didn't eat any of the groceries. They seemed caught up in the behavior of the past, as if the program had been so hard-wired into their skulls that not even losing their souls could erase the ritual of going to the grocery store.

And then suddenly the lights went out. Whatever had kept the generator going was defunct. "What do we do now?" asked Albert.

"Take advantage of the situation," I said. "This is fortuitous. We should have put the generator out ourselves. We can pass easier for zombies if they don't see us. They're too stupid to do anything about the dark."

If there is ever a Famous Last Words Award, I'm sure that I'll receive sufficient votes to make the final ballot. No sooner had I made my confident assessment than flickering, yellow light filled the store. Dozens of candles were lit. I could imagine Fly saying, in his I-told-you-so tone of voice, "If they can still shoot their weapons, they can do a lot of other things."

It was bad enough when Fly was right so often in person. Now I was carrying him around in my head to tell me when I made a mistake!

Not everything the zombies lit was a normal candle. Some gave off a heavy smell of burning butter or fat. I didn't want to think about some of the items they might be using for torches.

"I wonder how long before they burn the store down," said Albert.

"They haven't yet," I said. "Let's get those lemons and get the hell out of here!" As we went out into the throng, my heart was pounding so hard that I worried some of the creatures would hear it. Then they wouldn't need to smell us out or see our TV-commercial-smooth complexions to turn us into today's lunch special.

Matches still flared as zombies looked for items to light up. A "Price-Buster" banner suddenly caught fire and went up in flames. It didn't set anything else on fire. For the first and probably last time in my life, I was grateful to be among zombies at that moment. Real, live human beings would have freaked and caused a panic more dangerous than a fire. The zombies didn't care. And of course they didn't bat an eye.

To be fair to Fly, he never overestimated zombies; he just didn't want me underestimating them. For what Albert and I had to do now, we had to count on zombie stupidity. I made my way over to a pile of hand baskets and took one. Albert stuck behind me a lot closer than Peter Pan's shadow.

I passed him the basket and noticed that his hands were shaking. I sure didn't blame him. In fact, I had the strong feeling that he'd be doing a lot better in full combat against the monsters. With his religious background, bodies of the reanimated dead had to be heavy stuff.

If I remembered correctly, and I always do, the Mormons had a more old-fashioned idea of the body. One thing I could give Fly's nuns—the Catholic Church didn't make you worry about what happened to your body in a war zone if your soul was in good shape. The more spiritual the faith, the more popular I figured it would be in the atomic age, where we can all be zapped out of existence in the pulse of a nucleus.

20

Albert's fear sort of made me more daring. After I got my award for Famous Last Words, I'd use it to join Psychos 'R' Us. This situation was so insane that I started to think it might work.

We turned a corner and saw a zombie-woman sitting on the ground. She had two candles, a bag of charcoal, and a cigarette lighter; four items, two hands. She couldn't decide which two items to hold. So she kept picking up two of them, dropping them, and picking up another random pair.

I looked over at Albert and tried a little telepathy. As usual, the results were nothing to worry the neighborhood skeptics. Since Albert wasn't picking up on my silent message, I stepped forward and waited for my opportunity. The next time the zombie-girl dropped her candle and lighter, I simply reached down and picked them up.

Now that I'd solved the zombie's quandary, she got up and stumbled vaguely down the aisle with the other candle and the charcoal. I started to pass the lighter to Albert, then changed my mind and gave him the candle, which I lit. I preferred keeping the thing that actually made fire.

Playing somewhere in the back of my head were all those old horror movies where the one thing monsters fear is fire. When I was a kid, sneaking those movies late at night when everyone else was asleep, I never thought I was boning up on documentaries. At least I hadn't used a hammer and stake yet in fighting these bastards; but I intended to keep my options open.

We staggered down the aisle, trying to look suitably undead, and headed for the produce section. We quickly grabbed plastic bags and filled them with the most disgusting remains of lemons and limes we could find.

The limes weren't even a little green any longer; they were dull gray with black splotches. Although the lemons were still yellowish in spots, the other colors were dark and unwholesome. They were the sort of colors I preferred ignoring.

Other zombies began gathering around us and just standing there. Maybe our purposeful actions were too purposeful. Did these idiots have the brains to recognize nonzombie behavior?

I tried to think and look stupid, but that wasn't what was required. Pretending to be *mindless* is much more difficult. I let my mouth hang open and tried to work up a good supply of drool. Albert picked up on the idea . . . the fact I found him immediately convincing shouldn't be taken as a put-down. But, man, did he look the part when he put on his goggle-eyed stare.

The act seemed to help a little. Some of the zombies left us alone and found other things to stare at. One large black man—what had been a black man—dressed as a high school coach, continued to block our way, staring at the basket of rotting produce instead of us. He started to get on my nerves. When I moved either to the right or left, he shifted slightly . . . just enough to suggest he was willing to block us if we wanted to move up the aisle.

We might very well want to move up the aisle because the crowd was starting to press in behind us, cutting off that avenue of escape. I couldn't remember if we had closed the door behind us when we sneaked in the back. Other zombies could be coming in that way, dead feet shuffling forward, guided by dead brains to regain a fragment of the living past.

A sound came out of nowhere. It was so strange that I didn't even associate it with the walking corpses hemming us in. It was sort of a low mewling sound, coming deep from within chests where no heart beat. A humming, rasping, empty, lost, mournful, aching sound . . . a chorus of the damned calling out to any living humans left in the world, as if to say:

Come join us; life's not so good! Come and be with us. We are lonely for company. You can still be yourselves. The habits of a lifetime do not disappear only because life has spilled out. If you loaded a weapon in life, you can still do it in death; the routine will survive; all that will be burned away is the constant worry to prove yourself, make distinctions, show pride. Judge not; there is no point when you're dead.

I wanted to scream. I wanted to take my 10mm and start firing, and keep firing until I'd wiped them all from the surface of the Earth. Aboveground was for the living! The dead belonged underground, feeding the worms, who still had a function to perform.

The zombies were the pure mob, devoid of intelligence and personality. Staring at them in their own flickering candlelight, trying to pass, reminded me how much I hated Linus Van Pelt, who said he loved mankind, it was people he couldn't stand. Earlier, I read a book by H. L. Mencken, who said he had no love for the human race as a whole, but only for individuals.

Individuals. The whole point of evolution. Individuals. The only justification for the American revolution, for capitalism, for love. There were only two individuals in this cemetery that used to be a grocery store, and I was one. The other gestured at me that the basket of rotten citrus was full and we should be leaving, if we could find a path through the wall of pale, stinking, shambling flesh.

Albert took the lead. He picked up one of the limes and threw it up the aisle. It was a long shot, but it paid off when an ancient memory reached out fingers like a groping zombie and touched something in the coach's brain. He turned and shambled after the lime like it was a thrown ball.

We followed in the wake left by the big zombie pushing through the crowd. By the time the coach reached the lime, he had forgotten about us, which is saying it stronger than I intend. We were merely a series of impressions, of light and sound distracting the zombie for a brief moment.

The front door beckoned. It was standing wide open, so we didn't have to worry about the power. A fire was burning somewhere down the street, marking the path we would take if we made it outside.

Our last obstacle was the long line at the checkout, believe it or not. A zombie-woman stood at the cash-register, responding to old job conditioning as the others had fallen into the role of shoppers. She stood behind the counter, banging on the keys of the register with a clenched fist. The sight was too much, too friggin' bizarre even after all that we had seen. I laughed. It wasn't very loud, and I managed to choke it off at about the half-chuckle point.

But it drew attention.

Maybe the shred of a brain that still functioned inside the ex-cashier's head was back from its coffee break, but she stopped banging the keys and looked at me. Then she opened her mouth, disgorging a cockroach that had been making its home there. A gap in her neck revealed the probable entrance to the bug condo.

Then the bitch made a sound. It was a brand-new sound, a kind of high wailing that drew the attention of the others. She was doing a call to arms, and the wandering eyes, listless bodies, jerking limbs, and empty heads responded.

They finally noticed us.

"Run!" I shouted, and I didn't have to tell Albert twice. There weren't very many between us and the door. Albert used his bulk to good advantage, and while he cleared the path I readied the AB-10.

I waited until we were through the door before spinning around to take care of business. Sure enough, some of the zombies of higher caliber followed us through the door. I expressed my admiration for their brain power by answering with my machine pistol.

It felt good to be killing them again. Most of the zombies in the grocery store didn't have weapons, but the ones who followed us outside were armed. I always thought there was a link between intelligence and defending yourself; apparently it even applied at this almost animalistic level. The zombies returned fire.

Albert saw I was in trouble and ran back to me, Uzi ready. "Keep running, it's all right!" I shouted as he took down a pair of Mom and Dads who took turns unloading the family shotgun in our direction. As they collapsed in a heap, other zombies I had shot got back up, fumbling with their weapons. Before they could get off another round, zombies coming up behind them fired, and the bullets tore into the front line of zombies. We booked.

The "Fly" tactic worked its magic; the front rank spun to return fire against their clumsy compadres. By the time we got behind a row of munched cars "parked" by the curb, the zombie melee was in full cry.

A bunch of spinys appeared from somewhere and had their hands, or claws, full trying to stop the melee.

"Good job," I said in Albert's ear.

"The Lord's work," he said, smiling. "I didn't know they were such a contentious lot." He quoted a line, I don't know if from the regular Bible or the Book of Mormon: "Satan stirreth them up continually to anger one with another."

"You said it, brother."

We had to get back to Fly and Jill; they'd be able to hear the ruckus and would wonder what hornet's nest we'd stirred up. And it was nearly 2200.

I thought about Albert as we made time. There was a lot more to this beefy Mormon than I'd first expected. Fly and I had done all right when he joined our team, or we joined his. I'd bet on all of us, even Jill.

The reasoning part of my brain ran the odds and concluded that we were screwed. It had done the same on Deimos where Fly and I had beaten the odds so often as to give a bookie a nervous breakdown. That was with just two top-of-the-line human beings against boxes of monsters. Now with four of us, we had the boxes of monsters badly outnumbered.

Albert and I entered the alley that felt like home after the grocery store. One advantage of fighting monsters was not having to worry about identification and who-goes-there games. There was a certain gait to a running human that the zombies lacked. They forgot a lot about being human.

Fly sighed and shook his head, somehow managing to say "I can't take you *anywhere!*" and "welcome back" simultaneously without speaking a word. We were together again.

21

Damn, I was glad to see Arlene again. After all we'd been through together, survival was getting to be a habit. If reality took her away from me in blood and fire, I wouldn't mourn until I'd finished avenging her on the entire race of alien monsters. If by some miracle I was still alive when it was over and she wasn't, I would mourn for the rest of my life. Maybe she felt the same, but I couldn't afford to think about that.

As Albert dropped the grocery basket of rotting lemons right in front of Jill—who made one of her patented "ick" sounds—he tossed a quick glance back at Arlene, and it seemed to Yours Truly that the aforesaid returned it with interest. Compound interest. Well, stranger things had happened, especially lately. But I would never have imagined any chemistry between . . . well, it didn't bother me if something were cooking between them. All that mattered was the mission, I told myself.

"That caterwaul was you?"

"Like the good old days," said Arlene, "when we were young and carefree against a bloodred Mars filling up the sky."

"Huh?" said Jill.

"Uh," said Albert.

When Arlene waxed poetic, she was a happy camper. "Mission went well, did it?" I asked. "All right, let's apply the beauty treatment."

Albert bravely set the example, squashing several of the lemons and a lonely lime between his big hands then applying the result to his face. Arlene followed suit, and I, after taking a deep breath, dug in. There were plenty to go around. Then I noticed that Jill was hanging back.

"You're going to have to do this," I told her in my friendly voice.

"Yeah, yeah, I know," she said, only the second time she'd pulled the sullen bit around us. I could well imagine her giving this treatment to the President of the Twelve full-time. I wouldn't fault her for that.

"It's not that bad," said Arlene, rubbing one down the side of her own leg. Staining camo wear was a nonproblem.

"Okay, okay," Jill said, picking one up and tentatively applying it to her nose. "It's gross," she said with heartfelt sincerity.

"Here, let me help," I said, becoming impatient. I took a lemon in each hand, squeezed, and then began rubbing the results in her hair.

"Hey!" she said, backing away.

"No time to be belle of the ball," I snapped, continuing the operation on her face.

"Hey!" said Arlene, coming over, taking one of the lemons out of my hands and brandishing it under my nose as if it were a live grenade. "What do you think you're doing?"

"Doing my bit for truth, justice, and the American way."

"Uh-huh," said Arlene, reeking of a lack of conviction. "Fly Taggart, I need to explain this to you so that you will understand." Smiling pleasantly, Arlene stomped on my right foot.

While I was digesting all the implications of her argument, she whispered in my ear, "She's a woman, not a child."

"Don't treat me like a child!" Jill chimed in, as if she could hear.

"Don't act like one." I leaned close, ignoring Arlene, and spoke to Jill as I would to one of my squadron Marines who was acting out. "Listen up, *ma'am.* When you've got a set of butter bars, you can start thinking and making decisions. But until then, you do what *I* say, and *I* say this stuff is going on now.

"We've done your hair and face; next step is the rest of your body. You want to do that yourself, or do you want to give me a thrill by having *me* do it?"

She stared, then took the lime I held out. Test time was over for now.

We finished applying the lemons. Jill made faces but did fine; I hoped she wouldn't stay pissed for the rest of the mission. Arlene lemoned the backs of the rest of us where we couldn't reach, and then I did the same for her. After that, we bid farewell to our alley and moved out.

Albert took point and led us toward the railway station. I took the rear. Fortunately, now that we smelled like zombies, we could walk openly and carry our weapons. We rounded a corner and found ourselves in a mob of the previously mentioned. I could see Arlene start to tense up—understandable after what she and Albert encountered at the grocery store. But a moment later she was putting on a good act, probably better than mine.

For a moment I worried about Jill's performance: arms straight out like a bad copy of Frankenstein's monster, legs too stiff and jerking as she walked . . . too exaggerated. She'd never make it on the legitimate stage. But the zombies didn't seem to notice.

We passed through an archway and suddenly we were surrounded by imps, hell-princes, and bonys, with those damned rocket launchers strapped to their backs. I watched the bonys walk with a jerking motion so bad I could imagine strings pulling them as if they were the puppet skeletons I'd seen in Mexico during their "Day of the Dead" festival. If I hadn't already seen one in action in the truck, I'd think they were fake. One thing: they gave me new appreciation for Jill's performance as a zombie.

Then came that lousy moment when the Forces of Evil unveiled yet another brand new, straight-off-the-assembly-line monster. This one wasn't inadvertently funny in the manner of the bonys. This one was just plain disgusting.

The word fat barely described the awfulness of this sphere of flesh. We passed close enough to smell years of accumulated sweat, a neat trick considering how new the model had to be. The thing made me think of a planetoid trapped in Earth's gravitational field, only this hunk of flesh comprised fold upon fold of nauseating, ugly, yellow, dripping, flaccid chicken flab.

Of course, that was only a first impression. As it came still closer, I decided that it was a lot worse than I first imagined.

All I could think of was a gigantic wad of phlegm carved by flabby hands into a semblance of the human form with two beady pig's eyes sunk deep into the grotesque face. At the end of each tree-trunk arm was a massive metal gun, starting at the elbow.

In a choice between being blasted by those guns or

touched in any way, there was no contest. I could imagine a lot of names for the thing, and I was sure Arlene would have some ideas; but I wanted Jill to have the honor of naming this one. She'd probably come up with a better name than the different terms for excrement unrolling in my mind.

There were plenty of other monsters and zombies through all this, more than enough to keep us all on our toes and plenty scared. But this thing was just too much for my stomach.

The two steam-demons looming up before us were more dangerous; but there was something almost beautiful about them in comparison. They were well-shaped, with good muscle tone showing on the parts of them that were flesh instead of machine. Even their metal parts seemed clean and shiny compared to the dingy, rusty-looking metal tubes sticking out of that fatboy. I knew I was in trouble when I started making aesthetic judgments about the monsters.

I didn't like the way the zombies hemmed us in. I pushed left and right, trying to lead my troops out, but always shying away from the vigilant hell-princes and bonys; they kept getting underfoot . . . whenever I'd try to ghost, there they were.

It took some moments for the penny to drop: *we were being herded like cattle.* By the time I realized it, it was too late to get out; the zombie mass funneled together, headed toward a large building. My heart went into overdrive, and I was already starting to calculate the odds of bolting, when Albert leaned close and rumbled into my ear, "Here's some luck—they're driving us into the train station."

I looked, and by God if he wasn't right. They were putting us on a bloody train!

A man's heart deviseth his way: but the Lord directeth his steps.

The only possible fly in the ointment would be if the damned train were headed east; but I had a gut feeling it was headed straight into Los Angeles.

We couldn't avoid the steam-demons; they were standing at the boarding ramp to the open cattle car that was already starting to fill. Well, we'd decided to take the first opportunity to get aboard, and this surely was some sort of sign.

Those old nuns of mine were receiving a lot of prayers from me lately. I could never imagine saints or angels; so when I got in one of these moods, those withered souls in black and gray habits played across my memory. I used to think the nuns that taught me were ugly old crones. With what I'd been seeing lately, they had taken on a new beauty in my mind's eye.

My prayer was simple. Don't let fatboy get on with us, please; pretty please with a Hail Mary on it.

It was easy to stay together; there wasn't any room to be separated. We were packed in like the Tokyo subway at rush hour. Of course, I realized that if we *were* separated, we'd have the devil's own time trying to get back together.

When all this was over, I thought I might give religion another shake; as the door to the cattle car closed, I saw that we weren't going to have to put up with fatboy: it got onto another car.

"It's open in the back!" said Jill in surprise. At first I made to silence her for fear we would attract attention, but there was so much noise going on around us that our words wouldn't be noticed over the roaring and growling filling the narrow space. We were being pushed toward the rear of the car, where instead of a solid wall, there was an arrangement of vertical wooden posts with horizontal metal slats running through them.

"That's some window," Arlene commented.

"I see that none of you were brought up around livestock," I said caustically. "It's a cattle car."

With a grinding sound, the train started forward with a great lurch, throwing us into our rearward neighbors, who growled and pushed us back. The former humans who were now zombies did not behave nearly so well as humans would have; some responded to being jostled by firing off a few shots.

"Great!" shouted Arlene.

"If this escalates, we'll be wiped out in here!" I hollered back.

"What can we do about it?"

"Nothing!" I admitted. Time again to trust to luck. The nuns must have been working overtime, because the shots suddenly ceased. I glanced over and saw Albert with his eyes closed, moving his lips silently. I supposed that if praying was going to save us, this was a job for the pro.

Jill grabbed the back of my pants; it was a good idea—I grabbed Arlene, and she caught Albert.

We traveled past several small towns that evidently held little of interest. The night sky had a weird glow, but I still preferred it to the return of day, if that sickening green sky was waiting for us. It was too dark to make out details, but occasionally we saw fires burning on the horizon, funeral pyres to mark the passing of humanity. We finally came to a violent stop and there was more jostling. Our luck was still with us; the gunshots did not resume.

"Damn, I wish we could see through the door," I said. Behind us was a splendid view of a smashed building and a nice stretch of barren countryside; but heavy sounds in front of us indicated some action.

"The designers must not care if the cows are well-informed," said Arlene.

As if in answer to my request, the heavy wooden

door in the side of the train was pushed open to unpack some zombies, and we were greeted by a sight you don't see every day. A contingent of steam-demons was being herded by a spidermind. They were guarding what appeared to be a truck dolly in which a human form was wrapped up in bandages from head to toe. There was a slit for his eyes, but that didn't help tell us anything about the man or woman propped up on the dolly; we could only assume this was a human because there were straps across the figure—a dead giveaway that he was a prisoner.

The sight made me remember Bill Ritch. The only human they would take care to preserve with his mind intact was a human with knowledge they needed and couldn't extract without destroying . . . which meant that here was someone else we should either rescue or kill. He couldn't be left in the hands of the enemy, giving them whatever they needed. They marched forward out of sight, the steam-demons tramping in eerie, mechanical lockstep.

"Are you thinking what I'm thinking?" Arlene bellowed at me.

"Loud and clear!"

"They've got their tentacles on another of our tech lads!"

"Listen up!" I screamed. "Have plan!" They gave me their undivided attention, easy to do in such cramped quarters. "Grab guy! Run!"

Arlene rolled her eyes, unimpressed.

"How—move?" shouted Jill.

"Slowly!"

While we considered the strengths and weaknesses of our position, the monsters took the bandaged figure toward the front of the train. Although we couldn't see very well, it was easy to figure out what happened next.

The train started up again, having received its important cargo.

"Forward!" I screamed. "Make path!"

Jill wriggled her hand slowly out to where she was able to extend her fingers and . . . the best way to describe it was that she goosed the zombie-woman in front of her. The nervous system of a zombie isn't great shakes compared to when it was alive, but there were sufficient sparks left to kindle into fire.

The zombie-woman didn't jump or make any sort of exclamation; but she did move forward with sufficient force to dislodge the smaller male taking up space right in front of her.

Jill let Albert get in front of her. He had a lot of mass and widened Jill's narrow opening. The objective was clear: push forward to the connection between the cars. With the speed of a snail we inched forward. I figured that so long as we didn't piss off any of them enough to shoot at us, we were doing all right.

Just about then, one of the zombies took a potshot. I didn't see any particular reason for it; but what was I doing, trying to apply reason to zombie behavior?

The bullet struck another zombie in the throat, and it went down gurgling. We were packed so tightly, like Norwegian sardines, that further attempts at argument by projectile would probably annihilate the population of the cattle car.

Jill drew the small .38 caliber revolver we'd given her and looked scared and determined both at the same time.

"Hold your fire, Jill!" I shouted. She didn't make me repeat it. The zombie with the itchy finger kept firing wildly and suddenly connected with a point where a metal slat and wooden post came together. A heavy zombie near to the point of impact fell back against the weakened spot and suddenly went right through, leaving a huge hole big enough for even Albert to fit through.

"New plan!" I bellowed.

22

By now the train was up to speed again, smoking along at 300, 320 kilometers per hour. At this speed, the wind could be considered a refreshing deluxe feature for the typical bovine passenger. As I attempted to squirm through the opening, I quickly learned that a typhoon-strength head wind could slow down the most dedicated Marine.

The main thing was not to drop my shotgun as I climbed on the sill, leaned out into the hurricane, and stretched up until I reached the railing along the outside top of the train. I hoped the zombies wouldn't pay any attention to this latest change in their environment. At some level they were still human enough to resent this ridiculous crowding, or they wouldn't be exchanging shots. Maybe our team would rate zombie gratitude for giving them elbow room.

While standing on the sill, leaning forward into the wind, holding the railing, I reached down to help Arlene. Her slim, dry hand slipped into my sweaty paw, and I noted that it was cold. Arlene always had trouble keeping her extremities warm. I hoisted her out and up to the roof, where she hooked her legs to hang on so she could lean back down. Then Arlene helped me take care of Jill.

I didn't blame Jill for being terrified. But I was surprised when she started shaking. Or maybe it was just the train rocking violently back and forth. I guess this would be an experience to write home about, if there were still a home. No matter how brave and grown-up this fourteen-year-old wanted to be, she was having one wild-ass situation after another thrown at her and had to handle each without benefit of training.

The terror in her eyes didn't prevent her doing what she had to do, and I didn't pay attention to the tears. The angle was bad, but Jill weighed almost nothing—and I heaved a sigh of relief as I finished handing her up to Arlene.

Albert was a problem. He was a big guy and not as gymnastically oriented as Yours Truly. Arlene and Jill attached webbing to the railing, then attached it to Arlene. The webbing is extraordinarily strong, able to hold tons before ripping. We didn't go into hell without taking some decent equipment! No way was Arlene going to fall with that stuff on her.

Now Arlene and I could help Albert up. It was a lot easier than blowing away a steam-demon.

We might even have enjoyed our time on the roof if not for the hurricane head wind. It smelled a whole lot better than inside.

We lay on our bellies, and a ferocious gale battered us. But we weren't blown off; in fact, we could stand shakily, leaning into the wind. I figured there must be some sort of air dam up front, otherwise, 300 kph would have swatted a standing man off the top of that train like finger-flicking a fly.

"Listen up!" I shouted against the gale. "Single-file! Forward! Slowly! Don't fall!"

Arlene put her mouth right up to my ear. "How far L.A.?"

"Two hours—dawn—rescue human or kill him!"

"What?" screamed Jill, clearly horrified. She was plenty loud enough to be heard. There was no need to explain to two old soldiers like Arlene and Albert. I'd stopped thinking of Jill as a young teen, but there was no getting around the fact that she was a civilian.

"Death better than fate!" God only knew how much she heard, but she clenched her teeth and said nothing more. The brutal arithmetic inside my head could wait for another time; I hoped she would never have to decide who lives and who dies. Sometimes I envy civilians.

There was nothing else to say. Besides, we'd all be hoarse from shouting if we didn't shut up.

I went first; it was my party. I set the pace nice and slow. It took nearly a quarter hour to crawl the length of the train; fortunately, the track through Arizona was pretty straight. But the natural swaying of the cars could still hurl any of us to certain death; the rails were laid for cargo, not passengers.

I looked back frequently; we didn't lose anybody. Next stop: Relief City! Two cars ahead was the flatcar with a complement of one spidermind, one steam-demon, and one human wrapped like a Christmas mummy and strapped down tight. The spidermind was between us and the human, the steam-demon on the other side.

It occurred to me that these superior examples of alien monster-building might sniff us out better than the lesser breeds; and the wind did a lot to erase our lemon odor. In our favor, we were *way* downwind. The wind was so damned loud, I didn't think they could hear us either.

I gestured to Arlene. Time for the Deimos veterans

to do their stuff. We crawled closer, where I could see a very narrow gap between the cars . . . too narrow for the adults.

I noted the fact that the spidermind was so big, a couple of its right feet dangled limply over the side of the flatcar . . . and that gave me an idea.

But it was too narrow for the adults. *Only Jill could fit.*

Oh man, this was my nightmare come true. It was never supposed to be a walk for the kid—but this? Throw the raw recruit, not even driving age yet, into the meat grinder against a spidermind *and* a steam-demon? It was criminal . . . homicidal!

But what were the options? Not even Arlene could squeeze into that slender space; she probably out-weighed Jill by forty pounds. They were like two different species, and thinking of me or Albert down there was a joke.

Feeling my gut clench, as well as another part of my anatomy, I said to myself: *Time for the recruit to do her stuff.*

The levity didn't work. I still felt sick.

We crawled back and huddled with the others in the gap between two cattle cars full of zombies, where we could hear each other, at least. I felt like a class-A creep giving Jill her assignment; but nobody else could do it. Anyway, the kid seemed eager, not afraid. She'd make a good Marine. Did I say that before?

This time, my plan had more details: Jill would shimmy down into the tiny gap between the two cars, using some of the webbing. "Just like Spider-man!" she said. Well, whatever. We'd use all the positive fantasy images floating in her mind. She had to believe in herself absolutely to pull this off.

If they spotted Jill, she'd be dead meat, and the rest of us with her. Once she made it into the gap, she would very carefully loop the webbing several times over the nearest limb of the spidermind and pull it tight—*without* allowing the spidermind to notice it was being hobbled. She would attach the other end of the webbing to the titanium grappling hook the President had included in Albert's gear. We could do that before she started out. We'd lose the hook and some of our webbing, but with luck, we'd lose the spidermind as well.

"If she makes it that far," I said, wrapping up, "she drops the hook to the ground beneath the wheels and ducks, waiting for it to catch on a tie or something."

"And that gross bug gets yanked off!" she said, grokking the plan immediately. "Gnarly idea, Fly!"

I let her savor the image of the alien brain scattered across the countryside. Slamming into the car behind at better'n 300 per ought to do the trick nicely, and "Spider-ma'am" would defeat the spider creep with a thick dose of poetic justice.

Now all we had to do was make it work.

While Arlene and Albert prepared the hook and line, Jill let me wrap it around her waist. She asked me to do it personally. That meant a lot to me. Then I gave her a gentle push forward and hoped Albert's God wouldn't choose this moment to desert us. I put in a good word for Jill with the nuns as well.

Jill climbed down the side of the car we were on, two cars back from the flatcar. So far, so good. I climbed down after her.

We crept forward at wheel level, crawling alongside spinning death so slowly, it made our previous trek along the roof seem like a drag race. Mother Mary, I thought, please don't let there be any fence posts too close to the tracks!

We very carefully worked our way around the wheels; but if we were any higher up the train, the spidermind might have us in its sights. Hunkering down at wheel level, we were hidden by the side of the car itself.

There was enough light to keep Jill in my personal viewfinder every step of the way. I imagined her knuckles were white. Mine sure as hell were. I kept pressed right up against her back, my arms on either side of hers to make sure she didn't slip. We finally got to the edge of the flatcar; now the show was entirely Jill's, and all I could do was hang and wait.

23

Cheese and rice, I felt like a weenie when he took me outside the train. I swore myself I wouldn't eff-up any more. For the mome, Fly respected me, and Arlene too. I didn't care so much about Albert, but he was all right for one of the LDs.

Now was my chance to prove to everyone! Maybe I almost wrecked the truck when those missiles went through, and maybe they don't know how close they came to being hosed. But if I pulled this off, I'd make up for everything! Plus I'd pay back one of those crawly bastards for what they did to my mom. And Dad.

He was right, the slot was a tight fit, even for me; but I could wiggle through. I don't know what they would have done without me for this. As I slid along, I got grease on me. Gagged me out at first, but then I was glad, cuz it made me more slippery. Huh, like to see one of those wimp LD girls do this! She'd faint, and the human race would lose the war.

Suddenly, I saw a thin, silver thing sticking over the edge. Got wide on the end. I didn't recognize it at first, seeing it so close up. Then I gasped—it was a spidermind foot! It was bigger than I thought. It was bigger than *I* was!

The end of the foot fluffed out like bell-bottom pants, like my grandparents wore, like on the *Brady Bunch*. God, I was glad they didn't live to see the monsters kill their children.

I stretched, flipping the webbing, trying to loop the foot; but I couldn't reach that far! That PO'ed me—I was going to dweeb-out just cuz my arms weren't like an orangutan's.

Then the leg twitched. I screamed and jumped—and fell.

I slipped down, banging my knee and barely catching the edge of the flat thing . . . *my face was an inch from the tracks.*

Oh Lord—the wind blew off the ties, freezing my cheeks, and I smelled smoke. I think I even . . . well, peed my pants. Shaking like a leaf, I hauled myself back up. I spared a glance back at Fly; he looked like he might have peed *his* pants too. I shrugged—sorry!

I'm sorry, but hacking systems would never seem serious after this. Just a toy. This was *real.* I knew I was taking a big chance, but there was no way else to reach the foot: I rested my knee on the bed of the flatcar and stretched higher, and then I could reach the leg.

The spider moved again! I wasn't able to get back down before the leg pinned me back against the firewall of the car behind. I was stuck like a fly in the spidermind's web.

I didn't make a sound; I could barely breathe, but I didn't panic this time—I didn't have any you-know-what left. It didn't know I was there . . . so I hung.

It would kill me the second it realized I was there, same way I'd crush a bug; I was still alive because I was hidden from view by the huge leg itself. 'Course, it might kill me without ever knowing I was there; if it put its weight on that foot, it would pulverize me.

The place where it had me firmest against the wall was at my knee. The upper part of my body could still move. I still had a good reach. So I did what I came to do. I didn't let myself think what would happen if I failed.

I passed the webbing four times around the leg. My heart froze each time. I was in Girl Scouts once; the only thing they taught me that I still remember was how to tie a square knot. I tied the best buggin' square knot of my whole life!

Great. What next? Next you die, girl.

I thought I would cry, but my eyes were dry. My mouth was parched and my heart raced, but that was all. When I thought about all the stupid things we cry about, like boys and grades and losing a best girlfriend, it seemed strange I didn't cry *then.*

Then something happened inside. I felt calm for the first time since I saw the monsters. I didn't mind dying if I could take one bastard with me. A big one.

I unslung the grappling hook and let it dangle between the cars. Pinned against the wall, I wouldn't be able to duck down. Once I dropped the hook, the spider would be yanked to a stop as the train kept moving, and I would be crushed to a grease smear.

Thought about my new friends. Thought about what if Fly *had* kissed me. Thought about wishing I was anywhere else. Then I let go of the hook.

24

I didn't know what was going on with Jill, couldn't see a thing. She fell and screamed, and I'd popped around and seen her half under the track; then the spidermind shifted and I had to leap back. Now I didn't dare show myself—I'd get us both killed.

I thought Jill would have finished by now. I'd bet money she wouldn't lose her nerve. Either she was still waiting for an opening, or something had gone wrong.

Then I heard the heavy thud and metal-scraping sound that could only be the hook dropping under the train. It bounced up and down, over and over, while I waited and waited and *waited* for that big mother with the brain and the legs to be yanked into oblivion.

What happened next was so stupid and unlikely, it was like crapping out ten times in a row: the damned hook bounced up and hooked onto the train itself!

The little voice in the back of my head I hadn't heard from recently chose this moment to speak to me in the voice of an old kids' science show: *So, Flynn, what have we learned from today's experiment?*

Well, Mr. Wizard, we've learned that if the train is moving at the same speed as the spider-bastard, absolutely nothing will happen!

I humped back hand over hand, ducking down to check under the train, looking for the hook. Saw it! I slid through the train's shock absorbers. Time for more help from the nuns. If we hit a bump, the shocks would slice me in half. Suddenly, the train itself seemed like one of the monsters.

I made it through, then slid along the undercarriage on my back across the covered axles, under the train, until I could reach the flippin' hook. The damned thing was caught on an Abel.

I reached for the sucker and succeeded in touching it. Yep, there it was. Touching it was a cinch. I could touch it all I wanted without falling onto the track and being ground to hobo stew.

Getting it loose was the problem.

Once upon a time, I won a trophy in junior high gymnastics; there were only five of us, but I was the best in that class. I thought I was pretty hot stuff that day. Looked to be the moment for an encore performance.

I went looser with the legs, increasing the possibility of falling but giving me a longer reach. I didn't want to perform this trick more than once.

Not only did this stunt run the risk of my becoming part of the track, there was the extra worry of losing the duck gun dangling precariously from my back. Not having my weapon could be as close to a death sentence as getting run over by the Little Train that Could.

I got my hand around the hook, heaved, and yanked it free. I did a war whoop worthy of a Comanche . . . then I shut my eyes—I hate the sight of my own bloody, mangled corpse—and dropped the thing to the ground.

This time the law of averages was enforced by the probability police. The hook caught on a spar and held. I gripped my perch and braced for impact.

I clenched my whole body as the webbing tightened—then the freaking stuff *broke*. It wasn't supposed to do that! The end whipped like an enraged snake, lashing across my back. But I didn't let go.

I waited for the sound of that massive body being yanked to its doom. Still there was plenty of nothing. This was becoming irritating. But there was something: despite the howling of the wind and the machine pounding of steel wheels on steel rails, I heard a high, piping squeal. It sounded like a scream from hell.

As I began clambering back through the shocks and up the side of the train, I heard explosions. Something was happening. I climbed faster . . . to be greeted by the scene of the steam-demon shooting its missiles at the spidermind. The latter was at a disadvantage, listing as it moved, badly off balance.

The webbing had torn one leg off the monstrosity. It didn't take a rocket scientist to figure out what happened next. Losing a leg would put the spidermind in a bad mood. It wouldn't be philosophical about it. No, it would fire a burst from its guns at the only target in sight: the steam-demon.

For all their power, these guys had a weakness as deep as the ocean. Conquerors and masters need *some* self-control.

My primary goal now was to find Jill and get her out of here; but I didn't see her from this angle. She was probably still hugging the other side of the flatcar where she had lassoed the spidermind's leg.

The train hit a bad bump, exactly the impact that would have left me beside myself when I was doing my Tarzan of the shocks routine. The two monsters took the bump personally and increased the ferocity of the battle. I realized the high piping sound was from the spider—it probably made the noise when it lost its leg. The steam-demon emitted more human-sounding screams.

The wind seemed to be picking up, but neither contestant paid any attention to the weather. As I watched the spidermind tear up the steam-demon with a nonstop barrage from the Gatling gun, I remembered how difficult Arlene and I had found taking one of these down before. The demon was nothing compared to the other.

But if there were a cosmic bookie keeping tabs on this one, the final decision was still in doubt. The steam-demon followed the optimum strategy for his position, firing missile after missile at the robot exterior to the spidermind's brain. Cracks were beginning to appear.

I stayed put, praying for the best possible outcome. By the time the spidermind's brain case finally exploded, the steam-demon was so ripped it could barely stand. Under the circumstances, things were working out better than the original plan. After all, if the spidermind had been eliminated as intended, we would still have had to contend with the problem of the steam-demon.

While I was congratulating myself on the turn of events, the train took a sudden turn and the tottering, cybernetic creature nearly fell off the flatcar. That would have been the perfect climax to the duel of the titans.

Dawn started to streak the horizon with a sickening shade of green. The improved light made it much easier to pick out details of the local terrain; such as the high rock gorge we were just then passing over, thanks to a narrow bridge. This would be a splendid place for the steam-demon to take its final rest. The perfect end, as I'd already thought, to the perfect battle. Then I could find Jill and congratulate her on a mission well done.

The only flaw in this scenario consisted of a single claw—the claw the steam-demon used to grab hold and save itself as it fell right next to me. Right next to me!

It was bad enough seeing the demon this close up. Far worse . . . *it saw me.* As weak and near death as the thing was, it recognized a living human a few inches away. Very slowly, it raised its missile hand.

It was slow; I was a whole lot faster. I back-drew my double-barreled shotgun and fired both barrels, one-handed, squeezing both triggers simultaneously. Quite a kick. The blast tore off its entire hand at the wrist . . . the gripping hand.

The steam-demon plummeted off the car to the ground, exploding noisily as it got off one last missile shot that went straight up through the track ahead of the train, in between the rails, right on a curve in the bridge.

The train didn't bother slowing as it rolled over the missile-damaged point. I could imagine a cartoon demon with an engineer's cap, throwing back a shot of the good old hooch and not worrying about the condition of the track ahead.

As we passed, I saw in greenish daylight growing brighter by the minute that part of the inside rail was bent up from the blast. If it had been the outside rail instead, we would have plunged into the gorge. The President of the Twelve would've needed to audition a new act.

"Jill!" I howled. "Jill!" Climbing up to the flatcar was easy, but I suddenly had a cramp deep in my back. It was so bad that it paralyzed me for a moment.

I wouldn't let something like that stop me now. I twisting around trying to loosen up, still calling, "Jill, Jill!"

Where the hell was that kid? I was starting to worry.

I reached the end of the flatcar, looked down . . . and saw her there, gazing up at me with wide eyes. "You all right?"

She nodded, but not a word came out. Maybe she was suffering from shock. I reached down and she took my hand. I didn't care about the twinge in my back now. I hauled her up.

"Great!" I said.

"Alive?"

"Of course!"

"Oh." She still seemed not entirely sure.

I grabbed and hoisted her. Now my back felt fine, and for a crazy moment the sick-o green dawn looked beautiful.

I put her down. The mummy and we were alone on the flatcar now.

A warm glow spread through me, not unlike the warm jet of a hot tub. My old voice spoke, something good for once: *The debt is nearly paid.*

What debt? Oh. The debt of my stupidity in bringing assault onto the enclave.

That debt.

"Wait here." I could have sent her up the ladder to signal the others to join us, but she had earned a rest as far as I was concerned. Her vacation from hell might not last longer than a few minutes, but I wanted her to enjoy every second before I ordered her to face death yet again. I got them myself, bringing them to the cacophonous flatcar.

Arlene and Albert looked as exhausted as Jill, and as tired as I felt. Next time, we'd fly.

Arlene bent over and began unwrapping, revealing the face of another human in a world where being human was something special.

Huddling against the forty or fifty kilometer per hour wind that leaked around the engines and air dam ahead of us, remnants of the 300 kph hurricane two meters either left or right, we crouched over our mummy, staring. We saw the features of a black man, mid-thirties. As we shifted him around on the platform, I estimated his weight at about sixty-four kilos. Not a bad weight for 1.7 meters.

"What done him?" Jill shouted. A good question, though I could barely hear her small voice over the roar of train and wind. Computer and electronic jacks were all over his flesh, stuck like pins into a doll. He was unconscious. There were so many jacks, he'd probably be in extreme pain if awake.

Arlene pulled the lid back from his right eye, revealing a cloudy white orb, so completely glazed over that you couldn't make out a pupil. Even after encountering a who's who of monsters, fiends, and other denizens of hell, something really bothered me about seeing this helpless man before me.

He didn't reek like sour lemons, thank God. He was no zombie.

I still hadn't discussed with Jill or Albert what Arlene and I had mulled over—namely, the possibility that the Bad Guys were trying for more perfect human duplicates. Practice makes perfect. We had no idea how the zombies were created. Sometimes I thought they really were the reanimated dead; but other times I could buy the idea they were transformed while still alive. However the enemy was doing it, the lemon stink was a by-product of dealing with real human bodies.

If the enemy ever made perfect human copies from scratch, there would be no lemon smell, or anything else to give them away.

Arlene tried various methods of waking up the man, even slapping him in the face, but nothing worked. She looked at me and shrugged.

Jill reached out and gingerly touched one of the

jacks sticking out from the man's flesh. She managed to look crafty and thoughtful, even with her red hair whipping around her face like a brushfire.

She fingered the jack again and scowled.

Then Jill looked at me and mimed typing on a keyboard. She raised her brows. What . . . ? I blinked; light finally dawned on marblehead. She wanted to *hack* this guy's brain?

Well why the hell not?

We all crowded around the mummy, making a windbreak for Jill. Leaning so close, I could actually make out a few words. "Need—jack—find out what—wants to fight—can't promise it'll—might be the break . . ."

I couldn't hear everything, but I got the gist.

The real question was what on earth was inside that brain that was worth the protection of a spidermind and a handful of steam-demons? Back on Phobos and Deimos, the alien technology we had seen was different, biological somehow. They used cyborgs, combination biological-mechanical, like the spidermind itself. Was that what this dude was, some sort of link between humans and alien technology?

Or the other way around?

Well, whatever. We weren't going to find out anything in a wind tunnel . . . somehow, some way, we simply had to get this guy off the damned train. Somehow I doubted we could just ring the bell and say "Next stop, conductor."

I hoped the cybermummy would be enough of a son of a bitch to join us when we unwrapped him.

"Vacation over!" I bellowed over the gale. "War on!" Arlene gave me a dirty look, so I knew that the awesome responsibility of command still rested on my shoulders.

The man seemed physically manhandled and

bruised, but not seriously damaged, except for their attempt to transform him into an appliance. The question was, how would we get him off the train?

If we waited until we rolled into the station in L.A., I could imagine a slight difficulty in persuading a large contingent of, say, steam-demons into helping us with our cargo. The absence of the spidermind from the flatcar would take a bit of explaining as well. We lacked the firepower to make our argument completely convincing.

"Suggestion," rumbled Albert. It was hard to pick out his words; the timbre of his voice was too close to the throb of the engines, and he wasn't a good shouter. No practice, probably. I only caught some of what he said and wasn't too sure about what I did catch.

"Father—trains! Trick or treat—Jill's age—incorrect car—aggravates—emerging break . . . !"

I stared, trying to parse the incomprehensible "plan." Trick or treat? Jill's age aggravates the emerging break?

Or was that *brake*—emergency brake! Something about an emergency brake.

He tried again: "Couple of cars!" he hollered. *"Couple—car!"*

Couple of car. Cars? No, car . . . couple-car.

I smacked my forehead. Decouple the car. Which must *activate,* not aggravate, the emergency brake. Jesus and Mary! What a nightmare; a loud one!

That seemed like a plenty good plan to Yours Truly.

Hauling the mummy up to the semiprotected roof, we staggered overhead toward the last car; that's the one we would decouple. The train was going as fast as before, but we humped a lot faster along the roof this time. Killing the spidermind and steam-demon worked wonders for our self-confidence. Jill's attitude was so changed that I could probably dangle her over the edge, holding onto her ankles, without her showing a quiver, though I was glad we didn't require such a demonstration.

There were three cattle cars, which we had to pass by creeping along the sides, centimeters away from staring zombies. I thought sure they'd start shooting at us—what a time to die! At least the demons wouldn't keep their mummy.

But the reworked humans merely stared with malignant stupidity. They'd been given no orders, you see . . . just like bureaucrats at the Pentagod.

When we reached the last car, an enclosed cargo car, I looked down through the slatted roof to see that the interior was stuffed with zombies. As expected. Albert slid down between the cars in search of the emergency decoupler. After checking it, he climbed back up and shouted, "When?"

Another good question. We didn't want to be stuck in the middle of the desert. If we hung until the suburbs of L.A., we should be able to hold our own combatwise and be close enough to supplies, shelter, and other transportation.

I tried to remember the L.A. geography. "Riverside!" I shouted. That is, assuming the train passed through Riverside. If not, any eastern bedroom community would do.

Seeing was considerably easier in the daylight, even in the pale green light. For the moment, I didn't even mind the greenish hue of an alien sky. Get rid of these damned invaders, and we could look up at the natural color of blue minus the gray haze for which L.A. was famous. It would take a lot of work increasing the population to get everything back to normal, but it would be a satisfying challenge.

"Single!" hollered Albert. Why was he telling me

that? "Single in couple!" Whoops—*signal* when he should *decouple* the car. He climbed back down.

Arlene tossed me a faint nod and half smile, then gingerly slithered down the ladder and joined him.

25

Fly was too good a friend for me not to be honest with him. But I was so surprised how fast things were going that there wasn't anything for me to say. Who could talk in this breeze, anyway?

Fly, like most guys, made certain assumptions about women. When we decided just to be friends, I expected a certain strain. But we were pals, buddies, comrades. I liked it that way.

But bring another man into the picture, and there are consequences. Fly was a big brother. He never did take to Willie; and I don't think he ever thought there'd be the slightest chance I'd ever fall for a religious dude—especially a Mormon!

"Fall" was a bad image. I squeezed down between the surging cars, watching the river of brown streaks racing below us as the ground sped past. Albert stood on the metal tongue-thing that held the cars together; he kept switching his grip back and forth as the cars shimmied. I never realized they moved that much.

I was *falling* for Albert. Crazy, buggin', retarded.

Nothing short of the end of the world could have brought this about.

One "end-of-the-world," order up! Maybe we could reverse what had happened and give the human race a reason to go on living. Survivors. Those who refused to go down until the fat monster sang.

On Phobos, I thought I might be the only human being left alive in the universe. Then on Deimos, I thought Fly and I might be the only *two* human beings.

However few there were on Earth to stand against the invader, all that mattered was that Fly and I were no longer alone. And looking down on the wide shoulders of my new friend, I hoped I'd be "un-alone" in other ways too.

Drawing near, I saw his lips moving, reciting words that could have been from the Bible for all I knew. Some kind of prayer, I reckoned; it seemed to calm him, give him courage. Guess there's some good in religion after all, if you knew where to look.

I wondered if he had the entire Book of Mormon memorized, or just the "good parts," the passages that suited his prejudice? I knew, somehow, that Albert wasn't like that—maybe the first guy I ever met who guided his lifestyle by his faith, instead of the other way around.

He stopped, looked up at me and smiled. With an opening like that, he could hardly blame me for taking the next step farther down the ladder.

"Albert!" I shrieked. He said something, but I couldn't hear him. I was probably embarrassing him. That was nothing new for me when it came to interpersonal relationships. "I find you really attractive!" I bellowed romantically, secure in the knowledge that he couldn't hear a damned word. Then I shut up and listened to the train wheels.

"Something mumble something," he said. Damn,

he *was* embarrassed. But he pressed on, as brave with me as he'd been with the monsters. Now why did I make such a comparison? Typical, Arlene, I said to myself; always your own worst critic.

I don't mean to make you uncomfortable, I silently mouthed into the maelstrom.

He shook his head and shrugged, which might have meant, *I don't have the faintest idea what you're saying* . . . but I preferred to interpret it as *Nonsense, darling; my religion is really important to me, but so are you—and I know how you feel about it.*

He had me there. I didn't want to say anything right then. Physical combat can be so much easier than the other kind! I listened to the steady rhythm of the train wheels pounding in my skull like a .50 caliber machine gun, drowning out even the 300 kph typhoon we rolled through. The irregular rattling sound of the coupler, waiting for Albert's hands to reach down and seize it, sounded like ground-to-air artillery.

I looked at the ground unfurling beneath us like a giant banner; then I looked up at blurs that might be trees or telephone poles, shading a dawn green as a lime before it rotted and became zombie lotion.

"I can't give you what you want," I said at normal speaking volume. Even *I* couldn't hear me.

He said nothing, but looked up shyly at me.

I liked him calling me beautiful. With his eyes, at least. I liked it a lot. Being honest came more easily now that we were both admitting our mutual attraction. Well, you know what I mean—this wasn't exactly the best spot for a romantic conversation; but I knew what he would be admitting if I could hear him.

It wasn't only that I had problems with his religion; I didn't like *any* of them. I don't like turning over moral authority to a bearded ghost that you can't find when everything blows up.

Besides, we might not be compatible in other ways. Hah, how pure Arlene that was! Telling the man I wanted all the reasons why it would never work. I was grateful that it was so noisy down here that Fly couldn't hear a word. Time to shift from negatives to positives.

"But Albert, we could give it a try," I said, not caring that I was basically talking to the wind and the wheels. He wasn't even looking at me at the moment, concentrating on keeping his balance and not losing a finger in the metal clacking thing.

"We could, like, date. You know, spend a few nights together, if we live through this. Who knows? Something might happen."

Again he left me to contemplation of the train and the terrain. He was obviously struggling over what I'd said. It was pretty obvious that four forces were fighting in him at this moment: morality, manners, *moi,* and volume-comma-lack of.

Finally he worked up his nerve, craned his neck again where he could look me in the eye and said, "Something rumble something question mark?"

Now that was a conversation stopper. But I only let it stop us for a moment. "You mean, you're a virgin?" I asked, incredulous.

He tilted his head to the side; was that a yes?

"But you're a Marine!" I howled in amazement.

I burst out laughing at my own outburst. The Church of the Marine loomed larger in my mind than any competing firm.

Of course, there are Marines who remain loyal to their wives or abstain from sex for religious reasons. Hey, fornication is not part of the job description!

Amazing, but true. Still, the odds were against the clean-living Marine. "You ever heard the phrase, 'There are no virgins in foxholes'?" I asked.

He watched my animated, one-sided dialogue—it wasn't really a monologue—in puzzlement, tortured soul that he was. I couldn't give up that easily. What about the various ports and landing zones he must have visited on his sea tour? Bombay, Madrid, Manila, Hong Kong, Calcutta, Kuwait City!

Albert smiled at me again. Progress! I had an admission. I knew how I would conduct the cross-examination: "So tell me, Mr. Marine Corps sniper, did you never visit any of the local sex scenes? The cages of Bombay that hang over the street, where you have sex with a pross in full view? The port-pros in Manila? The Hong Kong sex tours, where a soldier with a few bucks in his pocket can visit a dozen knocking shops in a day and a half? Kefiri City, with more glory holes than any other . . . ?

You don't know? Uh, you place your you-know-what through a hole in a wall and somebody on the other side does, you know.

Yeah, maybe it was morals. Maybe he just didn't want his gun to turn green and fall off.

The angle was probably tough on his neck, but he swiveled his body a little so he could almost face me. "Something jumble something interrogative?"

Me? Well no, not exactly. He stared at me awhile longer. No, those places tend to be attractions for a male Marine. What would I do with a glory hole, for Pete's sake?

Heh, I could work the other side, theoretically. All right; he might have been naive in some ways, but he was a man of the world in others. The contradictions in this big man appealed to me. He contained multitudes.

I reached out and touched his cheek, glad he didn't pull away. I was afraid he might have been ready to write me off as a Marine slut. No dice; I was a responsible girl . . . responsible behavior in today's world meant carry extra loads and sleep with both eyes open. To quote everybody's third-favorite weird German philosopher, Oswald Spengler:

> Life, if it would be great, is hard; it demands a choice only between victory and ruin, not between war and peace. And to the victors belong the sacrifices of victory. For that which shuffles querulously and jealously by the side of the events is only literature.

Hey, that could be our first date! We hurl quotations at each other from thirty paces!

26

Riverside was coming up fast, so I took another look down at Arlene and Albert. They seemed to be carrying on a deeply meaningful conversation, though the Blessed Virgin only knew how they could possibly hear each other over that racket. It seemed impolite to stare, so I focused my attention on the horizon. There was a war to fight, a war to fight.

"Albert! Now!" I boomed at peak volume as the town raced up to greet us. Albert and Arlene started yanking on a lever atop the coupler. They heaved again and again, until I thought we'd be cruising into Grand Central before they got the bloody thing unhooked. Then it cracked open and the cars separated with an explosive bang.

The pneumatic brakes activated automatically, slowing the loose car we were on while the rest of the train sped on, oblivious, impervious. I wondered if the aliens would even notice that a car was missing. We destroyed the spidermind; did they have enough initiative even to count?

We braked toward a stop, more or less terrifyingly. The rails screamed, the car rocked and rolled. Jill held on for dear life, looking as green as the sky. Arlene and Albert kicked back, cool to the max. I was too busy watching everybody else to notice whether I was cool or freaked: I didn't want one of my crew to fall under the wheels and be crushed to death without me being instantly aware of it.

I couldn't bring myself to abandon the car without expressing an opinion on the zombies sardine-canned below. I positioned myself and fired a bunch of rounds through the roof slats. This riled them up, and they behaved in the approved manner. They attacked each other with mindless ferocity.

As the car came to a complete stop, Albert and I managed the cybermummy between us quite easily. We hopped down and bolted for cover in an alley.

The streets of Riverside were like the valleys of a lost civilization or the canyons of a mysterious planet. We beat cleats up and down to throw off any alien patrols.

Although deep in the heart of enemy territory, surrounded by more monsters than at any other time since returning to Earth, it was a relief to be off the train. I didn't know about the others, but I was grateful for solid ground underfoot again.

There was no way to tell what were the mummy's requirements for life support. Perhaps with an IV he could survive indefinitely in his present condition; but there was no way for us to be certain without direct communication.

Meanwhile, Arlene and Jill took point and tail, respectively. We were at the part of the mission where we were truly interchangeable, except for the necessity of keeping Jill alive until she could do her computer trick. Nowhere was safer than anywhere else.

We whisked through street and alley, avoiding patrols of roving monsters. We ran, carrying the mummy like old bedclothes between us. Putting the mummy down for a moment, Albert pointedly asked of Jill, "Are there any safe houses around here?"

Digging into her pack, Jill produced that small, portable computer, the CompMac ultramicro, more compact than any I'd seen before.

"Where'd you get that?" asked Arlene.

Jill answered with a lot of pride: "Underground special—built by the Church. You can get inventions out fast when you don't have to worry about FCC regs and product liability lawsuits."

She called up her safe-house program and then told all of us to look away. I doubted that I'd turn to stone if I didn't comply. Anyway, I complied . . . and listened to her type in about thirty characters—her key code, obviously. When she was finished, I looked at her again as she scrutinized her screen.

She nodded and pressed her lips firmly together, a sure sign in my book of Mission Accomplished. "There's a safe house about a mile from here on Paglia Place," she said. Then she called up a map of Riverside and showed the rest of the route the program suggested.

"I see a problem with part of this," said Arlene.

"The route goes within a couple of blocks of an old IRS field office where I used to deliver papers while I was a courier."

"Courier? What for?" asked Jill.

"For two years of college."

"Whadja get?"

"Minimum wage. Fifteen per hour, OldBucks."

"No, I mean what degree!"

"Oh. A.A. in engineering and computer programming," answered Arlene, embarrassed. I could imagine why. Arlene's degree must seem awfully trivial compared to what Jill had picked up on her own.

Jill nodded. "Hip," she said, without dissing my pal, for which I was grateful. The gal was a pretty grown-up fourteen-year-old, astute enough to recognize that Arlene was very touchy about only going to a two-year college. She couldn't afford any longer.

We followed the revised route Arlene traced.

I had some advice that nobody wanted to hear: "Fly's prime directive is not to use firearms unless ab-so-lute-ly necessary!"

Jill was the first critic. "But Fly, it's not like they're human."

"Using martial arts might only entertain them," Arlene added. "I'm not even sure a shiv would bother them, assuming you can find their ribs to stick it between."

"Is everyone finished?" I asked, a bit impatiently. "I'm not getting all liberal; I mean the wrong noise at the wrong moment could bring down a horde on our heads."

"Oh, why didn't you say so?"

I wished there were a quick course I could take in monster aikido; failing that, I'd settle for learning where they kept their glass jaws, so a quick uppercut could do the trick.

We padded up dark alleys and narrow streets,

trying to stay out of the sun. After a couple of klicks, Arlene suddenly stopped cold. When the Marine taking point does that, it's time for everyone to play Living Statue. We froze and waited.

Jill, for all her fighting instincts, didn't have the training. She started to ask what was wrong, but I clamped a hand over her mouth. Arlene continued facing forward but gestured behind her for the rest of us to backtrack. We did it very slowly; whatever it was hadn't noticed us yet, and I aimed to keep it that way. We backed up about a hundred meters before she let out her breath.

"Remember the fatty we saw back at the train depot?" she asked. "We just bumped into its older, wider brother."

We'd been so busy that I never got around to getting her to name that mobile tub of lard; but I instantly knew the creature she meant. I'd hoped that maybe the thing was an exception to the rule, an accident rather than a standard design. I preferred fighting monsters that didn't make me sick.

"I thought it was a huge pile of garbage," Arlene whispered intently.

Blinking into the darkness ahead, I finally made out a huge shadow shifting among the other shadows. The thing roused itself with the sound of tons and tons of wet burlap dragged across concrete. It stood to a height of two meters, only my height actually, but weighing at least four hundred kilos. The density and width of the thing was incredible.

The fatty—if we lived through this one, I hoped I could talk Arlene into a better name—made slush-slush sounds as it moved. It was probably leaving something disgusting behind it, like a snail track. In the massive, shapeless, metal paws that encased or replaced its hands, the fatty held some kind of weird, three-headed gun.

The thing wasn't facing us. It stood sideways, trying to figure out from which direction had come the noise disturbing its repose. Then it turned away from us, giving us an unobstructed view of its mottled, disgusting back. It made a horrible, rasping noise that I guessed was the sound of its breathing.

I pointed in the other direction . . . but just then we heard stomping feet approaching up the block that way. A troop of monsters. Just what we needed!

They were led by a bony. If we didn't know how dangerous it could be, it would seem sort of funny, leading them with that jerking-puppet gait.

There was nothing amusing about being trapped between a fatty in front and the Ghoul Club behind, between hammer and anvil, with no side streets or doors to duck into.

Albert sighed. I watched his shoulders untense. He unslung his weapon with casual ease, as though he had all the time in the world; which in a way he did. He was ready to die for the "cause," whether that was us or the rest of whatever.

Me, I was ready to live for mine.

Jill's face went utterly white, but she didn't give any indication of bugging. After the flatcar, she was a seasoned vet. Like the rest of us, she had that special feeling of living on borrowed time. She clutched the ultramicro to her chest, more upset about failing than dying. She contemplated our mummy with regret; she'd never get the hack of a lifetime!

Arlene whispered "Cross fire" a nanosecond before it occurred to me. Darting into the middle of the street, we had the bony in our sights. It stopped and immediately bent at the waist and fired its shoulder rockets. I hit the deck and Arlene dodged left. The rockets sailed over my head, one of them bursting against the big, brown back of the fatty.

Enraged, the fatty located the source of this scurrilous, unprovoked attack. It raised both arms and fired three gigantic, flaming balls of white phosphorous at the bony.

The center ball hit, but the other two spread, striking other members of the bony's entourage, frying them instantly.

The surviving members were no happier than the fatty had been earlier; they opened fire, and the bony forgot all about us, firing two more rockets at fat boy.

Meanwhile, my crew were very, very busy lying on their bellies and kissing dirt for all they were worth, hands over heads. All except me: I kept my hands free and rolled onto my back, shotgun pointing back and forth, back and forth, like a fan at a tennis match.

I didn't want to call attention to our little party, but neither did I want us to be noticed by a smarter-than-average monster who wanted to spill our guts to celebrate its position on the food chain. I wished it were still night.

The bony ran out of rockets before the fatty ran out of fireballs. The bone bag blew apart into tiny pieces, white shards so small they could be mistaken for hailstones, were this not Los Angeles.

The fatty kept firing. There were plenty of troops left to take out, and the walking flab seemed to have an inexhaustible supply of pyrotechnics. Maybe he got his stuff from the same shop used by the steam-demon.

At last, any troops left intact were no longer moving. The fatty kept firing for a while into their inert bodies.

When it stopped, nothing moved anywhere in sight—assuming those little pig eyes could see very far. We lay as still as we could; I wished we could stop the sounds of our breathing. A lump of congestion had settled somewhere in my head, and I wheezed on every second breath, but I was afraid to hold my breath for fear I would start coughing.

Of course, the monster's hearing might not be any great shakes. I could see small black holes on either side of his lard-encrusted head. If those were ears, they seemed minuscule. I lay still, rationalizing and wheezing, hoping the thing would do anything except—except exactly what it did next.

The fatty was badly shot and cut up, like a giant, spherical hamburger patty that had fallen apart on the grill. It rumbled and began to shuffle directly for us. If the monstrous thing stepped on one of us as it passed, it would be a messy death.

27

I decided if one of those massive feet were about to descend on any one of us, I would open fire. There might be a military argument for letting one of us die if the others were passed over, anyone but Jill, but—forget it. Not like that!

As fat boy stumped slowly in our direction, I realized with a sinking feeling that it was another genetic experiment copying the human form. The whole design was clearly functional, another killer-critter. But if they could make creatures this close to our basic body type, then they could do copies of us in time.

As these thoughts raced through my mind, the thing took one ponderous step after another, coming closer and closer—allowing for inspection of its nonhuman qualities. The skin was like that of a rhinoceros. Feed this lumpkin an all-you-can-eat buffet (with a discount coupon), and it might top out at half a ton. The bald head looked like a squashed football; the beady eyes took no note of us as it came within spitting distance. It *had* to be nearsighted. Now, if it were deaf and unable to smell, it might just miss us.

Good news and bad: if fat boy continued walking a straight line, it would miss us all. Alas, Jill's ultramicro lay directly next to her, and the fatty was about to step on this critical piece of equipment.

There wasn't time for anyone to do anything, except for Jill. All she had to do was reach out with her right hand and grab it. I saw her raise her head and start to move her hand, but she froze. What if it saw her!

With only a second to spare, she worked up her nerve and yanked the computer out of the way before the monster would have crushed it flat. By waiting so long, she solved her problem—the fatty couldn't see its own feet. The bulk of the vast stomach obscured Jill's quick movement.

Fat boy slogged on without further mishap.

I was ready to heave a sigh of relief, clear my throat, maybe even enjoy a cough or two. Jill started to get up. Arlene and Albert weren't moving yet, waiting for the all-clear from Yours Truly. I almost gave it when a blast of machine-gun fire erupted behind the fatty.

I was too damned tired to curse. We could use a short rest before taking on new playmates!

The fatty wasn't happy about the turn of events

either. It screamed with a sound more piglike than the pinkie demons.

The bullets sprayed in a steady stream, so many that some were surely penetrating that thick hide to disrupt vital organs—however deeply those organs were hidden underneath a stinking expanse of quivering flesh.

As the machine gun cut the monster to ribbons, I heard bug-wild, crazy laughter, the kind made only by a human being. The laughter continued, the bullets continued, until at last the fatty made the transition from hamburger to road kill. It made a wet, flopping sound, collapsed into itself and died.

We weren't playing statues while this was going on. Guns at the ready, firing positions, we faced . . . what looked like another human being. A very large human figure.

I almost called out, but I checked myself. Despite my gut-level joy at seeing another human, my innate suspicion held me back. After all, some real, live humans *cooperated* with the alien invasion. Sure, this guy shot the fatty; maybe he was on our side. But we couldn't be sure of that; and if he didn't come into the alley, he wouldn't see us. The alley was in deep shadow, hidden from even the pallid green light of a reworked sky.

Unfortunately, Jill was not a Marine. She was a young girl, and like most teenagers, she sometimes acted on auto pilot.

"You're human!" she yelped. Then she stopped suddenly, hand over her mouth, as if trying to push the words back inside. She realized what she had done. As to the consequences, she'd learn those in the next moment. So would the rest of us in the black alley.

The figure lifted a hand to its head and flipped back a visor over its helmet. The face underneath seemed human enough, from what I could see. He wasn't smiling. Jill made as if she might run, but she was thinking again. She wouldn't lead him back to us.

"It's all right, little girl," he said, scanning, trying to locate her. "I won't hurt you." He took a tentative step in her direction, and she held her ground, not making another sound.

Silhouetted against the light gray wall of a carniceria, he was an impressive sight. But whose side was he on? This deep into enemy territory, we couldn't let anything compromise us, not even common sense or basic instincts.

Fighting monsters was so black-and-white that there was something clean about it. This man was not a monster. Were we about to have the firefight of our lives, a new ally, or a Mexican standoff?

He didn't have a flash; probably figured he wouldn't need one in the daylight, such as it was. In the dark alley, however . . .

Silently, slowly, I slid my pair of day-night goggles out of my webbing and slipped them on, flicking the switch as I did so.

Now I could make out more of his gear: .30 cal machine gun, a belt-fed job; backpack full of ammo; radio gear; a flak jacket that screamed state-of-the-art body armor; and a U.S. Army Ranger uniform, staff sergeant. "Come on out, little girl; let me see you. It's all right." He raised his hand as if scratching his chin stubble . . . but a crackling sound followed by a rumbling voice made it clear that he was talking into a handheld mike.

I also saw one more twist: he had a pair of distended goggles himself on his helmet—night-vis goggles, they had to be.

When Jill said nothing, he reached up for them. My heart pounded; as soon as he put them on, he would see all of us crouched in the shadows.

As if she sensed the danger—or maybe she knew she'd blown it and was trying to redeem herself—Jill stepped forward into the faint illumination reflected from the dragon-green sky by the pale wall of the Mexican meat market. "H-Here I am, sir," she called.

"Are you alone?" he asked.

Jill was a trooper. "Yes sir. I'm alone, sir."

Slowly, the man lowered his machine gun right at her small, narrow tummy. The universe became a still picture of the man, the gun, Jill . . . and my hand tightened on the trigger of my avenger.

"Take it nice and easy," he told Jill. "You're comin' to meet the boss."

"Who's that?" she asked, her voice firm.

"We'll get along a lot better," he said, "if you get it through your head right now, bitch, that you don't ask the questions."

"What if I don't want to go?" she asked.

"Then I'll drop you where you stand," he answered. The machine gun had not shifted an inch. "Now move it or lose it," he said.

Jill moved all right, slowly and deliberately so he wouldn't suspect anything. The gun followed her, and the sergeant turned his back to the alley; and I guess that's what she intended all along, for she took a dive as soon as his body blocked the line of fire.

I needed no second chance. Mister Mystery Ranger didn't have the proper attitude toward "little girls." Not by a long shot.

Unloading both barrels into the guy's back got his attention. Arlene opened fire with her AB-10. Between the two of us, we gave him a quick and effective lesson in good manners.

He staggered, but managed to turn around. That armor of his was something! He started firing wildly while Arlene and Albert pumped more lead.

I slammed two more shells home into my trusty duck-gun and let them go into the son of a bitch's head.

The fancy headgear cracked like a colorful Easter egg and spilled out its contents. Surprise, you're dead!

None of us moved for at least a minute, listening for the sound of more aliens attracted by the noise. There were no footsteps or nearby trucks, but we did hear sporadic gunfire in the distance. Probably zombies.

"Jill," Arlene called out. Jill returned with an expression that could only be described as sheepish. The girl was covered in dust but didn't have a scratch on her.

"I'm sorry," Jill volunteered; "I feel like a total dweeb." The apology didn't save her from Arlene.

"That was a stupid mistake! You could have iced us all!"

Defiantly, Jill turned to me, Daddy against Mommy. I didn't say a word, didn't stop Arlene, didn't change expression. *Sorry, kid—I'm not going to undermine my second just to save your ego.* I didn't think it was that dumb a mistake; she was just a kid. But Arlene had chosen to make it an issue . . . and whatever I thought, I'd back her to the hilt.

Jill started to blink, angrily holding back tears. She turned to Albert, but he was suddenly really busy wiping his gun barrel. Well—about time she learned: no hero allowances, and I guess no kid allowances, either.

"All right," she said, voice quavering. "What do you want me to do?"

Arlene stepped close, lowering her voice so I could barely hear it. "There's nothing you *can* do. You owe me, Jill; and before the mission is over, *you are going to pay.*"

When Arlene stepped back, Jill's eyes were wide. The bravado and defiance were gone. She was scared to death . . . of Arlene Sanders.

The shock treatment seemed to work. Jill focused on something more important than her own shortcomings. "God, is the mummy all right?"

While Albert and Jill went to check out our recruit from the bandage brigade, I did an inventory on the soldier with the lousy manners.

Arlene joined me. "Was he a traitor?" she asked of the inert form at our feet; "or did we just kill a good guy?"

"Or worse, A.S. Is this that perfect genetic experiment we've been half-expecting ever since Deimos?"

"If he's Number Three," she said, "we'll have to—to give him a name." She kicked the side of the machine-guy with her boot. "I'll call him a Clyde."

"Clyde?" I asked, dumbfounded. "That's worse than fatty! It's just a name."

"Clyde," she declared, with the really irritating tone of voice she only uses when she makes up her mind and can't believe anybody would still be arguing.

"But Clyde?" I repeated like a demented parrot. "Why not Fred or Barney, or Ralph or Norton?" I suspected that I might be spinning out of control.

"For Clyde Barrow," she explained . . . and I still didn't get it. "You know," she continued with the cultural-literacy tone of vice, "Bonnie Parker and Clyde Barrow—Bonnie and Clyde!"

"Oh," I said, finally ready to surrender. "Jesus H., that's really obscure!"

At the precise moment that I invoked the name of the Savior, good old Albert decided to rejoin us, reinforcing a theory I've had for years that if you call on the gods, you are rewarded with a plague of believers. Not that I was thinking of Albert as part of a plague just then. The plague was out there, beyond us, where it belonged—in the heart of Los Angeles.

28

I thought you had a Christian upbringing," said Albert, annoyed at Yours Truly for the blasphemy.

"Catholic school," Arlene answered.

"Oh, that explains it," said Albert, which *I* found a bit annoying.

Further discussion seemed a losing proposition. So I resumed investigation of the Clyde. Which reminded of the earlier discussion about nomenclature. "Hey, Jill," I called out. "We decided to name this bastard a Clyde."

"A *Clyde?"* asked Jill in the same tone of voice I had said "Jesus H."

"Yep."

"What a dumb name!" I decided to put her in my will. Make fun of *my* religion, will they?

I went back to my close study of the Clyde. As I'd noticed before, he appeared fully human, if a bit large. Frankly, I didn't think he could be a product of genetic engineering; the results had been too crude up to this point. Most likely, he'd been recruited by the aliens.

I was sorry the man was dead, because I'd like to kill him again. It made me furious that any human would cooperate with the subjugation of his own race. I kicked the corpse.

Arlene was a good mind reader. "You think he's a traitor," she said.

"What else could he be?"

"You already suggested it."

"What's that?" asked Albert. Jill was all ears, too. The time had finally come to lay all the cards on the table.

"We've been considering the possibility that the aliens might be able to make perfect human duplicates," I told them.

"He could be one," said Arlene, pointing at the man. "Maybe the first example of a successful genetically engineered human. First example we've seen, anyway."

"I don't buy it," I said.

"But what makes you think it's even possible?" asked Albert, obviously disturbed by the suggestion.

Arlene took a deep breath. "On Deimos we saw gigantic blocks of human flesh. I'm sure it was raw material for genetic experiments. Later, Fly and I saw vats where they were mass producing monsters."

"In a way," I interrupted, "even the boney and the fatty are closer to being 'human' than the other genetic experiments—hell-princes, steam-demons, pumpkins."

"And now they've succeeded," said Arlene, looking down.

"Hope you're wrong," I said. "It's too much of a quantum leap, Arlene. Even the clothes are too good!"

"You have an argument there," she admitted.

"Those stupid red trunks on the boneys were awful." We looked at the spiffy uniform on the man.

"He talked like a real person," Jill observed. I hadn't thought about it before, but everything about his manner of speaking rang true, even the threatening tone at the end. If he hadn't been such a total bastard, I wouldn't have enjoyed killing him so much. Making a monster was one thing; cobbling together a first-class butthead was a lot harder, requiring tender loving care.

"OK," said Albert. "He looks, walks, talks and smells like a human being. So maybe he was one."

"Whatever he was, he's good and dead; and that's what matters right now," I tried to conclude the issue.

The way Arlene kept looking at the man meant that she couldn't shake the disturbing idea that he was a synthetic creation. I didn't doubt that they could do stuff like this in time. My objective was to prevent them having that time.

Arlene shuddered, then shook her head hard, as if dislodging any nasty little critters that might have snuck in there. "Well, if they did make him, he's only a staff sergeant. There's a lot of room for progress before they hit second lieutenant and start downhill again."

Albert laughed hard at that. She gave him an appreciative glance.

In a way, it was kind of strange to nit-pick over which was more likely to be true: human traitors or human duplicates. Either possibility was disturbing.

I let my mind wander over the uncertain terrain where treason sprouts like an ugly mushroom. If U.S. armed forces were cooperating with the aliens, were they under orders from the civilian government? Had Washington caved in immediately to become a Vichy-style administration? And what could the aliens offer human collaborators that the humans would be stupid enough to believe?

I didn't doubt for one second that the enemy intended the extermination of the human race as we knew it. Zombie slaves and a few human specimens kept around for experimental purposes didn't count as species survival in my book.

I must have been carrying worry on my face, because Albert put his hand on my shoulder and said, "We needn't concern ourselves over the biggest possible picture. One battle at a time is how we'll win this war. First, we destroy the main citadel of alien power in Los Angeles. Then we'll stop them in New York, Houston, Mexico City, Paris, London, Rome—ah, Tokyo. . . ." He trailed off. Already quite a list, wasn't it?

"Atlanta," said Jill.

"Orlando," said Arlene. "We must save the good name of the mouse on both coasts!"

"You know," I mused, "I wonder how much of the invasion force Arlene and I destroyed on Deimos."

"Oh, at least half," boasted my buddy; but she might not be far wrong. We killed a hell of a lot of monsters on the Martian moons. Each new carcass meant one less demonic foot soldier on terra firma.

"You know," said Jill, her voice sounding oddly old, "I could kill every one of those human traitors."

"I'm with you, hon," I agreed; "but you've got to be careful about blanket statements like that. Some were threatened, tortured. Hell, some could have been tricked. They didn't go through what we did on Deimos! They might have been told that the mass destruction was caused by human-against-human and now these superior aliens have come to Earth with a plan for ultimate peace."

"I'll bet you were a pain in your High School debate

society, Fly Taggart," said long suffering Arlene. "But you know damn well what she means!"

"Put it down to my practical side, if you want," I said. "I like to know the score before I pick a play."

Albert added a note. "Anyone can make a terrible mistake and still repent before the final hour."

"It's possible," I said.

"I'm sorry I made that crack about your growing up Catholic."

The two atheist females acted suitably disgusted by our theological love-fest. "The girls don't believe in redemption of traitors, Albert," I said.

"I'll pray for anyone," he said; "even traitors."

"Fine," said Arlene. "Pray over their graves."

While we failed to resolve yet another serious philosophical issue, Jill squatted over the corpse. In a very short time she'd become hardened to the sight and smell of carnage. Good. She had a chance to survive in the new world.

"Are you all right?" Arlene asked.

"Don't worry about me," Jill said, following my example and kicking the corpse. "They're just bags of blood, and we've got the pins. It's no big thing."

No one was joking now. Arlene looked at me with a worried expression. This was no time to psychoanalyze a fourteen-year-old who was doing her best to feel nothing. This sort of cold attitude was par for the course in an adult, a mood that would be turned off (hopefully) in peacetime; but hearing it from a kid was unnerving.

The words just out of her lips were the cold truth we created. Do only the youngest soldiers develop the attitude necessary to win a war? Until this moment, I wouldn't have thought of Arlene and myself as old-fashioned sentimentalists; but if the future human race became cold and machine-like to fight the monsters, then maybe the monsters win, regardless of the outcome.

Recreation time was over. Jill went to the cybermummy and started to lift him; he was really too heavy for her to do alone, and we got the idea. Albert helped her, and Arlene and I returned to battle readiness. The next goal was obvious: find the safehouse. We couldn't make good time sneaking through the dark carrying a mummy.

We were only ninety minutes away. All we ran into along the way was a pair of zombies, almost a free ride. I popped them both before Arlene even got off a shot.

"You have all the fun," said Albert. "This guy is starting to weigh!"

"You don't hear Jill complaining, do you?" asked Arlene. Jill said nothing. But I could see the sweat beading on her forehead and her breathing was more rapid. Arlene noticed, too. "Jill, would you like to switch with me?" she asked.

"I'm all right," she said, determined to prove something to someone.

Jill managed to hold up her end all the way to the door of the crappiest looking rattrap in a whole block of low rent housing. She heaved a sigh of relief as she finally put down her burden.

This stretch of hovels didn't seem to have been bombed by anything but bad economic decisions. The house was one-story, shapeless as a cardboard box with a sheet of metal thrown on top pretending to be a roof. The yard was a narrow stretch of dirt with garbage piled high. It looked worse than any apartment I'd ever seen and gave the scuzziest motels a run for the money, if anyone with a dime in his pocket would be caught dead there.

The final perfect touch was a monotonous cacophony of dumb-ass, psychometal "music" blaring through the thin walls.

"Let me take it from here," Albert volunteered.

"Be my guest," I said.

He knocked on a flimsy door covered with streaks of peeling, yellow paint; I half expected the whole structure to crash down in a shambles. I figured we'd wait a long time before any denizens within roused themselves. Instead, the door opened within a few seconds.

It was like stepping back in time to the late twentieth century, when post-punks, headbangers, carpetbangers, and other odd flotsam of adolescent rage had their fifteen minutes.

There were two young men standing in the doorway: one was blond, the other was darker, black-haired, and possibly Hispanic. Rocko and Paco, for the moment.

Rocko didn't say anything, staring at us with glazed eyes, mouth partly open. The only good thing to say about them was that there was simply no way they had been taken over by alien invaders! Even monsters know when to give someone a pass.

"May we come in?" asked Albert.

"Stoked," said Rocko.

There seemed no alternative to going inside; there was no escape rocket in sight. Albert braved the cavern of terrible noise first, then Arlene, then Jill with our buddy. There was nothing left but for me to go inside and witness . . .

The living room. The place was stuffed with what looked like the world's largest and bizarrest crank-lab. There were chemicals of various colors in glass containers balanced precariously on the ratty furniture. A large bottle of thick, silver liquid looked like it might be mercury. I wondered if these guys would blow us up or poison us.

Jill laid the still-wrapped cybermummy on the ground. Then Albert stepped forward. Without saying a word, he flashed a hand-signal. I recognized it: light-drop hand signals, based partly on American Sign Language, heavily modified.

Earth, said Albert.

Man, responded Paco.

Native.

Born.

I blinked. Albert flashed a thirteen-character combination of letters and numbers, and Rocko responded with another. I raised my brows . . . a hand-signal "handshake."

All of a sudden, Rocko's demeanor changed as his face melted into a different one entirely. He gestured to Paco, who closed his mouth. Both suddenly looked fifty IQ points brighter.

Rocko went to the stereo, a nice, state-of-the art system out of place in these surroundings, and turned down the music. "Let's talk," he said, voice still sounding like a stereotypical carpetbanger.

Things got too weird for Yours Truly. While Rocko rapped in a lingo full of terms relating to drugs and rock'n'roll, he produced several pads and pencils, enough for each one of us. The real conversation took place on the pads, while the duo spoke most of the mind-numbing nonsense, occasionally helped out by Albert and Jill, who could talk the talk better than Arlene or I.

The only part of the conversation I paid attention to came off the pads.

Our hosts filled in more details of this Grave New World. Rocko was actually Captain Jerry Renfrew, PhD, U.S. Army and head of one of the CBNW (chem-bio-nuke warfare) labs. His buddy was Dr. Xavier Felix, another chemical warfare specialist.

But why did they pretend to be crystal-meth dealers?

Innocuous, no threat, explained Felix with a scribble.

Civilian DEA, Felix wrote. **Pose crank cooker stuck fake crim recs into Nat Crime Info Cen comptrs.**

There was a noise halfway between a scream and a laugh. It was Jill, and she was jumping up and down. Out loud she said, "I haven't heard that group since I was a kid!" The music was still blaring in the background, even though reduced to a volume that didn't turn the brain to cottage cheese.

On paper, Jill wrote: **I did that!!!!! Mightve done your's!**

Too young, challenged Renfrew, erasing her apostrophe.

Judge/book/cover, argued Felix, added a circle slash around the triplet, the international no-no symbol.

We passed all the notes around to everyone; but each person got them in more or less random order. It took me a while to make sense out of the jumble. When everyone had seen a note, Felix or Renfrew touched it to a Bunsen burner. The notes were written on flash paper, and they vanished instantly with a smokeless flare.

According to Dr. Felix, the DEA, under alien control, was still staffed by traitorous humans, even now. They went hunting for people who could produce the "zombie-brew" chemical treatment used to rework humans into zombies.

They specifically hunted for the more sophisticated drug-lab chemists. It made sense that Captain Renfrew and Felix, both infiltrating from opposite ends, would come together.

When Felix's hand needed a rest, the captain jotted down: **lab I headed one of few not overrun.** He escaped with all his notes and some of his equipment, grew his hair long, and returned to alien territory to infiltrate.

Felix was already undercover, already infiltrating the alien operation, and that's where it got tricky: DEA knew Felix was really an agent; but they thought he was spying on the aliens for DEA—who were cooperating with the aliens in exchange for the promise of all drugs off the street.

In fact, Xavier Felix was a double-double agent, really working for the Resistance . . . unless he was a triple-double agent, or a double-double-double agent, in which case we were all sunk.

Don't aliens investgt horrible noise? I wrote.

They allowed themselves to laugh out loud. At any point in the music discussion, a laugh fit like a corpse in potter's field.

Evidently, excessive noise was not a problem aliens cared much about.

Something was torquing me off. After wrestling with myself, I finally wrote it. **How humans make zombie brew, help aliens evin infiltrating?!?!**

Renfrew stared, absently correcting something on my note. Don't know what. He looked wounded, in pain. **Delib scrwng up recipe. Neurologic poison slow kills drives mad. Makes useless.**

The captain bent over me and read along. He flipped his own sheet over and added: **we're only hot chems. Others druggies cooks FDA that kind of crap.**

Everyone else seemed satisfied, so I dropped it. I was the only one, I guess, who spotted the Clue of the Horrible Admission: even if they were screwing up the brew so the zombies died or went mad—weren't they still turning humans into zombies in the first place?

How did they live with that?

We showed them more about the cybermummy. They had the reaction of any scientist with a new toy.

If there were a solution, they were going to bust humps finding it.

They took us into the basement, where the music from upstairs was merely loud, not ear-splitting. I was surprised a house in Riverside had one, especially this piece of crap. Then it hit me like a bony's fist: they probably dug it themselves. Whatever the case, we were in the hands of impressive dudes.

"You can talk quietly down here without fear of surveillance," Felix whispered.

"Hooray," said Arlene, but kept her voice low.

"Amen," said Albert.

We left Felix and Renfrew and went downstairs, where we rested a moment. I was so tired I felt like the marrow in my bones had turned to dust; or maybe I was having trouble breathing down there. Without intending to, I dozed off on a thick leather couch.

When I came to, the others were unwrapping the mummy. It was embarrassing to have passed out like that.

"You okay, Fly?" Arlene asked over her shoulder.

"Yeah, must have been tireder than I thought," I said. "Sorry about that."

"No problemo," said Arlene, yawning. "I'll take the next nap. You up to joining us?"

I nodded and moved in for a closer look.

The cyberdude was the same as before, still a young black man turned into a computer-age pin cushion. Earlier, we removed enough bandages to see his face. We uncovered his head and saw it was completely shaved, the smooth dome covered in little metal knobs and dials.

As Albert and Arlene continued unwrapping, Jill took a step back. The man wasn't wearing anything but the quickly unwinding bandages. As they started unwrapping below the waist, our fourteen-year-old hellion got embarrassed. Oceans of gore she could take without batting an eyelash, but a nude young man was enough to make her blush.

I was deeply amused and grateful I woke up in time for the entertainment—Jill's reaction, I mean, not the guy. The more nonchalant she tried to be, the more fun I had watching. She actually turned fire-engine red, her normally pale cheeks matching her hair.

I noticed Arlene noticing me noticing Jill. Ah, women!

"It's nothing to get worked up about," she told Jill.

"Maybe Jill should leave the room," suggested Albert.

"That's her decision," said Arlene.

"I don't want to go back upstairs with the . . . chems," she said. "At least we can talk down here."

"Don't let them tease you, hon," Arlene said. "Most everything you're told about sex when you're growing up is a lie anyway."

"You mean what they're told in school?" Albert asked slyly.

"I was thinking of the lies they hear at home," said Arlene, instantly regretting the reference. We didn't want Jill constantly fixating on the slaughter of Mom and Dad.

But the more serious tone affected Jill positively. She went back to the table and helped finish the unwrapping. She didn't look south more than about five or six times. Seven, tops. Being a professional, I was trained to notice details like eye movements.

"What time is it?" Arlene asked, yawning again. She definitely deserved some sack time.

"Ask Fly," said Jill, "he's got the cl-cl-clock."

"Why didn't they have our conference down here, where we could talk, instead of using the pads?" asked Arlene.

I shrugged. "Aliens might think it was weird if

'customers' come over and the cooks disappear down into the basement with them."

"Won't they think it just as strange if the customers disappear alone?"

"Well, let's hope not."

I turned to Jill. "Earlier, you said you might be able to communicate with him on a computer, through one of those jacks. What's the next step?"

She went back to examining the body with the proper detachment. "Can you do it?" I asked.

"Yes and no."

"Care to explain?"

"Yes I can connect, *if* you get me the cables I need. One has to have a male Free-L-19, the other a male Free-L-20, both with a two-fiber mass-serial connector at the other end."

I sure hoped somebody else knew what the hell that meant. "Where do you think we can get all that?"

"Try upstairs; if they don't have any, try Radio Shack or CompUSA."

After writing down the kind of jacks required, I took the list upstairs and showed it to the chem guys. They didn't have what we needed, but the captain produced an Auto Club map and pointed out the nearest Radio Shack.

Kind of reassuring that L.A. still had its priorities.

Back in the basement, I asked who wanted to go. And the result was predictable: "I'll go," said Jill.

"Anyone but Jill," I said. "Maybe I should—"

"Why can't I go?"

"I know there's not much to do in Riverside except shop," I admitted, "even before the demons came. But we've been through this already, Jill. We're still in the you're-not-expendable period."

"I'll go," said Albert.

"Fine," I said. "Now Arlene can get some sack—"

"I'll go with him, Fly," said Arlene.

"But you were yawning only a moment before!"

"I'm not tired now," she said, real perky.

I did what anyone in my position would do. I shrugged. If Arlene had surrender papers for me, I would have signed them on the spot.

29

Lately, I thought I was overdoing quotations from the Book. I'd never had so vivid a recollection for the Word until the world changed. I'd found time to read the scriptures once more in the new era, and now the words stayed with me, perhaps because the altered world made the tales of the Book seem more vivid.

The original Mormons were condemned not only for taking multiple wives, a behavior that might have been cause for sympathy instead of resentment. What upset other Americans of the nineteenth century was the claim that God would reveal a whole new history to newly chosen saints. The concept of Latter Day Saints was more offensive to the Christian majority of that time than any personal behavior or economic consequences.

My favorite Bible passage was John 21:25, the end of the Gospel According to Saint John, and it should have been the perfect shield against such prejudice; but most Christians pay little attention to the Word:

> And there are also many other things which Jesus did, the which, if they should be written every one, I suppose that even the world itself could not contain the books that should be written. Amen.

They liked those words just fine in theory; practice was something else again. The portions where the Book of Mormon disagrees with established Christian practices didn't help either. People got really upset when they were told they were not merely wrong, but *diabolically* wrong, on the subject of baptism.

Hell. Arlene and I were about to go back into hell. We were trying to save living babies from burning in the hell on Earth. She was a good friend and comrade. I liked her a lot and hoped I would not witness her death. But since becoming bold about her sinful interest in me, she was making me uncomfortable. I would find her a lot easier to deal with if I weren't tempted by her.

Or if she would consent to . . . Jesus! Give me strength! Am I really ready to contemplate holy union? I grimaced; it was a very big step, a life commitment, and I was too chicken to think about it yet. I didn't feel much older than Jill!

My soul was troubled because I *did* desire Arlene. A verse from Nephi kept running through my mind, like a public service announcement:

> O Lord, I have trusted in thee, and I will trust in thee forever. I will not put my trust in the arm of flesh; for I know that cursed is he that putteth his faith in the arm of flesh. Yea, cursed

> is he that putteth his trust in man or maketh flesh his arm.

"A buck for your thoughts," Arlene said, standing very close to me. We were taking our first rest stop in an alley. Lately, I was coming to feel safer in alleys than in open spaces.

"I was remembering a passage from the Book."

"You want to share it with me?" she asked. I looked deep into her bloodshot eyes, the prettiest sight in the world, and there was no mockery or sarcasm. I wasn't about to tell her how hard I was trying to resist temptation and that right now I spelled sin beginning with a scarlet letter A.

But there was an earlier passage from the Second Book of Nephi that spoke directly to any warrior's heart. I quoted it instead:

> "O Lord, wilt thou make way for mine escape before mine enemies! Wilt thou make my path straight before me! Wilt thou not place a stumbling block in my way—but that thou wouldst clear my way before me, a hedge not up my way, but the ways of mine enemy."

"Good plan," said Arlene.

"God's plan."

She touched my arm, and I felt relaxed instead of tense. "Albert, what if I told you I'd be willing to study your religion to see what it's about?"

I wasn't expecting that. "Why would you do that?" I asked, probably too suspicious. In the Marines, I got too used to being sucker-punched by antireligious bigots.

"I'm not promising to convert or anything," she told me, "but I care about you, Albert. You believe in these things, and I want to understand."

"Cool," I said; but I was still suspicious of her motives.

She dropped the other shoe: "So if I'm willing to study what you believe, would you be willing to relax a little and we could get together?"

I'd expected more subtlety from someone as intelligent as Arlene, but then again, Marines were not famous for an indirect approach. I had to close my eyes before shaking my head. I couldn't make the word no come out.

"I don't mean to make you uncomfortable," said Arlene.

"You may mean the best," I told her, "but it doesn't matter what we do or say. Unless we're married, we can't make love."

"You mean we can't even fool around?" she asked.

"I mean we can't have sex together unless we're married."

I could tell by her expression I was a more surprising phenomenon than the spidermind. "You're kidding," she said. "Not even touching?"

"Not sexual touching." I wished she'd let up!

She looked away from me, almost shyly. "I'm only talking about a little fun."

I tried a new tack. "How can you think of fun when the world is dying?"

"Seems like a good time to me," she said. "We could use a break."

"Arlene, any sex outside of marriage is fornication, even just touching. That kind of touching. The sin is in the thought."

She mumbled something. I could have sworn she asked, "How about *inside* marriage?" But she turned away and pretended she hadn't spoken. I suppose Arlene was as freaked about the thought as I was.

I didn't think I was making the best possible case

for my faith, but God isn't about winning a popularity contest. He doesn't have to.

"Albert, if you ever feel differently, I'll be there for you." I could tell she'd run out of things to say. At this moment, I probably seemed more alien than a steam-demon or a bony.

Fortunately, the rest break was over. I pointed to my watch and Arlene nodded. We could return to the far less dangerous territory of fighting monsters in hell. At least I knew what to expect from them.

Nothing else stood between us and the Radio Shack except the corpses of some dead dogs. We broke into the abandoned store, kicking in the inadequately padlocked door. We used our day-night goggles to hunt through the darkness, not wanting to use a betraying light. A number of large spiderwebs were spun across a wall of boom boxes, proof that one Earth life form might survive the invasion unchanged. I was surprised that the store didn't seem to have been looted . . . but then, what for?

"We should be able to find the jacks for Jill," said Arlene, who giggled right afterward. It took me a moment to recognize what was funny.

She was right, though. In the store's unlooted condition, we found the jacks very quickly. She pocketed them and headed for the front of the store, but stopped at a counter. Something had caught her eye; I couldn't see what.

"I need to ask you a question," she said.

"Ask away."

"Do you love someone?"

"That's a very personal question."

"That's why I'm asking," she followed up. "Do you?"

She deserved an answer. "Yes, but she's dead."

"You never made love to her?"

"She died before we married."

"Thank you for telling me," she said. "I'm not trying to probe you, Albert. I've succeeded in revealing too much of myself. Now let's get back before I say something else stupid."

She went out the door, and I glanced at the counter to see a demo music CD of Golden Oldies, led off by Carly Simon singing "Nobody Does it Better." I'd never heard the song but I could imagine the subject matter. Jesus help us; was this a divine retribution? I shuddered; I hadn't seen any rainbows since the invasion.

We didn't exchange another word on the way back. Her expression was grim, hard. She was probably angry with herself for opening up to me without finding out first how I really felt. Nonreligious people usually had this trouble with us. We really meant it. No wonder we came off like nuts. How could I tell Arlene that she was probably allergic to nuts?

30

I let Jill take the next nap on the couch. For a crazy moment I envied the mummy for sleeping so long. Jill didn't seem all that rested when Arlene and Albert returned, but any sleep had to be better than none.

Jill asked if there was any coffee, and it turned out that the chems stored it in the basement. Hot-tap coffee helped bring her around, and with dark circles under her eyes and still yawning, she got to work on the man who was no longer a mummy but still plenty cyber.

She attached the necessary wires, brought up her ultramicro and started hacking. I still had my doubts that this would actually work; but the more excited Jill became, the more I was converted.

Then she said the magic words, "Yes, yes, *yes!*" and got up to pump her arm and strut like a guy. I doubt that sex will ever give her that much excitement.

About a minute passed while she fiddled with the TracPad, listening to handshaking routines on the audio-out. She gave the first report: "I've made contact with his brain at seventeen thirty-two. His name is Kenneth Estes."

"Does he know where he is?" I asked.

Jill hesitated, and then spelled it out: "He thinks he's dead and in hell."

"Can we talk to him?" I asked.

"Yup," said Jill. "I can type questions, and you can read his answers. But you have to scan through the random crap; it's a direct link to Ken's brain."

"All right, you interpret," I replied. "The first thing is find out who he is and why he's important enough for demon gift-wrapping."

Arlene sat up on the couch where she'd almost dozed off. This could well be too interesting to miss. Albert sat in a chair, but he was wide-awake. Jill tapped for a long moment at her tiny keyboard, using all ten fingers, much to my surprise. I thought all hackers were two-finger typists, it was a law or something. She read the first part of the man's story:

"As I said, his name's Ken Estes. He's a computer software designer slumming as a CIA analyst. Low-level stuff, not a field agent or anything. He was born in—"

"No time for the family background," I interrupted. "Keep him focused on how and why he became a cybermummy."

Somewhere, water was dripping. I hadn't noticed it before, but it was very annoying while waiting for Jill to pass on the messages in silence. Finally, she spoke again: "When the aliens landed and started the war, Ken was told by his superiors that the agency had developed a new computer which the operator accessed in V.R. mode."

"What's V.R.?" Albert asked.

"Old term; this guy's in his thirties! Virtual Reality; we call it burfing now, from 'body surfing,' I think."

"Oh, the net," said Albert.

"We'll go back to school later," I jumped in. "Get on with it, Jill!"

"High-ranking officers within the agency induced Ken to accept the implants 'for the good of the United States.' Told him he'd be able to help fight the aliens. Instead, it turned out they were traitors within the Company—"

Jill stopped for a moment, swallowing hard. She took another sip of coffee before continuing. We were back to her deep disgust for human traitors. She made herself read on. She wouldn't be guilty of dereliction of duty.

The high-ranking officers had cooperated with the aliens, joining a criminal conspiracy against the country they were sworn to defend—and incidentally, against their own species. Ken "told" us more through Jill: *Company 'borged me, attached me to alien net, one not part conspiracy waited too long, tried to save killed conspiratora-tora-tora befora took him out . . .*

"How did the aliens intend to use him?" I asked.

Jill asked, and the answer came: *Hoped him conduit betwalien biotechputer netputer and webwide human d'bases crlsystems.*

"Jeez, it's like a sci-fi James Joyce," I said. "From now on, you interpret, Jill. It gives me a headache!"

"We live in a science fiction world," said Arlene, wandering over from the couch, wide-awake, as Ken's tale unfolded. "Fly, I'd like to ask a question," she said.

"Be my guest."

"Jill, would you ask him how much of the alien technology was biologically based?"

Jill asked and passed on: "Ken says that *all* the alien technology is biotech, except for stuff they stole from subject races, like the rocket technology for the flying skulls."

"Yes!" exclaimed Arlene, as excited as Jill at a moment of vindication. "We've been on the right track all along, Fly. The original enemy went as far with biological techniques as they possibly could. Perhaps the first species they conquered lived on the same planet, but had a mechanical technology they were able to adapt to their own use. Eventually, they conquered the Gate builders; we monkeyed with the Gates, turned them on, and the invaders poured through. That would explain why in any choice between organic and mechanical, they always opt for the biological."

"And it would also explain why our own technology shows up in odd places," I agreed, "and why they use firearms."

"They're pragmatic," said Albert. "Their study of us proves that, these demonic forms they take."

I tried to get the show back on the road: "Jill, can he tell us how they communicate with one another?"

There was a long stretch before Jill helped us out with our immediate communication needs. "He says it hurts to think about this, but he will. He . . . realizes we're free. I've told him a little about us and . . . he does want to help."

"Tell him we appreciate anything he can do," I said.

Another moment passed and he answered the question beyond my expectation: "There are neural pathways integrated into the computers. Psi-connections carry all the orders. The aliens don't need to *tell* their slaves what to do! They merely think the orders, but it's different than merely thinking. No word. Project? Psimulcast?"

"Does Ken know where the commands originate?" I asked.

"He doesn't understand the question," Jill answered quickly.

"Uh, I'm not asking if he knows where the ultimate leaders happen to be right now. But does he know how the chain of command functions for the invasion?"

Jill's forehead showed some extra furrows as she passed on my thoughts, probably doing some translating along the way. Finally, Ken passed on a detailed report, filtered through Jill.

"Question is meaningless; no hierarchy."

"Hive culture? Collective?"

"Nope; they just . . . huh? Uh, they just all do the same thing. The aliens themselves; the slaves—I think that means everyone not part of 'the people'—fight like crazy. That's why they're not 'the people.' "

"Can Ken issue commands?"

"Fly, that's what he was made for! Receive alien commands and convey them to human systems."

"I mean, the other way 'round?"

She tapped, stared. "He doesn't understand the question. It's like he's not allowed to think about it or see the question. Some sort of protected-mode thing firm-wired in. Wait, he's talking again . . .

"This 'invasion fleet' is actually an exploration fleet. Highest-intel aliens are the entities inside the spiderminds. Send out fleets, probe, when feasible conquer alien worlds, no reason other than raw power. Well, Ken can't understand the reason, if there is one.

"Slave masters with an expanding empire, but more interested in finding new genetic material to absorb into their web-of-life—which is how they think of it—than they are in having new individual slaves . . . especially short-lived, contentious slaves."

Jill stopped talking and took off the headphones, rubbing a hand across her forehead. "Are you all right?" asked Arlene.

"Little headache. I'll be all right," she said.

"You need to stop?" I asked.

"No. Hey, I just had a brainstorm! If we could get Ken jacked into one of the alien terminals and override the safeties, we could sabotage their net!"

"Brilliant idea," I said. "Why didn't I think of that?" I winked. "Maybe we could sabotage their entire technology base."

"There's a problem. When he's connected to the net, there are built-ins that override his human volition. The monitor can't take over the CPU."

"It can if it has its own chip set and special programming," muttered Arlene.

"The program that shuts off his brain must have a 'front end' somewhere *in* his brain," Jill said—to herself, I presumed. "If I can find it, I can disable it, or I'm not Jill Hoerchner."

"Are you?" asked my pal.

Jill glanced over at her and added, "I'd need a quiet place where I can be undisturbed for several days. Days, not hours."

There were several hundred questions I wanted to ask Ken; but we heard a loud noise from upstairs. It didn't sound like more of the headbanger music. It sounded like heavy feet thumping around upstairs. Maybe it was aliens coming to pick up their supply of zombie brew.

I was pissed that the chems hadn't warned us when these "guests" would pay them a visit; then I realized that the aliens wouldn't stick to any kind of set program. All the more reason for the captain and the doctor to maintain their act.

Very quietly, Arlene flicked off the one light in the basement ceiling. We sat in the dark. We heard raised voices; the chems were denying that they'd seen a human "strike team" or a human wrapped in bandages.

I heard the telltale hiss of imp talk; I held my breath . . . there were a *lot* of feet tramping around up there.

A new kind of voice spoke next, a grating, metallic monotone. It sounded like a robot from an old sci-fi movie, or something speaking through a vocoder.

Once this voice entered the conversation, our human allies sounded frantic. I had a bad feeling about this. Good agents would put on a believable act. Good agents would stick to the part, right to the point of death. But were they?

The next sound we heard was all too familiar: a powerful explosion shook the house, followed by the smell of fire from above. Before we could even think about acting, there was another explosion, and now smoke began to drift down the wooden steps to our hiding place.

We listened to the alien storm troopers start tearing the place apart. They'd convinced me of their sincerity in trying to find us. I huddled the others and said: "The bastards *will* find the basement. Our only hope is if the cooks dug an escape tunnel, one that exits from here."

Keeping the light off didn't make it any easier, but I

hadn't noticed a tunnel when we could see. If my pipe dream produced a real pipe, the opening would be hidden anyway. We rummaged through spare equipment, desperately trying not to make noise. The stuff was mainly metal, so the process wasn't easy.

The chems had stored their chemical stuff in the basement. Tanks of volatiles, glassware, a fire extinguisher, jars and jars of chemicals (and I was grateful the glass was thick). There were plenty of shelves and books. And nowhere behind any of this did we find a secret opening.

We hunted the walls, shaking bookcases that might be doors, checking fireplaces for hidden holes, anything at all! I was about to give up when my hands came to rest on a bookcase that seemed bolted down, unlike the others.

I started tugging on various books to see if one of them was a trigger mechanism. Two things happened simultaneously. First, I found a book that wouldn't move. Never had I been happier to find something stuck.

Second, with a triumphant howling, the imps found the trapdoor and flung it wide, letting light pour into the basement.

We froze; I was a statue holding up the bookshelf; Albert stood nearby, holding the naked Ken in a fireman's carry; Jill was part of that tableau, holding her CompMac ultramicro, still jacked into Ken; and Arlene was on the other side of the basement room, in the gloom. Of the five of us, Ken did the best job of playing dead, but he had an unfair advantage.

A *thing* dropped down the open trap.

This baby looked vaguely humanoid—oh, they were keeping at it—but definitely alien. The yellow-white, naked body maintained the hell motif so popular with the invaders. No obvious genitalia. The arms and legs were unusually small and thin. The most outstanding feature was the way the skin rippled like bubbling marshmallows over an open fire. I wondered if this might be one of their enslaved races.

As it came closer, it dawned on me why the spindly limbs were irrelevant to its effectiveness in battle. The new monster was hot. I mean, fires-of-hell-make-your-eyeballs-pop hot. No wonder the skin rippled from the amazing heat. He was like a mirage in the desert made into burning sulfur-flesh, the most "hellish" creature yet.

There were books on the shelf right next to it. They burst into flame from his proximity, lighting the room, and the wood of the shelf charred right before our eyes. Maybe it was an optical illusion, but it appeared that actual flames danced along the thing's skin. The little voice in the back of my head started shrieking: *Saved the best for last!* The trouble with the little voice was that it was so damned optimistic.

As the living torch moved closer, I saw its eyes weren't really eyes—more like a ring of flaming dots so bright that it hurt to look at them. I wondered how we might appear to this creature; I also wished I had a barrel of ice water to throw on the uninvited guest.

The others were as confused as their fearless leader. Arlene was able to fire off a short burst from her AB-10. The thing didn't even react, but Arlene's machine pistol became so hot she had to drop it. Then the fire-thing moved between the others and Yours Truly, focusing on me.

Having cut me off, the monster put on a little magic act. It was so bright, I couldn't turn away, no matter how painful . . . and I watched its body actually contract, becoming brighter as it squeezed together—like it was about to explode.

Training took over, the healthy respect we were taught for all kinds of explosives. I had no desire to become Marine flambé.

I dove to the side, screaming inarticulately; everyone got the idea, falling flat, trying to cover himself. Fireboy exploded, a blast lancing out and disintegrating the bookshelf where I had stood a moment before.

Albert threw himself over Ken's body, then left Ken on the floor and grabbed his Uzi clone. We had all the light we could use.

The big Mormon opened fire. The big gun actually sounded soft compared to the horrific explosion from the alien, but the result was the same as with Arlene. Did the thing generate a heat field around its immediate body surface, heat so intense that bullets dissolved before getting through?

One good plan was growing in my head: *run away!* This was a much better plan than it sounded. Rising shakily to my feet, I could see quite clearly the tunnel we'd been trying to find. The shelf I'd been exploring had indeed covered the exit, and the explosion had done a superb job of *open sesame.* I considered how to rescue the others, or at least Jill and Ken. The mission wasn't a burnout case yet.

For some reason, the fire monster seemed to have a thing for me; it targeted me again. I recognized the telltale signs. Looking right at me (if those black dots counted for eyes), it began to contract, powering up for another burst.

Before I ended my career as a piece of toast, Arlene came to the rescue. She got right behind the monster and opened fire from behind. Having learned her lesson about wasting bullets on this guy, she used the fire extinguisher.

Never discourage initiative, that's my motto!

She sprayed the thing, snarling, "Goddamned fire-eater!" It was the best name she'd invented in quite a while.

The monster screamed. The fire extinguisher was

actually extinguishing the fire! This suggested a whole new approach to dealing with the monsters: properly labeled household appliances could restore Heaven on Earth.

Arlene kept pouring the foam on the fire-eater, who was making a sound somewhere between a screeching cat and sizzling bacon. If the Marine Corps were around after we'd saved the world, I'd recommend a special medal for Arlene as master of unconventional weaponry: first the chainsaw, now the safety equipment.

I have the highest possible regard for women who save my life.

"Move out!" I bellowed to one and all, issuing one of my favorite orders. Everyone liked the idea just fine. Except for one imp, that is, without the brains to avoid tough Marines who had just stopped a monster compared to which an imp isn't fit to light cigars.

Imps aren't generally all that bright, of course, so I don't know why I was surprised. The ugly little sucker dropped through the hole and threw a flaming wad of snot that I refused to take seriously. On the other hand, one of those wads cashed the chips of Bill Ritch. The thought made me doubly mad, so . . .

I returned fire with my double-barreled, thinking how I actually preferred an honest, all-American duck gun like this one to the fascist, pump-action variety. Yeah! The imp split down the middle, the guts making a Rorschach test. Better than a riot gun, no question about it.

We hauled ass down the tunnel as I ran our list of liabilities. There was only one, actually, but it was big. If we'd gotten the shelf open and closed behind us, we'd have a decent chance right now. However, all the monsters in the world knew where we'd gone, and the hordes would be *hot* on our heels.

Reinforcing this idea was the hissing, growling, slithering, wheezing, roaring, shlumping, and thud-thud-thudding a few hundred meters behind us. There was nothing to do but run like thieves in the night.

Arlene brought the fire extinguisher with her; God knows why, unless we ran into another of our brand-new playmates. Albert and Jill were strapped, so their hands were free to carry Ken. Poor Ken. The way he was getting knocked around, bruised, and cut, he would have been doing a lot better if the bandages had been left on. If we got out of this, I promised to buy him a whole new body bandage.

The tunnel, winding snakelike, was terribly narrow, lined with raw earth and occasionally propped with wooden braces. The little voice in the back of my head insisted we were perfectly all right, so long as the passage wasn't blocked. This was the same voice that always told me to leave the umbrella home right before the heaviest rainfall of the year.

Now, it's not like we hit a real cave-in. If we had, we'd simply have died right there. But a partial cave-in we could deal with.

Albert threw his massive frame at the wall of dirt, and it shifted. We were slowed down by Jill and Arlene pushing Ken through, while Albert yanked from the other side. I guarded the rear with the shotgun loaded, ready for bear. No bears.

A few feet ahead, we hit the outside of a huge pipe and found a hole buzz-cut right through it. We opened it, and I wished I'd left my olfactory senses back on Mars.

"Ew!" said Jill, another unsolicited but insightful commentary.

Sewer main. We were assailed by the odor of methane.

"Dive in, the offal's fine!" said Arlene cheerfully. The sound of our pursuers only fifty meters back made the idea a lot more appealing. We could hear their raspy breathing.

We ducked into the sewers, very careful that Ken shouldn't accidentally drown. We'd come this far together, and he was starting to feel like a member of the family.

As we ran we heard the last sound anyone wants to hear underground: the roar and whoosh of a rocket. I crashed into the others, making Albert drop Ken. Something heavy, smelling of burnt copper, whizzed over our heads; a nasty little rocket that just started to curve, heat-seeking, but couldn't quite make the turn. It blew a hole in the pipe instead.

And I'd thought the tunnel smelled bad before!

I shook the dust out of my eyes and coughed, then lifted Jill from the ground. Tears were pouring down her face, but she wasn't crying; my eyes were watering too. Albert jerked Arlene to her feet, and they both checked on Ken, who was lying facedown with a pile of dirt on his head.

Jill opened his mouth, shoveled the dirt out, and made sure he hadn't swallowed his tongue. He coughed, and Jill got to her feet, handing Ken off like a sack of wheat. I loved watching a fourteen-year-old do what was considered criminal in the previous world: act like an adult.

"Over here," yelled Albert, pointing to a small hatch leading to a cramped corridor. The monsters were big; they'd have a hard time following.

Albert went first, probably not a good idea. I preferred Jill and Arlene in front. If we were ambushed from behind, the girls might still get through, and Albert and I could hold off the Bad Guys; the mission would go on.

But it was too late to do anything about it now. At least we knew that anywhere Albert went, the rest of us could easily follow. I brought up the rear, hanging back to delay, if necessary.

The corridor walls were lined with pipes. When I caught up with the others, they were trying to open a pressure hatch at the far end. I brought bad luck with me—the sound of another rocket.

Albert and I dived left, Arlene and Jill right, taking Ken with them. Our actions confused the heat-seeker: it turned partially starboard, exploding and rupturing several pipes. Again we had the fun of choking and gagging on a huge burst of methane.

Albert grunted as he turned the difficult pressure hatch; we heard the gratifying sound of metal grinding against metal. He didn't open the portal a moment too soon.

Looking back, I saw imps, zombies, and one bony. That answered the question of who'd been firing rockets. Bringing up their rear was either *another* fire-eater or the one Arlene had sprayed with the foam. If the latter, he'd be looking for payback.

Arlene stepped up, fire extinguisher pointed, ready for round two. I suddenly remembered something from my raucous high school daze. "No!" I shouted. "Get back! Get through the hatch right now!"

She got.

Coming out last, I slammed the hatch shut and spun the wheel. "That's not going to last," said Albert.

"Won't need to," I said, backing away. "Everybody, get *way* back!"

Albert's face was a mask of puzzlement; then it dawned on him what was about to happen.

"Hope you all *really* like barbecue," I addressed the troops. "Hey, Arlene. Remember when they built the L.A. subway?"

"Yeah . . ." she said, scowling, still confused.

The mother of all gas explosions rocked us off our feet, blowing the hatch clean off its hinges; the flying metal could have killed any of us in the path.

I staggered to my feet. It didn't take a lot of nerve to go over and check on the results; just a strong stomach. Nothing survived that explosion, not even the fire-eater.

As I peered into the maw of hell, I saw nothing left of the alien pursuers except shreds of flesh and a fine mist of alien blood. And of course the lingering odor of sour lemons.

"What happened?" asked Jill, stunned. At least, I assume that's what she asked; all I could hear was a long, loud alarm bell.

I'd counted on the fire-eater; thankfully, it was hot enough to set off the methane.

Jill was completely recovered from being stunned. She jumped up and down and shouted something, probably some contemporary equivalent of yowza.

We old folk were still a little shell-shocked as we continued along the sewer. After several twists and turns, it dawned on us we were lost.

Arlene had a compass, and now was the time to use it. "We've got a problem," she said; I was just starting to be able to hear again. "It shows a different direction every time."

"Electric current in the pipe switches," I said. "Take averages, figure out a rough west."

No matter where we were and what was happening, the watchwords must be "Go west, go west." We'd find the computer in L.A., so the President had told us; hope he knew what he was talking about. There, we guaranteed a reckoning the enemy would long remember.

31

We continued westward until we finally emerged several klicks from where we'd entered. Night was falling again. We'd had a busy day.

"Transportation," Albert pointed out. We beheld an old Lincoln Continental, covered in some kind of crud halfway between rust and slime, making it impossible to determine its original color. It probably had an automatic transmission; the mere thought made me shudder.

Albert went over and opened the unlocked door. There was no key. "I'll bet it still runs," he said, lying down on the seat so he could look up at the steering column. He did violence to the crappy housing and started fiddling with the wires. A moment later the engine coughed into life.

"You hot-wired the car," said Jill, impressed.

"Sure," he said.

"I'm surprised you'd know how to do that," she said.

"Why?" he asked, getting out of the dinosaur.

"Was that part of sniper training?" Jill wanted to know.

"Part of my troubled youth."

"I wish more Mormons were like you," she told him.

"The Church was good for me, Jill," he told her. "It turned my life around."

"Which way were you facing?" she asked jokingly.

"Toward hell," he said.

"You're still facing that way," observed Arlene, "every time you take a step."

"Yes," he agreed, "but now I'm able to fight it. I'd rather blast a demon than give him my soul."

We'd had this conversation before. I preferred opting out this time. Arlene didn't mind a dose of déjà vu, apparently, but then, she was sweet on the guy. "They're aliens," she said.

"Sure," he agreed. "But for me, they're demons too."

One man's image of terror is another man's joy ride. Speaking of which, the old Lincoln was enough of a monster for me. I was half sorry it still ran. A quick look at the gas gauge told the story: half a tank, plenty to make it to Los Angeles.

One thing about an old family car: there was plenty of room for our family, including Ken propped up between Jill and Arlene in the backseat. I was happy to let Albert drive. I rode shotgun.

Albert flipped on the lights in the twilight and triumphantly announced, "They work!"

"Great," I said. "Now turn them off."

"Oh, right," he said like a little boy caught playing with the wrong toy. We drove along without lights, heading toward the diminished glow of Ellay.

"Do you have a new plan?" Arlene asked.

Glancing in the rearview mirror, I saw that Jill was sleeping. "Of course," I said. "Always. I think we should hijack a plane, elude any pursuit—"

"Yeah," Albert interrupted. "I wonder if they have any aircraft? I haven't seen any."

"Maybe they're using zombie pilots," Arlene commented hopefully. Zombie pilots would not have fast reflexes.

"So, as I was saying," I continued, "we take our plane and hot-tail it to Hawaii. There we find the War Technology Center and take them Ken. With help from Jill, we plug Ken into the bionet and crash the whole, friggin' alien system."

"Good plan," said Albert.

"Ditto," said Arlene.

It was good to be appreciated. With a proper respect for Yours Truly, I might yet help Arlene to find God. I was certain that Albert wouldn't mind that.

"Wonder if there'll be monsters at the city limits," said Albert at length.

"Don't see why they'd have that much organization," I answered, "after what we've seen. What do you think, Arlene?" I asked, glancing into the rear-view mirror again. She'd joined Jill in the Land of Nod. Given the condition of Ken Estes, the backseat had become the sleeping compartment of this particular train.

"The girls are taking forty," commented Albert with a touch of envy.

"How are you holding up?" I asked.

"Driving in the dark without lights keeps the old adrenaline flowing."

"I know what you mean. But if you can use some relief, I'll spell you."

He risked taking his eyes off the black spread of road long enough to glance over. "You're all right, Fly. I see why Arlene respects you so much."

"She's told you that?"

"Not in so many words. But it's an easy tell."

We both tried to discern something of the road. The horizon was bright, in contrast to the darkness right in front of us. It was that time of day. I rubbed my eyes, suddenly starting to lose it.

"Why don't you take a nap?" he suggested.

"No. Should at least be two of us awake, and I want to make sure you're one of them."

"Right."

Exhausted but too wired to sleep, we made it into Los Angeles at night. We didn't run into any monster patrols on the way. Maybe they were saving up some real doozies for us at the Beverly Center.

At the outskirts of the city, zombie guards shuffled back and forth in a caricature of military discipline. Even a zombie would have noticed our approach if we'd had the headlights on. Score one for basic procedure.

Albert took a side road, but we ran into the same problem. "How long do I keep this up?" he asked.

"All night, I'd say, if I hadn't prepared for this."

"How?"

"I didn't throw out the lemons we didn't get around to using before. I wrapped them in plastic wrap from the MREs. We still have them with us."

"To borrow from Jill, ick!" he said. "Who's been carting around that rotting crap?"

"You, Bubba!"

"Just for that, Fly, you get to wake the girls." The man knew a thing or two about revenge.

We parked and I woke up Jill first. Then I let Jill risk tapping Arlene on the shoulder. Some tough Marines you wake with kid gloves—or better yet, with a kid. Arlene came to with a start, but she was good. Very good.

The night air felt pleasantly cool. As we spoiled it with spoiled citrus, Jill asked, "What about Ken?"

"Lime and lemon him too," said Arlene. "We've all got to be the same to the zombie noses."

"So, walk or ride?" asked Albert.

"Don't see any reason to give up these wheels before we have to," I said, amazing myself, considering how I regarded the old Lincoln. "With the windows down, we ought to pass."

"I look dead enough to keep driving," said Albert. We all piled back in, thought rancid, graveyard thoughts, and rolled.

As we approached the first zombie checkpoint, I started worrying. There hadn't been any other cars around. But we'd seen a fleet of trucks with zombie drivers back in Buckeye. I'd have felt a lot better if we weren't the only car.

Suddenly we were rammed from behind. A truck had hit us. It didn't have lights. One good view in the side mirror revealed a zombie driver. "Don't react," I hissed to everyone, fearing a volley of gunfire at the wrong moment. Everyone kept his cool.

"We weren't hit very hard," I said. The truck was barely tooling along, at about the same slow approach speed we were doing. "Everyone all right?" I asked quietly.

While I received affirmatives, the zombie driver demonstrated some ancient, primitive nerve impulse that had survived from the human days of Los Angeles. The fughead leaned on his horn. All of a sudden, I completely relaxed. Getting past the checkpoint was going to be a cinch.

"Shall I take us in, Corporal?" asked Albert, obviously on the same wavelength.

"Hit it, brother," I said.

The truck stuck close to our bumper through the totally porous checkpoint. After that, we just drove in typical L.A. style, weaving drunkenly between zombie-driven trucks, leaning on our horn, all the time heading for the ever popular LAX. I wanted to give the airport the biggest laxative it had ever had with Lemon Marine Suppositories. Cleans out those unsightly monsters every time!

32

We dumped the car in one of the overcrowded LAX parking lots. Lot C, in fact. There was real joy in not worrying about finding a parking place, and an even greater pleasure in not worrying about remembering it.

We only had to hop a single fence to get where we were going, in the time-honored tradition of hijackers, and Ken didn't weigh very much. A thought crossed my mind. "So, uh, one of us knows how to fly a plane, right?"

"Better than flying it wrong," Arlene said.

"No time for jarhead humor," I said. "Gimmie an answer."

"Funny," said Arlene, quite seriously, "but I was about to ask the same question. Really."

We both looked at Albert. "I'd been planning to take lessons, but I never got around to it," he admitted sadly.

"How hard can it be?" I asked, recalling the words of an old movie character.

We infiltrated the refueling area for the big jets, and I found the perfect candidate: an ancient C-5 Air Force transport, which could easily make it all the way to Hawaii. Assuming somebody could drive it.

Everyone was already doing a good zombie performance, although I still thought Jill was overdoing it. Ken was propped between Albert and me, and we were able to make it look like he was stumbling along with us. We prepared to tramp up the ramp, joining a herd of other zombies.

A pair of Clydes waited at the entrance. Damn the luck! We could pass for zombies among zombies, but I wasn't at all sure about these guys.

They were disarming each zombie as it entered the plane. It was a perfectly reasonable precaution, considering how zombies acted in close quarters when they were jostled, pushed, pulled . . . or damn near anything else. I couldn't blame the Clydes for not wanting the plane to be suddenly depressurized, but the idea of being disarmed was not at all appealing.

We did some shifting around, then hit the ramp with myself in the lead, the other four right behind me, four abreast with Jill and Ken on the inside. Jill did as good a job as I had of keeping Ken's end up. This makeshift plan could work if the Clydes were bored.

Sure enough, they barely paid attention as we simply took our heavy artillery and tossed them on the pile outside the plane. Bye-bye, shotgun. This left us with nothing but the pistols hidden inside our jackets.

We stuck close to each other, lost in the zombie mob, as the plane started to taxi; then we worked our way up front. The Clydes were in the back, huddled and talking about something. By the time the plane lifted off, giving me that rush I always get from takeoff, we were close enough to the front that we could duck behind the curtain leading to the cockpit door. I took it on myself to give it a gentle push.

The door opened inward, revealing a pair of imps

hovering over a strange globe, another product of alien technology, bolted to the floor. The monsters appeared to be driving the plane through the use of this pulsing, humming, buzzing ball. It gave me a headache just looking at it; biotech made me need a Pepto-Bismol. The glistening, sweating device was connected to the instrument panel.

The imps' backs were to us. They were so preoccupied with their task, they didn't even turn around when we entered. I closed the door quietly and locked it.

From the cockpit I saw Venus . . . we were going the wrong way, due east!

This simply would not do. I pointed at the imps, and then at Arlene. She nodded. We stepped forward, pistols in hand, and the barrels of our guns touched the back of imp heads at exactly the same instant.

The little voice in the back of my head chose that instant to open its fat yap and suggest that Arlene and I should say something to the imps, on the order of, "We're hijacking this plane to Hawaii. We never did have a proper honeymoon!"

But there was no way to give an imp orders, other than *Fall down, you're dead!* We'd simply take over the plane. After we killed the imps.

I'm certain that Arlene and I fired at the same moment. The idle thoughts passing through my mind couldn't have affected the results.

But something went wrong.

The imp Arlene tapped went down and stayed down. She put two more bullets in him, almost by reflex, to make certain that the job was good and done. I should have been able to take care of one lousy imp, after the way we'd exterminated ridiculous numbers of zombies, demons, ghosts, and pumpkins..

One lousy imp! At the closest possible range! The

head turned ever so slightly as I squeezed the trigger. Somehow the bullet went in at an angle that didn't put the imp down.

Turning around, screaming, it flung one flaming snotball. One lousy snotball. I dived to the left. Arlene was already out of the line of fire, on the right, taking care of the other one. Jill crouched, fingers stuck in her ears, trying to keep out the loud reverberations of the shots in the enclosed space. Albert could have done the same.

But Albert froze. As much of a pro as he was, he stood there with the dumb expression of a deer caught in the headlights, right before road kill. Maybe Albert had a little voice in the back of his head, and it had chosen that moment to bug him. Or maybe it was such a foregone conclusion that these imps were toast, he'd let down his guard, taking a brief mental rest at precisely the wrong moment.

The fireball struck him dead-center in the face.

I remembered losing Bill Ritch that way.

It didn't seem right to survive all the firepower this side of the goddamned sun, and then cash in on something so trivial. It made me so mad, the cockpit vanished in a haze of red. It was like I'd mainlined another dose of that epinephrine stuff from Deimos.

I dropped my gun and jumped on the imp, beating at it with my fists, tearing at it with my teeth. I was screaming louder than poor Albert, writhing on the floor holding his face.

Hands were on me from behind, trying to pull me off, little hands. Jill was behind me, yelling something in my ear I couldn't understand; but the part of me that didn't want to hurt Jill won out over the part that wanted to rip the imp apart with my fingernails.

Letting go seemed a bad idea, though: there'd be nothing stopping it from tossing the fireballs to fry us all. Then I heard Arlene shouting something about a "clear shot," and I suddenly remembered the invention of firearms.

The caveman jumped out of the way to give Cockpit Annie the target she wanted. She pumped round after round into the imp's open mouth. He never closed it. He never raised his claw hands again.

Of course, while we were encountering these difficulties, there was a commotion outside. I guess we had made a bit of noise.

One of the zombies tried the door. The lock held for now. Sanity returned, and I helped the blinded Albert get up, casually noticing that he hadn't taken any of the flaming stuff down his throat or nose. He might live.

In the distance we heard gunshots and curses. The Clydes must have been forcing their way forward, shooting any zombies in their way. Suddenly, I was grateful that the plane was a sardine can of solid, reworked flesh.

"Okay, moment of truth," said Arlene, the mantle of command falling on her there and then. It's not something I'd wish on my worst enemy. "Who's going to fly this damned thing?" she asked in the tones of a demand, not a question.

The gunshots crept close. We had perhaps a minute.

"I will," said Jill in a small voice; but with confidence. I remembered her stint in the truck with some trepidation. Then I remembered how she stayed behind the wheel after a missile tried to take her head off.

"You didn't tell us you could fly one of these," I said, getting my voice back.

"You didn't ask," she said. It sounded like one of those old comedy routines, but without a laugh track. It wasn't funny.

"Jill," I said, "have you ever flown a plane before?"

"Kind of."

"Kind of? What the hell does that mean?"

A zombie threw itself against the door, where Albert still moaned. He braced himself, still fighting, still a part of the team.

She sighed. "Okay, I haven't really flown; but I'm a wizard at all the different flight simulators!"

Arlene and I stared at each other with mounting horror. I hated to admit it, even to myself, but my experience bringing down the mail rocket—with a high-tech program helping every mile of the way—probably qualified me less to fly the C-5 than Jill with her simulators.

"All right?" I said to Arlene.

"Right," she answered, shrugging, then went to hook up Ken.

I helped Jill look for jacks on the glistening biotech. She was more willing to touch it than I was. She found what she needed and plugged Ken into the system. The operation went smoothly; he'd been designed for the purpose.

Jill called up SimFlight on her CompMac and tapped furiously, connecting it to Ken, then to the actual plane. A moment later she spoke with that triumphant tone of voice that rarely let us down: "Got it! We have control!"

The gunshots suggested the Clydes were getting closer, and more heavy bodies were beginning to throw themselves against the cockpit door. I was about to make a suggestion when Albert beat me to it. He was down but not out.

"Godspeed," whispered Albert, still covering his eyes. "Now, why don't you purge all the air from the cabin, daughter?"

Raising my eyebrows, I silently mouthed "daughter" to Arlene, but she shook her head. Albert obviously meant it generically. He was much too young to be her real father.

Faster and faster, Jill typed away . . . then the raging, surging sounds behind the door grew dimmer and dimmer, finally fading away to nothing. Modern death by keyboard. We were already at forty thousand feet and climbing; up there, there was too little air to sustain even zombies. And Clydes, human-real or human-fake, had a human need for plenty of O_2.

"Well done, daughter," said Albert. He could hear just fine.

Having come this close to buying it, I could hardly believe we were safe again. A coughing fit came out of nowhere and grabbed my heart. Arlene put her arm around me and said, "Your turn to sleep again." I didn't argue. I noticed that Albert was already snoozing.

Sleep that knits up the raveled sleave of care . . .

I felt too lousy, and too guilty somehow, to stay under for long. Less than a half hour later I was awake again. Jill had turned around, crossed the coastline, and was over the ocean. All was well with the world . . . for a few seconds longer.

"Holy hell, we're losing airspeed!" she suddenly screamed, jerking us all awake. "We're losing altitude!"

It's always something.

The engines strained and whined, making the noises they would if headed into a ferocious head wind. But there was no wind. With a big *fooooomp,* one engine flamed out. Jill wasn't kidding about the quality of her simulator exercises; she instantly dived the plane to restart it. Then she headed back, circling around to try again.

"Stupid monster mechanics," I yelled. "Dumb-ass

demon dildo ground crew! How the hell do these idiots intend to conquer the world when they can't even—"

"Shut up!" Jill shouted. I shut up. She was right. I could be pissed off all I wanted after she saved our collective ass.

Two more tries and she was white-faced. "It's some kind of field," she said. "We can't go west."

"So that's how they're conquering the world," said Arlene calmly. I took my medicine like a good boy.

33

Jill set the auto-pilot to continue circling, hoping no one had noticed the deviation yet. She typed away, accessing the biotech nav-com aboard. Then she smiled grimly. "Listen up," she said.

We sure as hell did; the mantle of command was hers while we were in the air. "Guys, we're going to have to dump you off at Burbank." She said it like Dante's Ninth Circle of Hell where the devil himself is imprisoned in ice, spending eternity chewing on Judas like a piece of tough caramel. I'd made good grades in my lit. courses.

"What? Why?" demanded Arlene.

"The force-field switch is located in the old Disney tower, near the studio."

"Is nothing sacred to these devils?" I asked.

"Night on Bald Mountain," said Arlene, "part deux."

"Sorry. No choice."

Jill altered course and headed northeast. We didn't speak for the rest of the short flight. None of us could think of anything worth saying.

Finally, Jill was bringing the plane low over Burbank International Airport. "Can you do a rolling stop?" I asked. "Slow down to about fifty kilometers per hour, then turn it into a touch-and-go?"

"Uh," she said. After thinking about it, she continued: "Yeah. Why?" I let the silence speak for me. She gasped and said, "You're crazy if you're thinking of a roll-out!"

"I'm thinking of a roll-out."

"What the hell," said Arlene. "I'm crazy too."

Jill shook her head, obviously wondering about both of us.

She cruised in over the airport, ignoring the standard landing pattern and dodging other planes, which answered my question about lousy zombie pilots.

We were low enough that the passenger cabin was pressurized again. Arlene and I went aft, picking our way over a planeful of zombies and two Clydes that were examples of the only good monsters. Jill kept calling out, "Are you ready?" She sounded more nervous each time. We reassured her. It was easier than reassuring ourselves.

"Open the rear cargo door!" Arlene shouted so that Jill could hear. We hit the runway deck hard, bouncing twice; the C-5 wasn't supposed to fly this slow. The rushing wind made everything a lot noisier. But we were able to hear Jill, loud and clear, when she said the magic word:

"Jump!"

We did just that, hitting the tarmac hard. I rolled over and over and over, bruising portions of my anatomy I'd never noticed before. I heard the sound effects from Arlene doing her impression of a tennis ball. But I didn't doubt this was the right way to disembark the plane; couldn't risk a real landing.

I got to my feet first. Jill was having trouble with her altitude. "Jesus, *no!*" shouted Arlene at the sight of Jill headed for a row of high rises.

"Lift, dammit, lift!" I spoke angrily into the air. There wasn't time for a proper prayer.

At the last second, bright, blinding flares erupted from under both wings, and the C-5 pulled sharply upward. A few seconds later we heard a roar so loud that it almost deafened us.

"What the hell?" Arlene asked, mouth hanging open.

"Outstanding!" I shouted, fisting the air. "She must have found the switch for the JATO rockets."

"JATO?"

"Jet-assisted takeoff!" I shouted. "They're rockets on aircraft to allow them to do ultra-short-field take-offs."

"I didn't know that plane would have those."

"She probably didn't either," I said, so proud of her I wished she could hear me call her daughter the same way Albert had.

We watched until Jill became a dark speck in the sky, circling until we could get the field down.

We tucked and ran, jogging all the way to the huge Disney building; the Disney logo at the top was shot up—somebody'd been using it for target practice.

"Ready?" I asked.

"Always."

I took a deep breath; pistols drawn, we popped the door and slid inside.

My God, what a wave of nostalgia! It was like old times again . . . back on Phobos, sliding around corners, hunting those zombies!

Up the stairwells—couldn't trust the lifts . . . I mean the elevators. Any minute, I knew I'd run into a hell-prince—and me without my trusty rocket launcher. Thank God, I didn't.

We played all our old games: cross fire, ooze-barrel-blow, even rile-the-critters. The last was the most fun: you get zombies and spinys so pissed, they munch each other alive.

Every floor we visited, we looked for that damned equipment. Nada. We climbed higher and higher; I began to get the strong feeling that we'd find the field generator way, way up, fortieth floor, all the way at the top.

It'd be just our luck.

We took Sig-Cows off'n the first two zombies we killed; better than the pistols, even though they were still just 10mm. The next one had a beautiful, wonderful shotgun. I'd take it, even if it was a fascist pump-action.

"Like old times," I said.

"Back on Deimos," she agreed.

"They die just as easily. I like my new toy."

"Hold your horses, Fly Taggart," she said. "Haven't you forgotten something?"

"Like what?"

"A certain wager."

No sooner did she mention the bet than I did indeed remember. There was only one thing to do. Change the subject: "Those zombies were probably the least of our troubles, Arlene. We can settle this later—"

"No way, Fly! I jumped out of a plane for you, and you're gonna pay your damn bet." When she got like this there was nothing to do but surrender. All the demonic forces of hell were like child's play compared to welshing on a bet with Arlene Sanders.

"Well, now that you mention it, I do have a vague recollection," I lied. "And that Sig-Cow looks like a mighty fine weapon at that."

"Good," she said. "You take the Sig-Cow. The shotgun is mine."

We resolved this dispute at just about the right moment, because a fireball exploded over our heads. We were under bombardment by imps. Now the new weapons would receive a literal baptism of fire.

Blowing away the spiny bastards, up the fifth floor stairwell, I turned a corner and found myself nose-to-nose with another Clyde. This close, there was no question: it looked exactly the same as the one we'd killed in the alley in Riverside, the same as the two who'd disarmed us getting on the plane.

There was no question now: they were, indeed, genetically engineered. The aliens had finally made their breakthrough . . . God help the human race.

He raised his .30 caliber, belt-fed, etc., etc.; but we had the drop on him. He never knew what hit him—well, it was a hail of bullets and Arlene's buckshot, and he probably knew that; you know what I mean! But now I had my own weapon; she looked envious . . . but she'd had her pick. The bet was paid.

As a final treat, thirty-seven floors up—Jesus, was I getting winded! I felt like an old man—we were attacked by a big, floating, familiar old pumpkin.

It hissed. It made faces. It spat ball lightning at us.

I spat a stream of .30 caliber machine-gun bullets back at it, popping it like a beach ball. It spewed all over the room, spraying that blue ichor it uses for blood.

"Jesus, Fly," said my partner in crime, "I'm going to lose my hearing if this keeps up."

"What?"

"That machine gun! It's almost as loud as Jill and her jets."

"What's that?" I asked, grinning. I was delighted with the results of my belt-fed baby.

She gave a "playful" punch on the arm, my old buddy. I yelped in pain.

"Where's an uninjured place on your body?" she asked.

"That's a very good question. I think tumbling down the airstrip eliminated all of those."

"Same here," she said. "But you can still make a great pumpkin pie." She kicked at the disgusting remains on the ground.

"Shall we find the top of the mouse house?" I suggested.

"After you, Fly."

In battlefield conditions, a proper gentleman goes ahead of the lady. If she asks, anyway. I was happy to oblige; but the nose of my machine gun actually preceded both of us.

At the very top we found a prize.

The door wasn't even locked. Inside was a room full of computers hooked into a new collection of alien biotech. This stuff gave off a stench, and some of it made mewling sounds like an injured animal. I wished Jill could be with us, plotting new ways of becoming a technovivisectionist.

"Got to be it," said Arlene.

I had trouble making out her words, not because my hearing was impaired, but because of the noise level. My machine gun contributed a good portion of it. So did Arlene's shotgun. And there were several explosions. A nice fanfare as we blew away unsuspecting imps and zombies tending the equipment.

I picked up a fiberglass baton off the body of an ex-zombie guard and used it to bar the door. I expected more playmates along momentarily. The idea didn't even bother me; not so long as I could buy us some time.

Arlene waved the smoke away and began fiddling with the controls on the main console. She frantically started flipping one push-switch after another, looking for the one that would kill the field.

"There has to be a way of doing this," she said, "or finding out if we've already done it.

"What makes you so sure?"

"Well, what if the aliens *wanted* to fly to Hawaii?"

I nodded. "I can just see a pinkie in one of those Hawaiian shirts."

"Damn! I wish we had Jill and Ken with us."

"Defeats the whole purpose, A.S. They're ready and waiting, forty thousand up, ready to blow for the islands as soon as we cut the bloody field."

"Most of the switches require a psi-connection to activate, and I can't do that!"

By now there was a huge contingent pounding on the door. The fiberglass bar was holding them . . . so far. These sounds did not improve Arlene's psychological state or aid the difficult work she was trying to do.

"I'm not getting it," she said. "I'm close, but I'm not getting it. Damn, damn, damn . . ."

"Is there anything I can do?"

"Hold the door. Hold the door! I'm sure there's one special button, but how will I know it even if I find it?"

As if to mock her, the entire panel went dark right then. She looked up and saw . . .

Me. Me, her buddy. Fly Taggart, technical dork, first-class. In my hand I held a gigantic electrical cord that I'd sliced in half with my commando knife. I knew that knife would come in handy one day.

"When in doubt, yank it out," I said with a smile.

She tried to laugh but was too tired for any sound to come out. "Did you learn that in VD class?" she asked.

I was saved from answering her because the door started to give way under the onslaught. Then the shred of a feeble plan crept into my brain. I ran across to the windows and smashed them open.

We were forty stories high, looking straight down on concrete, but it seemed better to open the windows than leave them closed.

"We took the energy wall down, at least," I said over my shoulder. "Jill's *got* to notice it's gone and tread air for Hawaii."

Arlene nodded, bleak even in victory. She was thinking of Albert . . . I didn't need alien psionics to know that. "The War Techies will track her as an 'unknown rider,'" added Arlene bleakly, "and they'll scramble some jets; they should be able to make contact and talk her down."

"Would you say the debt is paid?"

I didn't have to specify which debt. Arlene considered for a long time. "Yeah," she said at last, "it's paid."

"Evens?"

"Evens."

"Great. Got a hot plan to talk *us* down?" I asked my buddy.

She shook her head. I had a crazy wish that before Albert was blinded, and before Arlene and I found ourselves in this cul-de-sac, I'd played Dutch uncle to the two love birds, complete with blessings and unwanted advice.

But somehow this did not seem the ideal moment to suggest that Arlene seriously study the Mormon faith, if she really loved good old Albert. A sermon on why it was better to have some religion, any religion, lay dormant in my mind.

Also crossing my mind was another sermon, on the limitations of the atheist viewpoint, right before your mortal body is ripped to shreds. Bad taste, especially if you delivered it to someone with only precious seconds left to come up with a hot plan.

She shook her head. "There's no way," she began, and then paused. "Unless . . ."

"Yes?" I asked, trying not to let the sound of a hundred slavering monsters outside the door add panic to the atmosphere.

Arlene stared at the door, at the console, then out the window. She went over to the window like she had all the time in the world and looked straight down. Then up. For some reason, she looked up.

She faced me again, wearing a big, crafty, Arlene Sanders smile. "You are not going to believe this, Fly Taggart, but I think—I think I have it. I know how to get us down *and* get us to Hawaii to join Albert."

"And Jill," I added. I nodded back, convinced she'd finally cracked. "Great idea, Arlene. We could use a vacation from all this pressure."

"You don't believe me."

"You're right. I *don't* believe you."

Arlene smiled slyly. She was using the early-worm-that-got-the-bird smile. "Flynn Taggart . . . bring me some duct tape from the toolbox, an armload of computer-switch wiring, and the biggest, goddamned boot you can find!"